THE CONSTITUTION MURDERS

Conover Hunt

Cover: Design by Cynthia Newton. Produced by Caldwell Printing.
Torso figure used with permission of Anna Keiller/studio@anna-keiller.com

ISBN: 0692945040
ISBN 13: 9780692945049
Library of Congress Control Number: TXu 2-008-409

ACKNOWLEDGMENTS

My interest on James and Dolley Madison began in graduate school, when Miss Caroline Holmes Bivins, a genealogist from North Carolina, suggested that a student attending the Winterthur Museum graduate program use her notes about original James Madison possessions for a master's thesis. The thesis was completed in 1971, and in 1976-77 became the basis for a traveling loan exhibition and book on the subject, sponsored by the American Institute of Architects Foundation in Washington, D.C. In 1980-81, the Library of Congress sponsored another loan exhibition and book in conjunction with the completion of their Madison Library. I co-curated that project with historian Kym Rice.

In 1984, the National Trust for Historic Preservation was in the process of acquiring Montpelier, the Madison family home in Orange County, VA, in accordance with the wishes of its last occupant, Marian du Pont Scott, who had a life estate in the property. Her will specified that the Trust hire an expert in Madison furnishings to select objects from her collection that might be suitable for future use in the mansion. I reviewed her 300-page inventory, visited the house and later continued to consult to the Trust as it completed the purchase and prepared the property for admission by the public in 1989.

Fast forward to 2004, when the Montpelier Foundation, which took over management of the property in 2000, asked me to perform additional research and prepare an extensive report on furnishings known to, or believed to have been, in the mansion during the Madisons' 80-year occupancy. My seven-volume report, detailing some 300 objects, was submitted in the fall of 2005.

My notes represented more than three decades of research. Nevertheless, this was only a small fraction of the research completed by the Montpelier Foundation since 2000. The mansion has been restored to its original 1816 architectural appearance, and the interiors now resemble the Montpelier that visitors to the Madisons saw from 1817 to 1836.

Much work remains to be done, in part because Dolley Madison's son, John Payne Todd, sold the contents of Montpelier, piecemeal, in a series of sales in Virginia and Washington, D.C. The last significant sale of Madisoniana took place in Philadelphia in 1899.

I thank Marian du Pont Scott, the National Trust, and the Montpelier Foundation for ensuring that Montpelier was saved and will survive as a testimony, in bricks and mortar, silk and mahogany, to the life and legacy of the Father of the Constitution and fourth president of the United States. It also serves to reveal the warm, loving relationship between the scholarly Madison and the gregarious Dolley. In 2017, the talented Foundation staff completed a major study of the Montpelier slaves and bravely opened at new exhibit showing the dark realities of a plantation culture that relied on human bondage to survive.

Montpelier has become the magnet to bring long-lost Madison possessions home. If for this reason alone, my meager efforts since 1971 has been justified.

This book is a work of fiction, using important historic sites as a backdrop to examine the presence of the past in American life today. Mistakes are mine alone. I wish to thank Dr. William Seale,

White House historian, for reviewing the first draft and offering encouragement and a solid critique. Other colleagues have made valuable suggestions on content and style: thanks are due to Dr. Wythe Holt, Anne W. Henry, Calvin Mansfield, Calder Loth, and Christopher Naab. My editor Chris Guthrie of Open Book Editors gave shape to my first attempt at dialogue and provided keen insights on how to tighten up the narrative. Creative Spaces and its staff prepared the book for publication as an Amazon e-book and in paperback.

Too many Americans today are woefully ignorant about the Constitution or have lost sight of its critical importance in our lives. Perhaps by casting history as mystery some will take time to rediscover the miracle of the American founding.

Readers can follow me on my web site, ConoverHunt.com. Reviews, hopefully positive ones, can be sent to Amazon.com

Conover Hunt
Buckroe Beach, Hampton, VA

TABLE OF CONTENTS

PROLOGUE 2017 AND 2011

March 2017

Cary Mallory, proprietor of Cary Mallory Antiques, was pouring a first cup of coffee in her basement kitchen when the front doorbell rang. Checking her watch, she frowned.

Eight am, much too early for visitors. Maybe Connie has locked himself out again.

"C'mon Lizzie," she beckoned, and the giant brown dog followed her docilely to the main entry on the floor above. When they reached the door, Lizzie's back hair went up. Cary tensed, realizing it was a stranger.

She peered through the eye hole in the door and saw a bland-looking middle-aged man in a rumpled brown suit, briefcase in hand. He had graying hair and unremarkable features. Cary turned on the intercom and asked him for identification. Life had taught her to take precautions.

The man reached into his inside suit pocket and pulled out an identity card and badge, which he held up to the door. His name was Don Schulz. The badge identified him as a senior field agent with the Washington, D.C. office of the Drug Enforcement Administration.

After cautioning Lizzie to behave, Cary opened the door, introduced herself and invited the agent inside. Lizzie padded behind them as they descended into the kitchen, where Cary poured Schulz a cup of coffee. After they both sat down at an antique walnut table, Lizzie settled at the visitor's feet, eyeing him warily.

Agent Schulz put his briefcase on the table and slowly withdrew a sheaf of documents, which he placed in a pile in front of Cary. At this point, Conrad "Connie" Taliaferro entered the kitchen and headed for the coffee pot. Cary introduced him to the DEA agent as her executive assistant.

"I'm glad you are here, Mr. Taliaferro," said Schulz. "These papers also pertain to you. "

Cary had skimmed the documents and handed them to Connie. "It's a subpoena to appear before a new congressional committee about Operation Fast and Furious," she warned him.

Connie's eyebrows went up. "Why drag up that ridiculous operation now, for God's sake? I thought it was all settled in 2011-2012!"

Schulz smiled. "As you may recall, the Mexican authorities recaptured Joachín 'El Chapo' Guzman in 2014, and the Justice Department has extradited him to the U.S, to stand trial in five jurisdictions." El Chapo, perhaps the most dangerous drug dealer on earth, had escaped earlier from two high-security Mexican prisons, eluding the authorities for a decade.

Everyone knew about the drug king, head of the Sinalola Cartel. But Cary and Connie were still confused about the visit from the DEA.

"We know very little about Fast and Furious," said Cary. "Our case was an investigation into murders on American soil in 2011, but there was no direct connection to El Chapo."

"Ahhhh," said the agent. "After El Chapo's capture, the authorities found one of the Fast and Furious rifles in his arsenal." The duo still looked clueless.

"You may not know that the Zeta drug cartel was taken over by the Sinalola cartel. If you look back to 2011-2012, you will find that the former U.S. president used executive privilege to withhold about 20,000 Department of Justice documents relating to the failed Fast and Furious operation."

"And.....?"

"The newly discovered connection to El Chapo has induced a federal judge to vacate the old executive order." He explained the likelihood that a new House committee would reexamine the case, using whatever new evidence was contained in the documents.

Cary groaned inwardly. The Congress had a penchant for lengthy investigations that might not lead anywhere.

She asked the DEA agent, "How much of our time will you need for testimony?"

Schmid rattled on about 'what ifs' for a while and then admitted that it could take a week or more in appearances before the committee.

"We may be able to save ourselves and your committee some time," said Cary with a small smile.

It was the agent's turn to look confused.

"Connie, please get the document from the safe." The assistant left the room and returned with a CD in a manila envelope. He handed it to Agent Schulz.

"What's this?"

"The definitive story of our involvement in government business in 2011. It's all there."

Placing the CD in his briefcase, Schulz asked how many other copies of the document were in existence.

"Several." was the reply.

"Who's read it?" Schulz withdrew a notepad from a pocket to officially record the names.

"The principals from our group who were involved have all signed affidavits at the end of the narrative attesting to its accuracy."

Schulz demanded that all existing copies of the document be turned over to the DEA.

Cary flatly refused.

Schulz's face flushed and he started to shout. Lizzie placed a huge paw on his knee, raised her very large head and showed giant fangs, stunning him into silence. Chesapeake Bay retrievers are well known for protecting their owners.

The dog dutifully escorted the agent from the house and returned for a treat. Connie gladly complied while Cary picked up her phone to warn the others about this new development.

2011

My name is Conrad Taliaferro – Connie for short – reporting from Cary Mallory Antiques in Richmond, Virginia, the city of seven hills, among its many esoteric claims to fame. The surname in our parts is always pronounced *Tolliver*, an enunciation readily achieved by dropping most vowels and swallowing a few consonants. It has nothing to do with Italy.

Let me begin by stating categorically that on the morning of May 25, 2011, I had no idea that the proverbial shit was about the hit the fan. Nor did I ever dream it would fall to me to organize and pen the final narrative of what came to be known as the "Constitution Murders." I'm writing it now, even though most of the details are still *highly* classified. God only knows if the narrative will ever see the light of day.

We – meaning the principals in the events – have done our best to keep the details fresh so the tale can be published at some unknown future date, after a whole bunch of folks, including yours truly, have passed over into the Great Beyond. We've made a valiant attempt to protect ourselves against attacks by armed, stone-faced government goons who wear dark glasses and have little speakers hidden in their watchbands. Fictional identities are shown in the appendix.

As for my credentials as a scrivener; I'm merely a local boy. I attended St. Marks School (private) and the University of Richmond, where I majored in English. I think my parents' idea was that I would never, ever, need to leave the blessed womb of this city, except to travel each summer to our family cottage on the *Rivah* near Whitestone in the Northern Neck. Since most everyone else on the *Rivah* also hails from Richmond, my upbringing was somewhat sheltered.

I'm over the age of consent, six-feet-two, and aggressively slender. Hair is brown; eyes are hazel. No distinguishing marks. I have never married. For more than a decade I have been the indispensable administrative assistant to Ms. Cary Mallory of said Cary Mallory Antiques, a thriving business without a shop or shingle. The establishment is in the historic Church Hill section of the city on one of those seven hills mentioned above.

The basic story is true. Work on this tome began in 2011. I recorded my own impressions of the events and asked the other principals to write up reports on their recollections about the *case*, which was my boss's initial foray into the messy and unseemly world of violent death and terrorism. We decided to divide the narrative into chapters for ease of reading. You will find the main informational source of each chapter under its title.

While I continue to pray that Cary will refocus her attention on pricey Chippendale antiques rather than dead bodies, I hold out little hope for success. She is aided and abetted by a willing partner in crime, her old Sweet Briar roommate Virginia Eliza "VE" Shane, pronounced "VEE". The roomie is one of *the* Texas Shanes, who are about as rich as the Lone Star State is large.

And now, to the story....

CHAPTER 1

NORTHERN LIBERTIES, PHILADELPHIA – EVENING, MAY 24, 2011
Ray Goodson, Scribe

At a few seconds past 9:00 pm EDT, Ray Goodson's cell phone rang. A rerun of NCIS was playing on his television set and Goodson, security director for the Northeast Regional Office (NERO), National Park Service, was relaxing at home with a beer.

Goodson, 63, had worked for the Department of the Interior since college. Standing a shade under six feet with bright blue eyes, a craggy face, and a salt-and-pepper military buzz cut, he kept his weight under control by working out three days a week. The security chief was respected within the NPS for his calm demeanor, his broad experience, and his ability to work well on a team.

Ray was reaching into his pocket for the unit, when he realized that the ring tone was different. Sitting up with a jerk, he instantly muted the TV. It was the red SAT phone linking NERO to a special security unit within the government in Washington. The cell was always attached to his belt for easy access. Goodson answered by pressing a series of numbers, a prearranged code name. The screen lit up immediately.

"NAKED TORSO ON U.S.S. CONSTITUTION. NO ALARM, NO SUSPECTS"

Quickly, the agent pressed additional buttons that simultaneously told the caller to stay on the line, while sending the call to Washington. That chore completed, Goodson took the caller off hold and restated his code name. The party in Boston gave his own code, and only then did the two men begin talking.

"What's up, Glenn?" asked Goodson. "Some joker put a plaster cast of the Venus de Milo on board?" Donald Glenn was the head of security for the NPS Old Ironsides site within the Charlestown Navy Yard in Boston.

"No such luck little buddy," said Glenn, a timbre of high tension in his voice.

"What we got is a young female torso, buck naked, no arms, legs, or head, propped up against the double wheel house on the U.S.S. Constitution. Officer of the watch found it on his rounds less than two minutes ago. Shook him up bad."

No shit, Goodson thought. "Any witnesses?"

"Nope."

"Condition of the remains?""

"Bluish white, no blood, very cold, little odor." Glenn was confirming Goodson's initial suspicion that the body part had been kept in cold storage prior to its placement on board the ship. *How the hell had it gotten there?* He was completely mystified about the breach in security and asked Don to elaborate.

"Crude or surgical?"

"Very surgical," said Glenn, remembering the precise edges of the dissection.

"What the hell happened to security?" Goodson pressed.

Glenn explained that the Navy officer of the watch neither saw nor heard anything prior to the discovery. The airport-like security screening facilities at the visitor entrance ticket desk on land were operational, but no one or thing had triggered the alarm.

The Boston security man surmised that the culprits who left the torso had either arrived by water or dropped out of thin air to deposit their macabre gift.

"Don, stand by for a visit from Homeland Security within the next few minutes." Ray thanked the security chief and both men disconnected.

Goodson rose from his lounge chair and headed for the bathroom. As head of terrorist threats to all National Park Service-operated sites from Maine to Virginia, he was also the liaison to a special unit within the Department of Homeland Security that coordinated terrorist issues for all the NPS sites and National Historic Landmarks (NHLs) nationwide.

Ray had no sooner finished his business and washed his hands than the SAT phone rang again. This time the text message came from New York.

"THIRTEEN TEETH, SCATTERED, FLOOR, FED HALL, GW INAUGURATION BALCONY, TOUR HRS"

Goodson did not bother to greet the security chief for the multiple National Park Service sites in the New York City area. He had been friends with Gray Powell for decades. Powell's report was tense but comprehensive. Goodson could tell the officer was pissed off.

"During last tour of day, NPS interpreter noticed teeth scattered on floor near the remains of the balcony where Washington was sworn in as the first president in 1789. Damned fool thought it was spilled popcorn. Custodian nearly had a heart attack when she recognized the debris as human teeth and reported to me at 9:05 pm. Fortunately, she did not touch the evidence or clean the floor."

Ray was beginning to tell Powell about the impending DHS contact when the New York chief interrupted.

"Wait, we have word that a leg was left on the dining room table at The Grange National Monument. Discovery 9:10 pm after alarm. No suspects."

Suddenly, the SAT call waiting light came on. *Not again!* Goodson felt his gut tighten with apprehension.

This time it was George Curwin from Independence National Historical Park in Old City Philadelphia., about a mile from Goodson's home.

"HUMAN BODY PARTS 3 SITES: APS (HAND), 1BUS (LEG), FCPS (HEAD). ALARMS LIT, XCEPT 1BUS."

Goodson's mind raced while he madly entered code. *Holy shit! American Philosophical Society, 1st National Bank of the US and the Print Shop at Franklin Court had been hit.*

Time to bring in the big guns, he decided, and entered a separate code that would automatically link his cell to ring at DHS. It would also send an alert about major security problems to the NERO director. He had barely finished the chore when his SAT phone put out another alert. Goodson sent a secure code asking the caller to hold and switched to another secure line on his cell. As he dialed, he checked the time. It was 9:16 pm.

Hamilton Coles, the Department of Homeland Security (DHS) coordinator of threats against National (NPS) sites and Historic Landmarks (NHLs), began speaking as soon as he saw Goodson's code. "We've got it, Ray," he said. "Red alert kicked in when you hit the bypass on your phone." He asked the security chief to stay on the present channel and report in by text at least every ten minutes. Goodson agreed and rang off.

The national parks system is divided up into administrative service regions. NERO is heavy with both NPS historic sites and National Historic Landmarks. The Washington, D.C. area is a separate National Capitol Region within the larger east coast multi-state area.

Charlestown Navy Yard, The Grange, Federal Hall, and Independence National Historical Park (INHP) were all within NERO. In response to the red alert message from her regional security chief, Elizabeth Rodgers, the NERO director, called in to get a brief. Goodson had been able to document the calls as they came into the SAT phone and confirmed to the director that all incidents seemed to be confined to the region.

"Keep me apprised," Liz Rodgers said curtly and hung up. She needed to get to work on media control. *What the hell is going on?"* she wondered wildly, dialing her deputy.

CHAPTER 2

CHURCH HILL, RICHMOND –
MEET THE NARRATOR
Conrad Talliaferro

Connie here again. You can see the basic problem: we had a dissected, naked, unidentified woman whose remains have been deposited almost simultaneously at several national historic sites. Before I introduce the remaining characters, a little background information is in order.

I started with Cary in 1996 as a combination gofer and packer, graduated to the status of picker in 2000, and was named on-site manager a few years later. My title and estimation of value to Mallory are self-generated and entirely justified. There is absolutely no one else on earth who could or would perform the services I render with the loyalty and brilliance I provide, not to mention for the measly salary I receive for my efforts.

The shop is in a drop-dead charming restored mid-19th century cottage located on a bluff overlooking the James River. The neighborhood boasts a full range of historic architectural styles, from majestic columned stucco brick mansions, stiff with gravitas, to humble artisan frame cottages. Cary's Antebellum white frame cottage is just a few blocks away from 25th Street, the location of

St. John's Church, where our favorite radical, Patrick Henry, delivered his famous 1775 "Liberty or Death" speech on the eve of the American Revolution. Hence the name, Church Hill.

Cary's cottage sits on a hill that slopes down toward the river. It's arranged on four floors, with a basement kitchen, dining room, study and powder room, front and back parlors on the main floor, two bedrooms with one bath above, and a spacious dormered attic suite, also with bath. From the front, it appears to be a raised 1½ story cottage. You can only see all four stories from the rear, which has a flagstone patio.

I reside in the dormered attic and look after the business and the property while Cary is away, which is most of the time. Visitors with appointments access the house via a narrow L-shaped front staircase leading to a small porch held up with stylized Doric columns. The patio on the rear has a commanding view of the James River, which really ain't much to brag about, being a churning, muddy stream full of ugly grey boulders. Nevertheless, locals call it the "fall line of the Mighty James."

The parlors, guest room, kitchen, and dining room are furnished with fine American antiques and folk art, a few of them available for purchase. Cary lives upstairs but works in the basement study, buying and selling furnishings via the Internet and through her well-trained army of pickers. Most of her acquisitions never get shipped to Richmond but are transported directly from the point of sale to the new buyer, or stored temporarily until the sale is finalized.

She does not keep regular office hours, travels at will, and lives without the crushing overhead associated with keeping expensive inventory or having multiple sales personnel on hand daily to await customers. If I had not been the type of enabler who gave her the leisure to meddle in crime, none of this ghastly business would have happened. It was me after all; I let the dogs out.

Earlier in her career, Cary had an active shop. When she started out in 1996, Cary was a dealer, salesperson, head cook, and bottle washer. She operated in the commercial district in Church Hill kept regular open hours and endured clusters of browsers, most of them looking for flea market prices rather than investment quality works of art.

I slowly assumed more responsibility and eventually became her right-hand man. Some would use the term loosely. My late father had various euphemisms to describe his only son, including "gay as a goose," "flaming fairy," and "light in the loafers."

It's just as well that Dear Old Dad went to his reward in that exclusive NRA Gun Club in the sky before California Governor *Ahnold* coined the phrase "girlie man;" otherwise I would have been shackled with that moniker as well. Of course, times have changed. That was the era before Equality Virginia, regional LGBT – bet you can't name them all – business networking groups, festivals that draw tens of thousands of people of every conceivable persuasion, and our growing reputation for only putting money into the hands of open-minded corporations and political candidates.

Cary's move away from shopkeeper was evidence of a solid base of clients, a strong network of pickers locating good merchandise, and a record of sales cumulatively worth tens of millions of dollars. It takes several million to start up an antiques business, you know, particularly one dealing in early American decorative arts.

Cary cashed in on some of her inheritance in 1995 – what was left of it anyway – to set up the first shop. After a wobbly start, the business gradually stabilized. By 2011 she had several seven-figure sales under her belt and no longer even bothered to display at the nation's top antiques shows, New York and Philadelphia among them.

Fortunately, Cary made enough money to weather the collapse of the antiques market during the Great Recession. These days she still invests a lot of money subscribing to all the major and regional auction house catalogues and key publications on Americana. But she was never among the regulars on Antiques Road Show. The PBS production doesn't pay its appraisers after all, luring its experts with promises of publicity instead. Cary hates publicity and doesn't see much sense in doing much for free.

Onward!

CHAPTER 3

MONTPELIER, ORANGE, VA –
EVENING, MAY 24, 2011
John Abbott

I t was a quiet night at Montpelier. Ned Willis, director of security for former President James Madison's Virginia home, was seated at the main control desk in his office, watching the bank of 24 wall-mounted monitors flick from one image to the next in a continuous rotation. An electronic panel nearby glowed green, indicating that the 100-plus buildings on the property were secure. Montpelier's isolated location, situated on more than 2,650 acres about four miles south of the Orange County sheriff and fire departments, made up-to-date security a necessity.

Ned was a native of Orange, whose ancestors had moved into the fertile Piedmont of Virginia from the Tidewater during the mid-18th century to grow tobacco and farm. Tobacco was long gone as a crop, but farming remained the Willis family's main occupation. At 64, Ned had thick, grey curly hair perched atop a weathered face. He was only five-foot-seven, but he was strong, attesting to a lifetime spent working the land. A tractor accident four years ago had left him with a gimpy leg, so he applied for the security post at Montpelier, leaving agribusiness in the hands of his sons.

The security office occupied Montpelier's Victorian train station facing Route 20 South. It was built by William du Pont of Delaware, who purchased the former Madison home in 1901 and transformed it into a great country estate. Du Pont commuted each week to Wilmington, Delaware headquarters of the family's vast business interests. Guests would sometimes take the train out to Virginia for weekend parties.

The complex erected by William du Pont boasted a bowling alley, skeet range, pony barn, formal gardens, horse barns, and other amenities that made it almost self-sufficient. Many full-time employees had housing on the grounds, and there was plenty of room for guests in Montpelier's rambling 55-room mansion house. The Montpelier Foundation operates the site and returned the main mansion to its smaller, Madison-era profile in 2003-2008.

Marion du Pont Scott, William's only daughter, was the last family member to reside at Montpelier. After her death in 1983, it was acquired by the National Trust for Historic Preservation, which managed the site until 2000, when operations were turned over to the private foundation.

Thanks, in part, to a $20 million gift from the Paul Mellon Foundation, the house was restored to its appearance when Madison lived there in retirement, from 1817-1836. Significant rooms from the du Pont era were removed from the mansion and reconstructed in a new Visitors' Center elsewhere on the grounds. Curators and archaeologists stayed busy collecting original Madison-era artifacts and unearthing the remains of slave housing and other long-disappeared outbuildings on the property.

Ned noticed he was losing mental focus, so he rubbed his bad leg. As he was scanning the large electronic panel of monitors, a blinking red light appeared suddenly, showing a security breach on the rear, one-story portico, or colonnade, at the mansion house. He clicked the monitor nearest that location but did not see any movement. Quickly, he radioed Bill Shackelford, the roving security patrol on duty, to proceed to that sector to check things out. The breach automatically triggered silent alarms at the Orange County sheriff and fire departments.

Shackelford's jeep was not far from the mansion when he got the call. He quickly turned onto the main road leading to the front portico and swerved left, past the classical garden temple on the lawn, and around to the rear of the house, the location of the classical colonnade projecting from the center rear of the building. Bill stabbed the brakes, grabbed a flashlight in one hand, and slipped his fingers around his Glock with the other. He clicked his walkie-talkie over to speaker mode to communicate directly with Ned.

"Condition red, boss," he said. "Got the far north triple-hung window open about three feet from the bottom. No evidence of animals. Small break in the glass near the top of the lower window frame. Looks like we have human penetration." *Someone broke the glass to reach in and unlock the window, raising it to get into the house!*

Montpelier's most important buildings were wired inside and out, with contact alarms at all the doors and windows. Occasionally, a bird would fly into a window or a tree branch would break off during a storm and hit the building, either of which could activate the security warning. To minimize false alarms, Montpelier had arranged a seven-minute delay before Orange County sheriff and fire department personnel were dispatched to the site. This interval gave field security personnel enough time to reach the affected location and send out an all-clear code green if nothing was amiss.

Failure to activate the code within this brief window was an automatic red alert, called the *aw shit code* by local personnel. Montpelier security could also override the delayed alarm by pressing the red button at any time during the process.

Ned pressed the panic button the moment Shackelford reported "condition red," alerting all agencies that they should report to the scene ASAP. The security chief followed up with information about the location of the penetration.

Meanwhile, Shackelford had crawled under the open window and switched on one of the architectural floor lamps that were used to increase the interior lighting during tours at night or on dark, rainy days. He had entered the rear of the mansion's main parlor and quickly reported, "parlor empty." Then he hustled from room to room on the main floor, calling in status reports. Shackelford then ascended the staircase in the old, south wing to examine the bedrooms and old library above.

Montpelier had functioned as a duplex from 1799-1829, when Nellie Conway Madison, the president's mother, had died. Her late husband, Colonel James Madison, Sr. had built the original Georgian-style house during the mid-1750's and left her a life estate in the family home. The widow resided for three more decades alone in the original section of the residence. James and Dolley's many guests would call on the "Old Lady," as she was known, after her dinner and before theirs.

As soon as Shackelford reached the original library, he stopped. "Got a package on the floor over by the corner fireplace in the old library," he reported. This was the room, overlooking the mansion's front portico, where Colonel Madison, Sr. kept his books. Madison, Jr. had used the room to perform his research on the history of governments prior to the Constitutional Convention in Philadelphia in 1787. He also penned some of his essays for the *Federalist* papers there. Staffers were careful to use the term *old library* to distinguish this room from the *new library* on the first floor in the north wing that Madison added in 1809-1811, during the presidential years.

"It's rectangular," reported Shackelford, "about the side of a glasses case, wrapped in brown Kraft paper, no label." The guard knew not to touch the object and continued his search of the second floor. Finding no other evidence, he gave the "clear" signal and returned to the library to await assistance. Loud sirens told him that help was only seconds away.

Ned Willis had kept Sheriff David Leigh briefed by cell while the county official was in route to Montpelier. Leigh immediately dispatched some of his men to search the basement kitchens and storage rooms before coming up to the old library. Post-restoration, the mansion house was 12,500 square feet on three floors. Shackelford had followed procedure, searching all the main rooms first.

Sheriff Leigh and Patrick Shea, the fire chief, both responded in person to the alarm. They entered the upstairs library less than a minute before Foundation President John Abbott appeared in the doorway, hastily dressed but wide awake. The red alert had rung in his bedroom in the Bassett House on the estate grounds. Abbott had stayed on, with the new title, after the National Trust transferred management to the Foundation in 2000.

Someone raced in to report that the basement and all exits were clear. Leigh, Shea, Abbott, and Shackelford stared down at the little package on the floor, and waited. David Leigh was no slouch; he had spent twenty years on the Washington Metropolitan Police force, rising to senior officer before he retired to Orange for his current semi-retirement. He was well-versed in the special security procedures involved in the protection of national landmarks.

Ned Willis's report about the package had led Leigh to contact Steven Daniels, another Orange County "come here" who was a retired military demolitions specialist. Daniels had agreed to serve as liaison to the county in case a terrorist threat was ever directed their way. The bomb man was the last to arrive, carrying a case of tools he would need to deactivate any explosive device in the mysterious package.

Daniels asked if anyone wanted to leave the room before he examined the box. No one budged. After scanning the exterior, he reported that there were no active electronics inside, then removed the Kraft paper. Nothing happened, except a small, yellowed fragment of paper floated to the floor.

Leigh shone a light on the paper, noting that it was covered with handwriting which had faded to a mahogany brown color. One of Leigh's deputies stepped forward with an evidence bag, but John Abbott interceded.

"It looks like a historic manuscript letter," he said. "See if you can slide it onto another flat surface, just to keep it from falling apart." After rummaging through the evidence kit, the deputy carefully inserted the fragile paper into a glassine envelope with a firm backing.

Meanwhile Daniels inserted a probe into the package. By then they could see that the package was white plastic with a red *U* written in ink – or blood – on the top of the hinged lid. Daniels glanced up at Leigh. "I think you're good to go, Sheriff."

Leigh grasped the box in one gloved hand and carefully opened the lid. Shackelford turned his flashlight on the contents.

Both men gasped at once. Shackelford's light hit the floor and the room went dark. Leigh bobbled the box without dropping it, while Shackelford picked up the light.

A pair of milky brown eyeballs stared out from a nest of cotton padding inside the box.

Everyone had gathered around the grisly evidence when Abbott's cell phone rang. He glanced at the screen and saw the special code for the Department of Homeland Security. Turning away from the others, he activated the call.

"John Abbott here."

"Mr. Abbott, this is Walter Johnston from the Landmarks Protection Division at DHS. We want to alert you to the potential for a security breach at Montpelier." He went on to state that several landmarks and national historic sites associated with the era of the Constitution were reporting incidents.

"We have a pair of brown human eyeballs here,' Abbott reported, his voice lifeless. "We also have the fragment of a letter. They were left on the floor in the old upstairs library in the mansion. That the kind of incident you're talking about?"

"Yes sir, please hold," said the agent, leaving the Montpelier president to cool his heels for several minutes. Abbott's posture had slumped and he was staring at the floor when a female voice came on the line.

"Mr. Abbott, this is Agent Janet Casey. Are you in the old library? "

"Yes." Then, "Who the hell are you?"

"Assistant Director of the Landmarks unit," said Janet in a low, controlled manner. Abbott was to wait for a DHS agent to arrive and turn over the eyes, the packaging, the letter, and any other trace evidence found at the scene. She also asked for security tapes and contact information for Orange County personnel who responded to the alarm. Abbott handed the phone to Leigh, who had released his hold on the box.

"Sheriff David Leigh, here." The sheriff confirmed that all evidence was in his possession. Later, he told Abbott that Dover Air Force Base was handling the forensics for the eyes and the FBI would examine the letter and other pieces of evidence.

"I'm not turning over the letter," said the sheriff bluntly.

When Abbott heard squawking about the Patriot Act and national security from the phone, the Montpelier president grabbed it out of Sheriff Leigh's hand.

"Abbott here, Agent Casey." He explained that Montpelier was in the best position to authenticate the handwriting on the letter, which would be kept in its protective envelope until that process was complete and promised the authentication would be completed by noon the next day. Reluctantly, Casey agreed, but informed Abbott that a senior DHS agent would come to Montpelier to collect it.

Leigh and Abbott agreed to meet the following morning. The sheriff would keep the evidence overnight and check for prints.

Abbott would arrange for experts to authenticate the handwriting on the letter. The two men exited the mansion house together, leaving the others to clean up.

"I don't like this one bit," said Leigh, shaking his head in the cool, night air. "Minutes after the alarm goes off, the evidence is in place and the perp has vanished into thin air."

Abbott promised to double-check the alarm system the next day. If the Montpelier president thought the timing of the call from DHS was fishy, he kept it to himself.

CHAPTER 4

CHURCH HILL – MORNING, MAY 25, 2011
Connie

I t was nearly a month after the annual statewide Garden Club of Virginia Tour, show-casing immaculate and tastefully decorated historic and modern homes along with luxuriant, verdant gardens. The houses featured artistic floral arrangements made by the local garden clubbers, all designed to enhance the well-appointed interiors.

Let Connie Taliaferro assure you, tourists flock to Virginia every year for the two-week event. Some of the Commonwealth's most important historic mansions remain in private hands and are only open to the public during the tour. The Garden Club of Virginia applies the proceeds to good works like the restoration of historic gardens and archaeological investigations.

Cary was already sipping her morning coffee in the kitchen when I trotted downstairs for breakfast. I was feeling particularly sporty that day in a lavender seersucker suit with a sequined baseball cap turned backward in the manner of more masculine men. I flashed my wingtips, of course, no socks.

"How's business, sweet cheeks?" I asked, pouring cream in my designer coffee before taking a bite from a giant apple fritter from the Northampton Bakery, one of Richmond's great institutions.

"Connie, you look like a mutant lilac bush." Cary scanned me up and down, frowning, taking in my coordinated Nicole Miller tie featuring pink and lavender bunnies and the amethyst stone blinking in my ear lobe.

"Too much?" I sighed. "I feel so *boring* lately, you know? So old and over the hill."

"Face it, darling, you're not twenty anymore. You need to start paying for dinner if you want any action. At forty, your days as a kept man are over. Fortunately, your business success and that trust fund from your dearly departed aunt should ease your transition into the role of *older man*."

"Is that any way to speak to Conrad Taliaferro, your beloved assistant? *Honest to John, this woman has edges as sharp as broken glass.*

"Tell me about your current *enamorado*."

"Oh, Matt? Well, first off, he's *gorgeous* and has the most *divine* blue eyes. But the boy gulps down caviar like it's ranch dip." The phone rang, cutting me off just as I was getting started.

"Cary Mallory Antiques," I drawled before listening in shock at the sound of a deep voice from the past.

"This is Hamilton Coles. I'm calling about Montpelier. Is Cary there?"

"Hold on," I muttered, doubting Cary would even take a call from her long-ago lover.

Seeing the alarm on my face, she calmly put down her coffee. "Who died?'

"It's Ham Coles." I handed her the phone as she cleared her throat.

"Cary Mallory," she said, sounding professional as ever.

I tried my best to eavesdrop but only heard snippets of information: "*murder... meeting... Madison....*"

"Where?" Cary asked.

"*...body...Abbott...*" said Coles.

"Okay, I'll be there." She hung up, set the phone down calmly, and took a sip of her coffee.

I stared blankly at her. Then, rising without a word, I strode to the wet bar and began whipping up a Bloody Mary, all in a vain attempt to recover from the shock of Hamilton Coles' voice. I held the vodka bottle aloft as an offering, but Cary shook her head. She said she had to go to Montpelier for a meeting due to a mystery surrounding a murder. She said it might involve the Madisons.

As far as I knew, all the important Madisons had been dead for ages. *Mystery, murder, Madison, meeting, Montpelier, Ham Coles?* I took a giant swig and wiped my upper lip.

"Speak to me, Cary. I want to know everything."

But she said she hung up before getting any details.

Damn!

Cary left the kitchen and I heard her climb the stairs to her bedroom. At the top of the stairs I heard her mumble, "I wonder if this is about the missing papers?"

CHAPTER 5

CHURCH HILL – LATE MORNING, MAY 25, 2011
Connie and Cary

I followed Cary upstairs, Bloody Mary in hand and determined to learn more about the mysterious call from Coles. I perched myself on the edge of her bed and saw the irritation in her eyes at the sight of me, waiting patiently. I watched her as she rooted around for clothing, a briefcase, and accessories.

"What papers?" I asked, munching on a slice of lime I pulled out of the Bloody Mary.

Cary sighed and turned to face me. "Look, before James Madison died in 1836, he entrusted a packet of papers to his brother-in-law, John Payne, and told him they contained debts he had paid for his stepson John Payne Todd without his wife's knowledge. Then Madison instructed him to give the packet to Dolley after his death."

"So?"

"Well, Dolley's son Payne Todd had a reputation for gambling and drinking, with the result that the Madisons had to bail him out of jail and other unpleasantries for decades after the boy reached maturity."

"Well, did John Payne turn over the papers or not?"

"We *think* he gave them to Dolley shortly after Madison's funeral."

"Had John Payne read them?"

"We aren't sure. Accounts of Madison's last days vary, and only one contemporary observer stated that Madison offered to show them to Payne."

"And then what happened?

"Well, fast forward to Washington, D.C. in July 1849, when Dolley was on her deathbed. Todd had continued his wasteful spending after Madison's death, literally bankrupting his mother. He and his creditors tried to force the old lady into signing a new will, one that would leave everything to Todd and disinherit her adopted daughter/niece/companion Annie Payne, who had moved in with her aunt years earlier to look after the aging former First Lady. Dolley gave a carpet bag full of papers to Anna and Mary Cutts, another niece, and instructed them to remove them from her house."

"And?"

"Apparently the two girls raced away with the carpet bag to parts unknown, and that was the last we heard of the papers."

Cary excused herself and went into her bathroom, closing the door behind her. I heard the shower and tried to imagine that last scene in James Madison's life. It wasn't that hard. Cary was an expert on all things Madison and she always talked about it. I'd read several of her books on the subject and visited Montpelier with her many times over the years. In fact, she was still on contract there, this time updating the Montpelier files on original furnishings.

Although half the surviving classical mansions in Virginia have been attributed to the hand of Thomas Jefferson, in the case of Madison's home, Montpelier, the legend had teeth. Jefferson was Madison's best friend for more than half a century. Shortly before his election as fourth president of the United States, Madison began planning a major expansion at his family home. He wrote to Jefferson, asking for the use of some of the many workmen that Jefferson kept employed at Monticello and his country retreat, Poplar Forest, located outside Lynchburg.

A researcher cataloguing papers at the Virginia Historical Society had recently uncovered an 1808 drawing of the proposed 1809-1814 expansion to Montpelier with notations in Jefferson's own hand. Furthermore, the builders' accounts for the work survived, submitted by two well-known Jefferson workmen, James Dinsmore and John Neilson.

I heard gargling sounds coming from the bathroom and thought more about Madison. Jefferson had died a decade before Madison, who expired in June 1836. The "great little Madison," as he was known, had been born terribly frail and seemed to have spent a great part of his life on the brink of death. He was the eldest child born to wealthy Virginia planter Colonel James Madison, Sr. and his wife Nelly Conway.

Against all odds, the junior Madison managed to soldier on for 85 years before he succumbed to the ravages of old age.

I knew that the retirement years for many of the American Founding Fathers had been hectic, with scores of visitors descending on their homes like locusts. Virginia had supplied four of the first five presidents, all of whom had country estates. The absence of nearby towns with accommodations for these guests forced the ex-presidents to offer room and board to complete strangers. Some visitors stayed for only a day or two, but others settled in for weeks at a time.

As James Madison became increasingly infirm, a bedroom for him was created from a former tea room located in the back part of the mansion's first floor, overlooking the rear lawn. It placed Madison adjacent to the dining room, where he could converse through the doorway at meals with the many friends and strangers who came to Montpelier in all seasons. It also connected to his extensive *new* library in the mansion's north wing.

After retiring from the presidency in 1817, he and his flamboyant wife Dolley spent most of their time at Montpelier, carefully sorting his papers while Madison quietly edited his legacy for publication. Long before he became president, Madison was known as the Father of the Constitution.

Cary's many writings on Montpelier furnishings had given me a clear picture of the mansion's interior during the retirement years. Montpelier was a great deal spiffier than the usual country home of its era. No whitewashed walls for Jemmy and Dolley, no sir. Some of the main rooms sported printed and flock wallpapers, and Parisian carpets graced the hardwood floors. Louis XVI chairs were blended in with the work of the best American cabinetmakers, and more than a hundred works of art were featured on the mansion walls. The house even boasted a sculpture gallery.

Cary reentered the bedroom a moment later, fully dressed and ready to go.

"When were James and Dolley married?"

"September 15, 1794 at her sister Lucy Washington's house, in what's now West Virginia." She was rooting around for earrings in her jewelry drawer.

I recalled that Dolley had been a widow when he met James Madison. "Who was her first husband?"

"John Todd, Jr. He was a Quaker attorney in Philadelphia with a house on the corner of Fourth and Walnut Streets. Congressman Aaron Burr, later tried for treason, made the introductions."

"John Payne Todd was her son from that marriage?"

Cary nodded and picked up her purse. I hoisted her suitcase and we walked downstairs together. Cary gave me instructions to cover the shop for the next two or three days. I followed her outside and we trudged to her car.

"Wait, what killed John Todd, Jr.?"

She got in her car and rolled down her window. "You gonna put the suitcase in the car?"

I did as she asked and slammed the trunk.

"Yellow fever," she said. "It killed 5,000 people in Philadelphia in the summer and fall of 1793." With that, she was gone.

CHAPTER 6

WASHINGTON, D.C – LATE EVENING, MAY 24, 2011

W hen the first alarm hit the Department of Homeland Security (DHS) offices, an automatic page went to Hamilton Coles, the division coordinator. Fortunately, Ham was alone, having finished a dinner date with an attractive attorney in one of the many international law firms located in Washington. He was holding his secure satellite phone and en route to his office near L'Enfant Plaza when Ray Goodson set off the red alert within the NPS-NERO region, putting the matter under the direct control of DHS.

Coles parked quickly and sprinted toward his office, working out a strategy for an efficient delegation of authority, at least for the short term. He could hear the shouting and cell phones ringing when he was fifty feet from the office. *All hell must have broken loose.*

Coles shouted orders rapidly to his coworkers as soon as he entered the door. "Jones, you're in charge of NHLs and NHL districts. Get two assistants and start with the NERO."

Often called the "ladies in waiting," National Historic Landmark buildings, sites, and districts are deemed of high importance to the nation, but do not require direct federal management. Newly designated NHLs are added to the list almost every year. Coles racked his brain and figured there were about 2,000, probably more, in the entire country.

"O'Reilly, you coordinate with Goodson at NPS," he commanded. Nicki O'Reilly had come to DHS from the Park Service. She and Goodson already knew each other.

Ham then turned to Barbara Charlton, an agent who was familiar with the inner workings of DHS and the other federal intelligence services. "Get me a team of analysts who can explain body parts at historic sites to help us build a way ahead." She headed off, dialing her cell phone as she ran. Barbara had a raft of contacts among government intelligence agencies. Ham knew she would put together a good team to assist them.

He assigned individual agents to handle each incident and charged them to work closely with the coordinators. Ham then instructed an aide to set up a status board to record facts as they came into the office. Finally, he contacted the assistant deputy secretary of the protection division at DHS, his immediate boss, and asked for top-level media coordination for these incidents. William Shaw assured Ham that an expert would be in his office within minutes.

"Let's try to keep the lid on this thing, Ham," Bill urged.

Ya think? thought Ham as he turned to the status board. It was divided vertically into two halves beneath a large map of all NHLs and NPS sites in NERO. The left column listed the site and the time of the alert. The right column showed a list of body parts and additional details. Ham immediately saw that Mount Vernon in northern Virginia, an affiliated NPS site, was now on the board. Apparently, a tourist had placed a severed foot on a chair in the dining room during operating hours. Staff found it after closing. No alarm, no suspects.

"Guys, I want all body parts and potential DNA evidence to be sent directly to the forensics lab at Dover Air Force Base for

analysis." The armed forces lab in Delaware was charged with identifying the remains of soldiers blown to smithereens by incendiary
devices in the Middle East. Its equipment and expertise were state
of the art. Fred Schmidt was the man in charge there.

"Someone call Fred Schmidt ASAP!" he yelled.

A staffer was writing current information on the status board.

A severed arm had been found near the statue of Benjamin
Franklin facing College Hall on the campus at the University of
Pennsylvania. A student noticed it and contacted the campus police. *The university is not an NPS site,* mused Ham. He could not
recall if it was an NHL. *An astute NPS officer must have called over to
check, since Franklin had founded the Philadelphia university.*

Coles studied the board for a minute, his mind churning in
search of a connection among the sites. *The Constitution!* Ham
called an agent who seemed to be free and assigned him to check
in with all historic sites associated with the era of the Constitution.
Then he started naming them from memory:

The National Constitution Center, not historic but pertinent
Independence Hall
Montpelier, Madison's home in Virginia
Mount Vernon
John Jay's House, in New York
Roger Sherman – is there a Connecticut house or site?
George Mason's house…in Virginia…Gunston Hall was the name
Franklin – Franklin Court, Pennsylvania Hospital, the Library
Company, UPenn…hell, half of Old City!
The Grange, connected to Hamilton
First Bank of U.S., connected to Hamilton
Old Ironsides in Charlestown, the U.S. Constitution
American Philosophical Society
National Archives…"

All agents were fully occupied, so Ham called his superior and told him he was ready to brief. Barbara Charlton had assembled a small team of intelligence experts, who met DS Shaw and Ham in a conference room.

Bill Shaw was a veteran CIA administrator who moved over to DHS when the Department of Infrastructure Protection was created to oversee the safety of government property after 9/11. "Landmarks", or "National Monuments and Icons," as it was called within the department, was a small operation with a very high profile. Shaw was in his early 60s, pudgy and tough.

"First thoughts?" posed the assistant deputy secretary to the group.

"CIA thinks the body parts may be a dismemberment, possibly belonging to one victim. The Mexican drug cartels are fond of this type of mutilation."

"FBI can handle prints." It was the representative from the Bureau who spoke.

"Dover is ready to receive body parts and will be able to confirm the identity of the victim or victims and pre-or-post mortem dissection," said Ham. "It looks like the remains were frozen and then distributed."

"Are we sure we're dealing with one victim?" Shaw asked.

"Too early to tell," Coles said.

The agent explained that there had been ten invasions, all on May 24. Two took place during public tours near the end of the day. The rest occurred at 9:00 pm or shortly thereafter. Some alarms were bypassed. Ham concluded his brief by explaining his actions to alert all sites and landmarks associated with the era of the Constitution. Shaw nodded.

After checking again by cell with his office, Coles informed the group that the invasion total still stood at ten sites. "We may get more, since we're notifying potential sites and they'll be dispatching security to check." So far, the pieces added up to one body.

"Was Independence Hall hit?" The site had been on the books as a likely terrorist target since 9/11.

Ham shook his head.

"Can we shut it down?" asked Shaw.

"'Fraid not," said the agent, who then explained the potential problems with media in the event the public was barred from the famous building.

"*Shit*," muttered Shaw. He dismissed the agents from his office and grabbed his phone. It was time to notify the powers above him.

CHAPTER 7

WHO IS CARY MALLORY?
Cary and Connie

So, who is Cary Mallory? Well, over the years I've learned a great deal about my boss. She is a few years older than I am, a tall, angular woman with penetrating blue-grey eyes, long dark blond hair, a no-nonsense demeanor, and a nearly photographic memory of people, events, and objects amassed from books, auctions, museums, magazines, private collections, and antiques shows.

She has what the trade calls a *great eye* for the quality and proportion of antiques and can spot repairs and replacements with deadly accuracy. Her specialty is furniture, with a secondary focus on antique textiles and folk art. Cary avoids dealing in American glass – says there are more fakes than genuine examples – and eschews the *decorator* end of the business. Only serious collectors contact Cary Mallory. Rich people who merely want to decorate a room with a few antiques go elsewhere.

Some would describe Cary as beautiful, but, as I already noted, she has hard edges that lead most observers to conclude that she is handsome. She's far too independent for a proper Southern woman. She never became a Junior Leaguer and, so far, has never married.

Cary hails from Hampton, Virginia, an ancient village about 80 miles southeast of Richmond, located where the mouth of the James River meets the lower end of the Chesapeake Bay. Hampton has muddled along for more than 400 years without sinking into oblivion.

It is also known as *Crab Town* for its former main industry. For centuries, tough watermen there harvested blue crabs and oysters from the estuaries leading into the Chesapeake Bay. Local processing houses would buy the daily catch, then ship the fresh seafood to parts far and wide.

"Waterman" was a term for the commercial fishermen who worked along the Thames River in England during the Middle Ages. These sinewy, hardscrabble people brought their skills and traditions with them as settlers to Colonial Virginia, Maryland, and North Carolina, where they settled along the main waterways and plied their trade.

Working watermen have respect for Mother Nature and little else. They are an independent lot, hating interference from outsiders. As Cary's grandfather, Cap'n Johnny Mallory, told me more than once, "Most folks ain't worth the powder and shot to blow em all to hell, son, pure 'n simple."

Cary is the only child of John Mallory the Umpteenth – more than twelve generations had passed since the first John landed in the New World – and his filthy rich wife, the former Elizabeth Montague. Libby, one of *those* Texas Montagues, pronounced her name "Montage", with a flat *a* as in *vague*.

Cary Whiting Mallory was named for her grandmother, Anne Whiting Cary, the late wife of Cap'n Johnny. The Carys, Whitings, and Mallorys were all Old Hampton names of great longevity, some of them dating back to within fifty years after the town's founding in 1610.

They were already Old Hampton at the outbreak of the Civil War in 1861 and managed to survive the terrible conflict, still robust, but largely penniless. Local natives today will tell you that

Hampton is the oldest continuous English-speaking settlement in the United States. If hard-pressed, they might admit that San Augustine and Santa Fe are older but are Spanish-speaking, which seems, to them at least, to be less desirable.

They acknowledge the existence of Jamestown, founded upriver in 1607, but are quick to point out that it was never much more than a smelly, mosquito-infested swamp that did not survive past 1699. Finally, they remind all comers that the Puritans who arrived in Massachusetts on the Mayflower up north in 1620 missed the first boat to Hampton by nearly a full decade.

The city celebrated its 400th anniversary in 2010 with a series of events that garnered modest attention. Hampton's architecture does not do justice to its history, since the town burned smack-dab down to the ground every time there was a war, and a few times for good measure, in between them. Thus, most of its story is buried underground. Some wags proposed that Hampton celebrate its Quadricentennial by once again torching the town, but cooler heads prevailed. Instead there were parades, new historic markers, and some remarkably good books about local history.

Modern Hampton has a few buildings from the post-Civil War period, with most structures dating after World War I. The city's main asset is its extensive waterfront property, with vistas into the Hampton Roads harbor and the lower Chesapeake Bay. People like to say Hamptonians don't do much, but they seem to have enough scratch to keep very nice boats, live in manicured Williamsburg-style waterfront houses, send their kids to good schools, and get season tickets to the Redskins.

Cap'n Johnny Mallory, father of John the Umpteenth, was a working, *gentry* waterman seafood processor. That term meant that he owned his own dead-rise workboats and hired yeoman watermen to harvest the crabs and oysters that were sold for processing in his factory before the product was shipped to up and down the East Coast.

The Cap'n – pronounced *Cap-um* – sold enough shellfish to send his son to the University of Virginia, where the extraordinarily handsome son of the Old Dominion attracted the affection of Dallas Idlewild Club debutante Elizabeth "Libby" Montague. The Texas heiress had been shipped to Sweet Briar to complete her education and to broaden her horizons before embarking on a lifetime of spending her anticipated fortune with grace. Idlewild is the distinguished Dallas gentlemen's club that invites the top city belles to bow before society each year.

Libby and John had *the* wedding of the year in Dallas. There were sixteen bridesmaids in all, a week of parties in tony Highland Park, thousands of wedding gifts, and a reception at the Dallas Country Club that set a new local record for wretched excess.

The Montagues settled enough money and jewelry on Libby to keep her in the style to which she was accustomed, and the newlyweds produced a lovely baby girl within three years of the honeymoon. Little Cary divided her summers between the sprawling Montague ranch outside Dallas and the Hampton waterfront home of Cap'n Johnny, whose wife died when John the Umpteenth was little more than a boy. Cary usually spent winters with her parents abroad, accompanied by a combination governess/nanny, until the child was old enough to be dumped at a Swiss boarding school.

Bad luck struck the Texas family in 1980 when the Montague Lear jet, carrying the senior Montagues, the John the Umpteenths, and the pilot, flew into a massive freak thunderstorm over South Texas en route to a weekend black-tie-and-boots western art sale at an estate outside Houston. Everyone was killed in the crash.

Libby's older brother Bubba, known by some mean-spirited wags as "BB" for Bubba the Boozer, declined to take custody of his 13-year old niece, stating that Cary had inherited "enough damn cash to buy a whole army to raise her." Cap'n Johnny was not amused. He assumed guardianship of Cary and her inheritance, and arranged to bring his granddaughter home to Hampton from Switzerland.

Once he had his gangly, pimpled, and somewhat withdrawn granddaughter settled at Hampton Roads Academy – good academics, private but not snobby – Cap'n Johnny dutifully dug into the Montague family finances. He quickly learned they derived from the four basic Texas food groups: ranching, oil, banking, and real estate.

It would be years later before he told Cary the truth. "Sweetie, that Montague business smelled worse than two-day-old crab scrap in August." Apparently, anyone who had ever lived in Hampton immediately grasps the heavy significance of the analogy.

Cap'n Johnny dug out his best funeral suit, flew out to Texas, and met with Bubba and a plethora of lawyers and corporate executives. He demanded enough money up front to provide Cary with about $100,000 a year for the rest of her life. Then he tacked on the estimated costs of her future education, at a level to match or exceed Libby's, plus a six-figure down payment on her post-college debut season at Idlewild in Dallas. He then secured enough for pin money to ensure she had the cash for clothes and transportation to socialize with the *right* people until she reached age 25, when the corpus of her trust would become due.

Bubba must have been hitting the sauce early that day, because he asked about the costs of a wedding before the lawyers could muzzle him. *That boy's goofy as a huntin' dawg*, Cap'n Johnny thought to himself. But he immediately thanked Bubba for his insight, assured him that a wedding could be handled perfectly well, and more cheaply, in Virginia, and took home another $200,000.

The Virginia waterman left happy, but whiny voices from Texas were heard later to speak of the presence of an unpleasant odor during the negotiations. Bubba's people said it was crabs, but Cap'n Johnny only chuckled and said it smelled like money to him.

As it turned out, the old man was prescient. During the late 1980s the Savings and Loan scandal took down Bubba Montague, who was heavily invested in Texas's leading bank, numerous S&Ls, and a great many shaky development schemes in the New South. The banking and real estate busts were joined by a drop in the price of oil, sinking many Texas billionaires like stones. Bubba avoided jail time, but most of Cary's remaining trust fund vaporized.

Cap'n Johnny invested Cary's initial settlement quite well and could spend modestly on her education. He also bought the accoutrements required to maintain her status as a Montague and an FFV (First Family of Virginia). He even got to bank the money for the debut at Idlewild, because the young woman had absolutely no interest in such social trappings.

As I said earlier, Cary has never married, so the $200,000 investment toward her wedding was still accumulating interest. Prior to his death at 88, Johnny pronounced himself "happier than a pig in slops" about the way Cary's finances had grown.

The Mallory, Cary, and Whiting ancestors must have believed that the initial big sea voyage to Virginia from England was about all they could handle, because subsequent generations rarely moved farther than fifteen miles in any direction from Hampton. *Why tempt fate?* they probably asked.

Granddaddy Mallory decided Cary needed the comfort of relatives and his own close parental attention to help her overcome the bizarre foreign influences that surrounded her during her formative years. There were thousands of cousins living within a 30-mile radius of Hampton, with so much intertwined lineage that the young woman half expected to see relatives with six fingers, crossed eyes, genetic deafness, and other signs of long-term intermarriage. Cap'n Johnny made sure she met them all.

The scion of the Mallory family had a team of workmen to crew his boats and an adequate staff to manage the lucrative seafood processing business, so he had the time to devote considerable attention to Cary, who would accompany him on business trips when the school year allowed.

Johnny had an eye for antique furniture, much of it relegated to the barns and back porches of once-prosperous farms in the Virginia Tidewater. He would drive around in his pickup truck, pay a fair price for the pieces he liked, and sell them to dealers in the larger cities on the East Coast. Before long he was making a significant profit. Cary spent her vacations with Cap'n Johnny, visiting farms in Gloucester, Mathews, Poquoson, and other rural hamlets in counties nearby.

The old man had books on antiques, which she read avidly, and a choice collection of Americana. Cary studied this to train her eyes to discern variations in color, material, texture, or proportion that would differentiate quality original furniture from overly restored or made-up pieces. By her late teens, she could tell the difference between an exceptional quality antique and an average one. The Cap'n made sure she knew how to analyze construction and could spot repairs.

"Stand back and let it speak to you," Cap'n Johnny would command, encouraging her to get an overall impression of each antique before examining the intricacies of its interior

"Here, feel the plane marks," demanded Cap'n Johnny, rubbing his rough fingers along the wood grain on the back of an 18th century chest of drawers. Cary learned to use her nose to smell the faint odor of secondary woods that pointed to the region where an object was made.

"Does it sing to you, sweetie?" Cap'n Johnny would ask, urging her to use her senses to the fullest in her study of each antique.

Most of the Mallorys were short people, wiry in physique, with long noses, reddish tanned skin, and bright blue eyes. Cary got her coloring and height from her mother, and the rest, including a down-to-earth attitude from the Tidewater clan.

Her grandfather's profits from *pickins* helped pay her way to Sweet Briar, where she earned a degree in Art and American Studies. This led to a scholarship to Winterthur, one of the nation's top graduate programs in early Americana, operated jointly by the University of Delaware and the Winterthur Museum.

After earning an MA in Early American Culture in 1991, she joined the curatorial staff at the Division of Political History at the Smithsonian National Museum of American History. At least, that's what the museum used to be called, before the government sold the name to a millionaire for naming rights. It's now known as the Smithsonian Behring Center.

Cary still refers to her stint at NMAH as her *Gothic Interregnum.* Political history collections consist of memorabilia and objects associated with important political movements and leaders. Aesthetics are sometimes secondary when deciding whether to acquire them.

The Smithsonian based its operating approach on the old university model, and the strong practicality of the working watermen culture in the Virginia coastal region was a far cry from the rarefied quasi-academic atmosphere at the museum. Cary recoiled at long meetings, where colleagues espoused politically correct views championing their own small areas of specialization, with little attention paid to the educational needs or interests of the public.

"Why preserve Old Glory?" whined one such curator; "It has no relevance or meaning to Native Americans."

Cary found herself in a museum housing a great collection of artifacts associated with significant dead white men and women, being cared for by curators who seemed to reject them for the very paleness of their original owners' skin.

She argued in vain for exhibitions that would be culturally inclusive, only to see the curatorial committees vote in favor of spotlighting individual minority groups. The trend was to atone for the absence of balanced interpretation in the past, when white culture had completely dominated American historiography and museum education.

Cary embraced the need to balance out earlier omissions but feared that future generations would grow up ignorant of the basic foundations of American history and government. She fully expected someone to ask whose picture was on the $1 bill.

After more than three years of frustration, she finally blew up during a planning session for a major exhibition on the presidency. Since the NMAH (SBC) owned millions of objects under the stewardship of many different divisions, a curatorial department might get space for a major temporary exhibition only once or twice every twenty years. Political History was due for a big show, and the competition within the department was keen.

Several curators groused about having to focus on the presidency at all.

"How trite," sighed a specialist in military flags.

"I think we should focus on the presidential servants," said one curator.

"*Everyone* already knows how the presidents and first families lived."

Given the fragmentation in history education since the 1960s, Cary thought it was doubtful that many Americans could even identify the presidents, much less expound on how they lived. The curators of the First Ladies Hall weighed in for a show on first ladies and were promptly shot down, since they already had a permanent exhibit in the museum, an extreme rarity at the museum.

Jeannine Butler, the world expert on American political campaign memorabilia, delivered her spiel, but the others expressed their conviction that the boys "across the Mall" in the office of the Smithsonian Secretary would want something weightier than buttons and banners to attract millions of visitors.

The revisionists had their day. One curator proposed that the show examine how presidents have abused the Native Americans;

others wanted to show how chief executives had given short shrift to women, Negroes, European immigrants, Jews, Catholics, Asians, poor people, and the handicapped.

Cary had been continuing her Winterthur thesis research on James and Dolley Madison and proposed an exhibit on the Founding Fathers. There were gasps from around the table.

They were all white!

They were all men!

They all believed in slavery. Well, Franklin came around at the end, and Adams didn't have slaves, *but really!*

Were they even relevant?

"We have outstanding collections on the subject, and I believe that the Founders are extremely relevant to the American public," said Cary firmly.

"Public shmublic" sneered one colleague.

Sad and disgusted, Cary felt that her associates preferred to publish and exhibit for their own peers, using the public's money to pay for their research. In their eyes, projects for the public were pop culture, firmly beneath the level of their attention.

She walked out of the meeting, submitted her resignation to the chairman of the department, and drove back to Hampton to see Grandpa Johnny.

"Fuck the eggheads," Cap'n Johnny said. "Go out and make some money."

Cap'n Johnny had used some of Cary's inheritance to buy and sell some choice waterfront property over the years. He invested the profits and offered Cary an advance on her inheritance to stake her in the antiques business. She took his offer, bought the house in Church Hill when prices in the gentrifying neighborhood were still reasonable, and set out to acquire her initial inventory.

Again, Johnny came to the rescue, having set aside some important southern pieces in anticipation that his granddaughter would eventually come to her senses and want to go into a genuine business. He also contacted his network of fellow pickers and dealers. Cary notified her museum associates of her new venture, and soon Cary Mallory Antiques was up and running.

The market in southern decorative arts was growing rapidly when Cary hung out her shop sign in 1996. The important research conducted since the 1960s at MESDA, the Museum of Early Southern Decorative Arts in Winston-Salem, NC, had changed the museum and collecting fields' appreciation for southern craftsmanship, which sometimes attained a very high level of sophistication.

Curators at Colonial Williamsburg, who had earlier published on New England furniture in the collections, turned their attention to studies of regional production closer to home. New money in the sun belt showed a healthy appreciation for locally made antiques, spurring prices for the occasionally odd southern interpretations of English or northern American furniture Curators at the Mint Museum in Charlotte, the High in Atlanta, and the Dallas Museum of Art started buying up southern production.

The established northern museums like Winterthur and the American Wing at the Metropolitan in New York decided to reassess their existing holdings and expand into areas of production below Baltimore, an early and well-identified artisan center. Enthusiastic southern collectors were quick to remind others that Maryland stayed with the North during the Civil War. Baltimore was no longer truly southern.

Eighteenth century fine furniture from Boston, Newport, Philadelphia, and New York continued to bring the highest prices, but it was becoming increasingly scarce. The curatorial grapevine in American decorative arts was small and active. Soon the younger museums, particularly in the sun belt areas, were calling Cary in search of important examples of southern craftsmanship. She supplied these important clients and schooled newer collectors on the stylistic and technical nuances of the regional models.

A rise in interest in African American arts and craftsmanship worked equally well for Cary, whose knowledge of folk art of the South included many documented examples by black artisans. Southern homes with tall ceilings also became excellent display spaces for early American quilts or hooked rugs, both hung like modern paintings. Within four years, Cary could focus on a solid group of collectors and stopped having to keep regular office hours.

CHAPTER 8

MEET HAMILTON COLES – 1998-2000
Cary and Connie

Well, let me just tell you; hearing the voice of Hamilton Coles after an absence of a decade was quite a shock to *moi*, whose fate it had been to comfort poor Cary when the filthy bastard broke her heart in 2000 after a brief but intense affair.

The details of the earlier liaison have a bearing on our story, so I've consulted my old diary entries and can offer a credible summary below.

In 1998, Hamilton Coles was older than most students who matriculated into graduate school at the College of William & Mary, but his application came with impressive credentials. Firstly, he was what is known as a legacy, a close relative of someone who had attended W&M before. The Coles family had attended William & Mary for centuries, not just decades, before Ham's application dropped through the mail slot in the Graduate School Admissions office.

Secondly, Ham's family was of importance outside the cloistered walls of academe. The college was, after all, a state educational institution and had to look at the big picture, particularly with the General Assembly in Richmond controlling a sizeable chunk of the purse strings. His ancestor Edward Coles was a brother of Isaac Coles who served as Secretary to the sacred Thomas Jefferson, when the sage of Monticello was president of the United States. Nor should we forget that TJ himself graced the halls of W&M long before he founded the University of Virginia.

Edward Coles was also a close cousin to Dolley Madison – her mother was a Coles – and he served as secretary to President James Madison until well into his second term. Of significant note was his strong early position against the institution of slavery, and his emigration to the western frontier, where he bought land and freed his servants before taking on the challenge of ensuring that the recent territory of Illinois would remain slave-free. Coles won the battle and was elected second Governor of Illinois, but then suffered defeat in his next run for the office.

Historians at the Omohundro Center at the college, a national hub for studies in early American history, assured admissions officials that manumission was a *very rare occurrence* in Virginia at that time. Edward Coles, they said, was an important historical figure. College admissions decided that his actions would bolster William & Mary's policy of increased diversity and inclusion. Ham Coles' qualifications killed two birds with one stone, according to one member of the Admissions Committee.

The committee also noted with satisfaction that Coles was gloriously rich, and the only male heir to a manufacturing fortune amassed by his grandfather in St. Louis before his death at the age of 90. The reason for the industrialist's long life was attributed less to his living habits than to a stubborn determination to keep making money. Ham was his only grandson.

Candidate Coles' application came with impressive educational credentials. He had attended an outstanding eastern prep school before earning his undergraduate degree at Harvard. Invariably, someone on the committee pouted with disappointment that Coles was a product of the nation's oldest college, with William & Mary being the second oldest, but the dean of admissions stared him down. The college would reap the benefits of out-of-state tuition fees, a princely sum.

Then there was the communication that came from an undisclosed source in the government, indicating that the advancement of Ham Coles' education in history would serve the good of the nation. Upon reviewing the man's resume, the committee noted huge gaps in data, where Coles had disappeared for months, if not years, at a time.

Fortunately, a main training center for the CIA, known as Camp Peary, was within a few miles of the college. Locals were quite accustomed to seeing very intelligent and physically fit young men, and now young women, with sketchy resumes and a tendency to disappear into thin air without warning.

"Forget the resume," said the dean. "He seems to be retired, and we've never yet had a spook blow up the Swem Library. He's in."

Ham fit in well with his classmates, even though he was about ten years older than many other graduate students. He kept somewhat to himself, but many of his colleagues were pulling down extra jobs to make tuition and living expenses, so the atmosphere was more subdued than in undergraduate school. Most of the routine involved attending classes, writing papers, and giving presentations.

Classes were more infrequent, papers due weekly, and presentations a regular exercise before one's peers and the faculty. Ham considered the talks as preparation for a career in teaching.

Every graduate student had an advisor. Ham's was Noel Weekley, the Distinguished Professor in American History, who was also affiliated with the Omohundro. Coles had noted the number of capitalized letters in the scholar's long title, and rightly assumed that someone had assigned him a VIP mentor. He was appropriately humble and earnest when he finally knocked on Weekley's office door.

"How can I help you, son?" asked Weekley, puffing on a pipe and reclining with the smug officiousness of a priest in the confessional. Ham prattled about his classes and interests before mentioning his direct descent from Edward Coles.

"I know Coles!" exclaimed the academician, bolting upright in his chair. Within minutes, the professor decided that Ham should focus on Edward Coles for his MA thesis and Ph.D. dissertation.

Weekley announced grandly that he would personally oversee the work, naturally assigning a Teaching Assistant to handle the mundane day-to-day tasks. Doors would open everywhere for Coles; all would be well. Finally, Weekley assured Ham that the thesis would be worthy of turning into a book that would enrich the field of American history and, quite possibly, earn royalties for the college.

"Son," he said. "You have a million relatives." Coles didn't see Weekley again outside of the occasional class or lecture, until the old man showed up for a photo op in conjunction with the release of Ham's book, *Edward Coles, a Personal and Academic Reappraisal.*

Ham sailed through his coursework toward the doctorate, sometimes suspecting that the CIA, his former employer, had discreetly informed college administrators that *smooth sailing* was the watchword for all concerned. *Or else.*

The agency had given Ham a partial leave of absence in 1995 after his wife of three years was kidnapped, tortured, and murdered by insurgents he was tracking. He and Nancy Hicks had met at a spook party in DC. They felt an immediate attraction that led to their marriage after a courtship of only six months. The couple were apart a great deal of the time, but the bond was strong. Ham was devastated by her murder.

During the early days of his leave, Coles tracked down the leader of the insurgents, abducted him, tortured him, and finally killed him. The former American agent was amazed at the satisfaction he felt from the man's screams, his ragged pleas for mercy, and the appearance of his savaged and bleeding body. After he had disposed of the remains and thrown up everything in his stomach, he went to bed and slept for three days.

The CIA turned its back on the murder, cleverly manufacturing a story that blamed the criminals for turning against one of their own.

After a suitable absence touring several countries in search of a future direction, he was contacted by a representative of the CIA, who offered him a deal he could hardly refuse. Next stop, an advanced degree at William & Mary.

Over drinks at the Trellis Restaurant one evening with Annie Cooper, an attractive associate painting curator at Colonial Williamsburg, Ham learned that some of the foundation's art works had come from Coles relatives living in Pennsylvania and the Midwest.

"Someone named Robbins comes to mind," said Annie, nibbling on her Death by Chocolate. She was too young for Ham, but a welcome visual treat after the long hours spent reading historical volumes and barely legible stained manuscripts in the library stacks. He asked her to check the accession records at CW, and on their next date, she filled him in on her research.

"The family owned three of our portraits of early presidents," she said. "James Madison, Thomas Jefferson, and James Monroe." Madison and Jefferson, both by Gilbert Stuart, were gifts. The Monroe was purchased, but came from the same family. It was painted by John Vanderlyn in 1817. The Madison was done from life in 1804. The Stuart of Jefferson is extremely fine, but it has been deemed a contemporary copy after the life portrait at Monticello. All of them carry a history of having belonged to former president James Madison and hung at one time in his Virginia estate, Montpelier." Ham also learned that the Montpelier estate survived and was located not far from Charlottesville.

"Until 1984, Montpelier was privately owned, making it a public mystery," Annie said. "For many years, it was the residence of

Marion du Pont Scott. Unless someone was heavily into steeple-chase racing, he probably didn't get invited inside the mansion." Mrs. Scott, daughter of industrialist William du Pont, had been an avid horsewoman, but was known to be extremely shy with people outside racing and breeding circles.

"The portraits came to us during the 1940's." she added.

Ham told her that one of the donors to Williamsburg was one of his great aunts. He had not known of the gifts, which were made before he was born. They made a date to see the paintings, which were on display at the reconstructed Capitol building. After the tour, Ham took Annie to lunch in the elegant dining room at the Williamsburg Inn.

The curator told him that the Monroe had hung for many years in the Inn. "Monroe didn't figure prominently in the history of the Colonial Capitol when it was in Williamsburg," Annie said. He had gained prominence in Virginia and then national politics after the seat of government moved to Richmond in 1780.

Ham wondered if the absence of a strong connection to Williamsburg explained why Monroe had been consigned to spend decades of humiliation hanging on the wall in a hotel, but said nothing. The curator was curvy, intelligent, and available for future dates.

During the summer of 1999, Ham went to Illinois to research the Edward Coles Papers at the Chicago Historical Society. Then he moved on to the Coles holdings at the Historical Society of Pennsylvania, located in downtown Philadelphia.

He dutifully contacted family descendants asking for entrées to private holdings of manuscripts and ephemera. Many gave him a warm welcome and free access to their records. Of course, he perused the Madison, Jefferson, and other papers of the leaders of the early Republic, many of them housed in the manuscript division of the Library of Congress or the Alderman Library at the University of Virginia.

In a series of letters between James Madison and Coles, who was in Philadelphia during the late 1820s, the former president thanked his former secretary for intervening on behalf of Payne Todd, Dolley's son by her first marriage to Philadelphia Quaker lawyer John Todd.

Ham checked Todd in William Privale's classic biography of Madison and learned that Dolley Payne's first husband, Quaker attorney John Jr., and a second infant son, William Temple Todd, had died during the yellow fever epidemic that swept Philadelphia during the summer and fall of 1793. John Payne Todd, born in 1792, had survived.

Reading on in the manuscripts, he discerned that Coles had later arranged to get Payne Todd out of jail in Philadelphia on more than one occasion and had also paid some gambling debts there. His ancestor had handled the releases and repayments with discretion. *Early 19th century cover up*, thought Coles, wondering if there was more to the story and just how much Todd had been a burden to the early president and his wife.

Ham learned that Edward Coles' abolition beliefs had led to extensive correspondence on the subject with Madison, Jefferson, and others. Coles was aghast that Madison had not freed his slaves under the terms of his own will.

After retiring from the presidency, Madison had intimated to his Quaker friend that he planned to manumit his slaves upon his death. George Washington had freed his slaves, to become effective upon the death of his wife Martha. In a series of angry letters, after Madison's death in 1836, Coles expressed his shock and disappointment to Dolley Madison that the former president had changed his mind. He was further enraged upon learning that the widowed Dolley had sold some slaves almost immediately after Madison's funeral.

Ham paused to think about the many complex factors at work in the plantation-dominated South during the years prior to the Civil

War. Many states had drafted their constitutions with provisions to outlaw the importation of slaves, and the federal Constitution put a deadline of 1807 on the practice of direct importation.

But the growth of the new Cotton Belt after the 1793 invention of the cotton gin made Virginia slaves more valuable. The non-import law went into effect, but there was no prohibition against interstate sales. At the same time, tobacco, the traditional major Virginia crop for export, had exhausted the soil, leaving planters in need of cash, which could most easily be obtained by selling human property to the new burgeoning planter class in lower South Carolina, Georgia, Alabama, Mississippi, Louisiana, and parts of Kentucky.

Washington had died in 1799. Martha lived until 1802. Rumors had circulated that her life was in constant danger from slaves or sympathizers who would kill her to fully implement the terms of manumission in George Washington's will. Then there had been the quelled slave revolt planned by Gabriel in 1800 in Richmond, and the infamous 1831 slave insurrection in Southampton County, led by slave minister Nat Turner.

Turner and a group of followers had rampaged for several days through farms in the isolated rural area and murdered more than fifty white men, women, and children, using axes and whatever other weapons they could find. Turner remained at large for more than two months, keeping tensions at an all-time high for slave owners.

His confession was recorded by an attorney and published not long after Turner was tried, convicted, hung, drawn, and quartered. The Virginia General Assembly strengthened laws against free Negroes and slaves after the massacre, heightening growing support for abolition of the hated institution in many other, mainly northern, areas of the nation.

Edward Coles had carefully left his home in Virginia and reached the Illinois Territory before he freed his slaves. As to the debts of Payne Todd, Ham made a note to check for additional information in published books on Madison and in the collections at Princeton and other repositories.

Coles consulted the Dolley Madison collections at the Library of Congress, which included letters between the former First Lady, Edward Coles, and other family relatives. Ham also wrote to repositories with small Madisoniana holdings, receiving copies of the archival materials in their care. Nothing panned out.

That fall, Ham met with Annie Cooper again for dinner and discussed his research findings.

"You might as well make a trip up to Montpelier," she advised, giving him the name of the director and curator there. Ham contacted both and drove to Orange in October, when the fall colors were at their height. The road to Montpelier led north from I-64W at Zion's Crossroads, passing through Gordonsville on Route 15. The scenery was outstanding, with rolling hills, large estates set back from the road, and majestic foliage in a riot of yellow, red, plum, and orange colors.

Lots of money, here, he thought. *Even the horses look rich.*

Turning left at the small town of Orange, he continued south on Route 20, passing farms until he saw a Victorian railroad station on his left. Ham took an immediate right at the *Montpelier* sign across from the station and drove to a parking lot adjacent to a one-story visitor center. A frame building nearby held the Montpelier gift shop on the first floor and executive offices above.

Ham entered, climbed the stairs, and was seated in a small reception area while waiting for his appointment with John Abbott, the executive director of Montpelier, a property of the National Trust for Historic Preservation. After a protracted legal battle with the du Pont heirs, the Trust had purchased the mansion house and additional acreage and taken over management of the property.

Before too long, Abbott appeared in a doorway and motioned Ham into his office. After offering him coffee, they sat down to discuss Coles' research and the future of James Madison's home. Abbott was in his late 30s, of medium height, with thick dark blond hair just beginning to pale at the temples, a round face, and hazel eyes. He had the polished manner displayed by many senior administrators for the National Trust, the nation's leading membership institution promoting historic preservation.

"Much of the $10 million that Marion du Pont Scott left to the Trust was used to pay attorneys to clear the property for purchase," he said. "After that, there was little cash on hand to do more than emergency repairs and to keep the place running." He recounted that the Montpelier mansion had a copper roof that cost a cool $1 million to replace. The estate boasted ten miles of paved roads, hundreds of miles of fencing, nearly two dozen separate waste water treatment facilities, and more than 100 outbuildings.

Abbott revealed that the Trust had decided to preserve the du Pont additions to the main mansion in place and would try to bring James Madison to the forefront through its interpretive programs. He cited Winterthur, Hagley, Longwood, and Nemours in the Brandywine Valley of Delaware/Pennsylvania as outstanding examples of the important history and accomplishments of the descendants of E.I. du Pont de Nemours, the Frenchman who emigrated to the U.S. in 1799, establishing a gunpowder plant along the banks of the Brandywine River in Delaware.

Privately, Ham believed that the du Pont story had already been adequately told elsewhere, and that the main reason for keeping the additions in place at Montpelier was a lack of funds to bring Madison back to life in bricks and mortar.

Coles explained his thesis on Edward and summarized his research to date. "I want to get a better understanding of the Madisons and Edward Coles' ties to them," he said.

The director nodded and promised the assistance of his staff and access to the facilities under his control. "We don't have too much primary research material here," Abbott said, and was pleased to learn that Ham had already contacted the curator for an appointment.

Taking his leave, Coles walked over to the Visitor Center to explore the exhibits there. Regular shuttle buses ran from the center to the mansion house, and he wanted to get some context about the site before meeting with the curator, whose office was in the basement of the main residence.

Having read descriptions of Montpelier written during Madison's time in archival papers, Ham was struck by the magnificence of the views, the lushness of the overall setting, the spectacular fall color of the trees, and the intense blue-grey of the Blue Ridge Mountains in the distance. He recalled one visitor describing the atmosphere as *salubrious*, and decided it was apt.

Coles kept an eye out for the shuttle bus, which arrived about ten minutes later. The driver dropped him off at the base of the front portico. There was one other couple on the bus who also disembarked.

The house looked tired and worn, with a cracked stucco exterior in a bilious shade of peach. The front portico was constructed in the Jeffersonian classical style, with columns in the proper orders and a large federal-style, glass-framed front entry. Ham noted with some curiosity that the columns of the front portico extended all the way to the ground, rather than resting on plinths at the floor. A docent met him at the door and led him inside.

Ham told the guide about his appointment. She promptly pressed a button on the wall to call the assistant curator, assuring Ham that he would be met in the parlor in a matter of minutes. The graduate student took a moment to look around. They had passed from a small entry foyer into a large square parlor with elaborate classical trim and three large triple-hung windows along the rear wall. The giant windows let in light from the rear colonnade and garden beyond. The room was in poor condition, with bubbling plaster walls, an obvious sign of long-term water damage from the roof or windows. A handsome, carved marble fireplace surround on his left and a massive overhead chandelier were both clearly of the Victorian era. Some of the detailing looked Madison-era, some appeared to be from du Pont. Coles knew that the exterior of the house bore little resemblance to the original Madison homestead.

William du Pont's extensive remodeling after 1900 had involved adding a second story to the two wings adjoining the main block, and there were additional rooms projecting on the rear that encased, and visually dwarfed, the historic one-story portico centered on the back wall. Little was published about the appearance of the house during the Madison era since the property had remained in private hands.

Suddenly, a stunning, petite young woman entered from a doorway to the far right of the fireplace and offered her hand in welcome. "You must be Hamilton Coles," she said, smiling warmly. She gestured for him to follow her back in the general direction from which she had come, introducing herself as Sally Drennan, assistant curator, and they passed numerous rooms until reaching a door to the basement at the north rear side of the main floor. They descended to the basement, retracing their steps along a hallway to an office area. Sally entered and offered Ham a seat at a conference table loaded with research books and files.

The modern-day main mansion house was an architectural jumble featuring older Madison elements mixed into newer du Pont spaces. Restoration architects approached the puzzle in accordance with national historic preservation standards. The Trust began its work by researching written records of the various alterations and additions over the years before it physically penetrated the walls to reveal historic construction details within the structure itself.

"How did du Pont actually manage the estate?" Ham asked

"For many of the eighty-plus years of the du Pont occupancy, the property operated somewhat like a self-contained feudal village," said Sally. "Employees stayed from generation to generation, were paid in cash, and many spent their paychecks on supplies and groceries at a general store, also owned by du Pont. It's just out on Route 20 across from the rail station."

"I see."

"Yeah, the du Ponts really took care of their staff, including medical expenses. In a sense, the Trust acquired a property where the existing employees knew little about public health services or outside life in the 20th century."

Sally rose from her seat and invited Ham to accompany her on a private tour of the main house

He saw that the original house, built by Colonel James Madison ca. 1750-55 was to the south. After James Jr. married, he had added a thirty-foot expansion to the north in 1797-98 and built the classical portico on the front. During the last expansion in 1809-14, President Madison had enlarged the structure again with the addition of matching one-story wings with nearly identical basement kitchens, a rear portico, and a garden temple. The latter still survived on the front lawn and was positioned over a buried ice house.

The mansion completed around 1814 by James Madison was befitting of a president, thought Ham, as he walked onto the rear classical portico. Sally explained that the architectural research represented the early part of the second phase of what the Trust dubbed the *Search for Madison*.

Ham thought the designation was more than apt. *I hope they can find poor Madison in this sprawling Edwardian pile.* Back in the house, Ham saw architectural conservators examining lath and plaster behind discreet holes made in the walls. After a quick tour of the other rooms on the main floor and the second story, they returned to the basement.

Ham explained his work on Edward Coles and his interest in learning more about Coles' personal relationship with the Madisons, including additional information about Madisoniana that ended up in the hands of the Coles, and, finally, the activities of Dolley's son, Payne Todd.

Sally sighed.

"Well, it's safe to say that Payne Todd screwed up everything he touched during his miserable life," she said. It'll take millions of dollars and decades of work to figure out where the Madison's possessions went after they left Montpelier."

"You're obviously *not* a big Payne Todd fan," Ham said dryly.

"To know him is to despise him," said the curator, shaking her head. Then she added by way of total condemnation, "He was a complete ne'er-do-well."

Well, that's telling 'em sister, thought Ham, resisting an urge to smile. "Why does he bother you so much?" he asked.

"He made our jobs so much harder." She continued, elaborating about how he had hocked silver and sold furniture to neighbors from the back of an "old gig driven by a blind horse."

"Is there a simpler way to learn more about him? You know, without having to be a psychiatrist or a specialist in the decorative arts. I just need the big picture."

"Cary Mallory can explain it," Sally said.

"Who and where is he?"

"She's a woman. Cary's at Montpelier today updating her research files. She's working from the scholar's apartment located elsewhere on the grounds." Sally went on to explain that Cary had enrolled for a Ph.D. at the University of Virginia and was organizing materials for her dissertation, an extension of her Winterthur Master's thesis on Madisoniana. With that, she walked to her desk and buzzed Mallory, who invited her to send Ham along.

"She has extensive notes on Madison objects and a lot of re-search information," said Sally, adding somewhat ruefully that Cary Mallory was not particularly fond of the way the Trust was handling the estate. Cary argued that the mansion was unintel-ligible after the many du Pont additions and should be restored to its original appearance during the time the president lived here. Ham could sympathize with her view, based on his brief tour of the property.

Sally then drew a map leading from the main house to the apartment, which was located past the old laundry. Ham ambled down the hill behind the mansion along a road that led between an old laundry building on the left and a dilapidated greenhouse on the right. The road split in two directions at the bottom of the hill. On the right across the road, and a short distance up another hill, was a two-story frame house, obviously of the du Pont era. Ham strode toward it and saw Cary Mallory emerge from the front door just as he entered the yard. She appeared firm-jawed and handsome, her blond hair pulled behind her ears.

"Mr. Coles, I'm Cary Mallory. I apologize for asking you to meet me here instead of in the main curatorial office." She spoke with a deep Virginian accent, peppered with shades of something farther north. She appeared to be about thirty, of medium height with long blond hair, brilliant grey-blue eyes, angular features and a full mouth. She wore conservative dark slacks and a white silk blouse over her slender frame. Ham saw no jewelry except a pair of gold, pearl and enamel drop earrings, obviously from the Victorian era. He found her smile captivating.

"This building has been converted into a dormitory for visit-ing scholars and students of the Constitution," Cary explained, escorting him to a small parlor. Once seated, Ham outlined his research and interest in delving into Madisoniana and the per-sonal relationship between Edward Coles, the Madisons, and Payne Todd.

Cary sighed and looked away.

"I keep getting long sighs when I mention Payne Todd," Ham said.

Mallory laughed from deep in her throat. "That bad, huh?"

"You bet."

They agreed to meet the following week at her home in Richmond. Mallory gave him directions and asked him to bring whatever documentation he already had from his research.

"Sounds good," he said. "I look forward to it."

We'll see" said the Madison expert.

CHAPTER 9

RICHMOND – OCTOBER 1999
Connie and Cary

A week later, Ham made the 45-minute drive to Richmond from Williamsburg. The ride from the 5th Street exit into downtown and up to Church Hill put him at Cary's door at noon. He took in the asymmetrical layout of the antebellum house and admired the small, classically-inspired white porch. The front yard boasted a decorative iron fence, a design accessory for which Richmond was famous.

After Ham rang the bell, Cary appeared wearing dark slacks again and a loose-weave, aqua oversized sweater. A gargantuan Chesapeake Bay retriever sat at her side. She introduced her as "my baby Amanda." The beast shamelessly sniffed Ham's crotch and wagged her tail. Her gold eyes warning him to *behave or be lunch*.

Cary turned from the door and walked into the house. Ham stood stock-still in the doorway, waiting for the dog to issue a formal invitation. Finally, baby Amanda smiled. Chesapeakes are sometimes called "Smileys" for their unique grin, which was a combination of a sneer, a real smile, an attack of gas, and a show of giant fangs before an attack to the jugular vein. Ham knew the breed and sensed nothing untoward, noting that Amanda's tail was still

59

wagging. Then she turned and padded after her mistress into the inner recesses of the house. Ham followed Amanda cautiously.

"Coffee?" asked Cary from the kitchen.

Condiments and lunch fixings were already set out on an antique drop-leaf table in one corner, along with mugs and a plate of cookies.

"Yes, please," said Ham, taking her invitation to sit down at the table. The dog sat down next to Ham and placed its huge head, complete with a 30-inch neck, on his lap. Her eyes turned up to him expectantly.

You'll get the entire plate of food if you want it, girl, Ham swore to himself, praying that the dog was neither overbred nor overly hungry. He ignored the drool on his designer pants leg.

The kitchen was modern but retained its old windows, baseboards, and ceiling moldings. Cary was obviously a cook, since he saw an extensive array of gadgets, a small Vulcan range, a Sub Zero, and other appliances only a true foodie would need.

Ham saw that she had resisted the new trend for granite counter tops, opting for porcelain tiles with a dark mortar. The effect, with a tile floor, art on the walls, and the traditional architecture, was clean, handsome, and successful. The room was warm and welcoming, but ultimately functional. The sandwich bread seemed to be home made, not carry-out from Ukrop's or a local bakery.

"Help yourself," said Cary, making a half sandwich for herself. Ham carefully built his lunch, occasionally dropping pieces of meat and cheese for the dog. *Thanks be to God the Chesapeake is trained with a soft mouth.* She took the treats without removing any of Ham's hand or arm.

"Do you hunt her?"

"No, she's a house pet," said Cary, adding that her family had raised Chesapeake hunting dogs for decades. She admitted that she had only three months to train Amanda to mind her before the animal turned into a true threat to her owner and the world at large.

"My family taught me to realize that a 12-week old Chesapeake is already smarter than I am, and by four months will be stronger than I am. So, the initial training period is critical." She reached over to scratch Amanda's curly brown behind. The dog stretched her neck joyfully, lay down, and rolled over for a tummy rub.

"How does one train a Chesapeake puppy?" Ham asked. He only knew that water torture wouldn't do the trick. The breed seemed to like to break through ice to get to a duck in distress, if only to finish it off in its giant maw.

"Well, you have to get its attention first." Cary stroked her belly.

"How?"

"They say you get the attention of a golden lab by hitting it with a wet noodle between the eyes. A regular lab will respond to a rolled-up newspaper. A Chesapeake requires a good swat with a two-by-four."

"You hit her with a wooden board?"

"Well, actually a broom. It got her attention, and after that she responded well to verbal training. They're very physical dogs. We don't have them long, only about ten or twelve years."

Amanda shifted her golden eyes to Ham, who saw wisdom in her gaze. It was as if her eyes were making a statement while asking a question. *You're here and safe because she says it's okay. One wrong move and you will vanish from the face of the Earth. Any questions, mister?* Her tail thumped with contentment. She let out a breathy sigh that hit him like a foul gust of wind in a gale, then let her massive head fall to the floor for a nap.

"So, tell me about your dissertation," Cary said.

Ham exhaled and tried to relax. He covered the basics of his research and explained what he had found to date.

"Did you review the Payne Todd papers at LC?" asked Cary.

Ham did not recall them, but Cary filled him in. They were late papers – many of them between Dolley and her son after Madison died – and included a brief diary that Todd kept during the first half of the 1840s. Ham did not recall them, checked his bibliography, and found no reference.

"You need the papers," said Cary. "They're a part of the puzzle."

"Puzzle?"

Cary nodded and sipped her coffee. Amanda snored from the floor.

"Read the diary in LC. Double-check the Dolley Madison and Cutts family papers, particularly the late ones. Then get back to me and I'll tell you more,"

"That's it?"

"For now."

They rose from the table and shook hands. Cary invited him to call as soon as he was done. "Don't worry about Amanda," she added. "She never forgets a scent. You'll be welcome back."

—⟨+⟩—

Ham made a return trip to the Library of Congress and asked for the collections of manuscripts, which together took two days to read. Todd's diary was very disturbing. He had kept it sporadically between 1842 and 1844. It revealed a compulsive man who recorded his daily intake of alcohol, his bowel movements, his DT's, and his futile attempts to get himself under control. Ham saw that Dolley's son indeed had sold furnishings from Montpelier, carting relics around the countryside in an old "gig with a blind horse."

The papers, when combined with the late materials from the Dolley Madison collection, revealed the mother and son's frantic efforts to raise funds at the end of her life. They had planned to raffle off silver and art works, all testimony to the fact that Dolley had failed to heed her late husband's warnings to keep Todd's expenses in check.

What was wrong with her? Couldn't she see that what he was doing would ruin her?

CHAPTER 10

WILLIAMSBURG – DECEMBER 1999

Ham called Cary again just before Christmas break to ask for another meeting. This time she agreed to drive to Williamsburg.

"Seems only fair," she said over the phone.

They met on a cold December late morning at his apartment near the historic area. He had promised to take her out for a meal at Merchants Square, the location of several fashionable eateries in the area.

This time Cary wore a designer dress and low heels. She also wore light makeup, which set off the blue of her eyes. Ham thought she looked spectacular. The pearls at her neck and in her ears, were heirlooms. She wasn't a ravishing beauty, he thought, but an interesting one.

At lunch Ham showed her more of his research, pages and pages of notes along with primary sources and documents. He grinned as he placed the last of his notes on the table, proud of all that he had collected.

She nodded and handed him a microfilm. "This tape is from a small historical collection. You'll have trouble reading it. The copy's bad, but the originals are worse. There are some Payne family notes from the late 18th century, then two diaries Payne Todd kept, one of them dating back to 1818. They're partly in code.

"Code?"

"Yeah. If you haven't read the full correspondence between Madison and Jefferson, you won't understand the impulse Todd had for writing in code. It was his pathetic attempt to replicate the writings of his two role models."

"Okay."

"Look, I'm sharing this with you because it ties into the efforts that Edward Coles made later to save Payne Todd from himself, and to protect the Madison name."

"Why haven't you published it?"

"It contains little information about objects, and mostly I find it distasteful. You can credit me for leading you toward this collection in a footnote if you wish. Obviously, the archive must give you permission to publish."

Ham took the microfilm and placed it in his briefcase.

Ham saw that Cary had a healthy appetite, a trait he liked in a woman. She was intelligent and well-versed on many subjects. He realized she also had a dry sense of humor, was very self-effacing, and could tell stories in the best southern tradition. Ham laughed heartily at some of her tales of professional explorations and adventures in the antiques business. He began to open about his own life and shared some of his ambitions for pursuing an advanced degree in middle age, and his hopes for sharing his education with others.

Cary listened intently. Ham noticed that she rested her chin on her right hand, eating with her left.

"Southpaw? He asked, and she confessed that she came from a family of lefties, destined to live shorter lives because the world was designed to function right-handed.

Over coffee, Ham looked Cary in the eye.

"So, what else is there to this story, Cary?

She thought for a minute. "I guess something's missing. There are family secrets we don't know."

" What do you think? I mean, if you had to guess."

"Dolley's missing papers," she said. "She wanted some things hidden from history and went to great pains to see that they were."

"Tell me."

"On her deathbed, Dolley asked her two trusted nieces to take a carpet bag, stuff it full of personal papers and some family spoons, and remove it from her house, to keep the materials out of the hands of her son, Payne Todd. From there the two girls made off with the papers."

Ham nodded, unflinching and considering her blue-gray eyes.

"We can trace the spoons through the estate of Annie Payne, but little's known about most of the papers. I mean, the letters might be personal correspondence between James and Dolley, but the couple was rarely separated during their marriage. Also, materials from those brief periods survive in libraries and museum archives."

"So, what do your think's in those letters?"

"I can't help but think they have to do with the packet of materials Madison instructed John Payne to give to Dolley after his death. Madison said they contained evidence of nearly $20,000 in Payne Todd's debts that he had paid without his wife's knowledge. The family account about the packet also states that Todd's total debts through the years were upward of $40,000."

"A huge amount of money at the time."

"Right. One of the mysteries I've tried to solve is the actual source of the many artworks Todd purchased for Montpelier during his stay in Europe. The total cost to Madison was more than $6,500, a sum larger than the annual salary paid to the secretary of state. Did Madison order Todd to buy them or were they yet another unexpected debt? I'd like to know."

In Ham's studies, he had grown familiar with the politics of the time. In response to Russian Tsar Alexander I's offer to mediate a settlement to the war between Britain and the United States, Madison had appointed Albert Gallatin, John Quincy Adams, and James Bayard to the foreign delegation. Todd was named one of the secretaries to the commission.

"The notes say that Madison gave Todd $1000 for spending money during his European trip."

Ham had just read about this portion of history. Madison had believed that the peace commission would last about six months. *Ha!* The 300-ton Neptune, which sailed in the spring of 1813, carrying the commissioners, their attaches, and four servants, was at sea for six weeks. The delegation went first to Gothenburg, Sweden and detoured to Copenhagen before arriving in St. Petersburg late in July. The tsar was away at the time. Gallatin and the others were received by John Quincy Adams and the Russian Chancellor, Count Romanzov.

The Americans went to the tsar's summer palace at Tsarskoe Selo and had dinner with Count Ovarovsky. In late October 1813, the commissioners and aides were presented to the dowager empress Maria, Grand Dukes Nicholas and Michael, and the Court. In November, Payne Todd and another aide left St. Petersburg via Gothenburg for three weeks in Paris. In January 1814, Gallatin and the others left via Amsterdam for London.

Madison added Henry Clay and Jonathan Russell to the commission, who went off to meet the other commissioners in London. The delays in getting the British to agree to a location for negotiations had taken the better part of a year, and the English did not want to allow Alexander to mediate. They implied that this was a dispute between Great Britain and her colonies, making it a family matter. In doing so, they basically ignored the American Revolution and the 1783 Treaty of Paris that granted independence to the new United States.

Gallatin tactfully suggested that the negotiations be moved to Ghent, which was geographically closer to the site of the European

Congress in Vienna, where the European heads of state would divide up the territory earlier claimed by Napoleon for his Empire. Madison agreed to the change of venue.

Gallatin, the Swiss-born financier and diplomat, had arrived in London in the spring of 1814 and finally met with Tsar Alexander there in June. Delays in communications between the president and his commissioners played havoc with efforts to end the war. In October 1814, Madison had instructed Gallatin to give up most of the U.S. demands and see if he could achieve a peace based on the *status quo ante bellum*. In short, get us out of this conflict fast!

The British and U.S. delegations finally met at the table in Ghent on November 2. An agreement to return to the status quo was reached at last, and a treaty was signed by both commissions on Christmas Eve, 1814. Word of the Treaty of Ghent would not reach the U.S. until February 1815, when it was promptly ratified by the Congress.

Madison eventually heard from nearly every member of the peace commission about Payne Todd's increasing dissipation during the mission. There were early leaks about Todd's behavior in Russia, beginning in the fall of 1813. Payne was being treated like a prince. He had fallen in love with a Russian countess, they said.

"Madison must have gritted his teeth in sheer frustration," remarked Cary, before continuing the tale.

It was not until October 1814 that Payne Todd wrote to Madison to inform him that negotiations in Ghent were proceeding slowly and to commiserate about the August burning of Washington by the British. Also, in October 1814, George Dallas, an aide to the commission, arrived in Washington to deliver dispatches to the president, telling him the negotiations had accomplished very little. Dallas told Madison that Payne Todd, had left for three weeks in Paris and had remained there for three months, delaying his return to the delegation in hopes of being presented at Court to the French king. Gallatin had tried to intervene and failed.

After the peace, Madison awarded some of his commissioners with new diplomatic postings in Europe, and the rest returned to the U.S. William H. Crawford of Georgia was serving as Ambassador to France during the period and left England with Commissioner James Bayard earlier in the summer of 1815. The two men had Payne Todd's luggage with them. Todd missed the boat and did not leave England until the end of July, accompanying Albert Gallatin. It was Crawford who wrote to Madison in August 1815, informing the president that Todd's luggage had arrived with them when their ship landed in New York. There was much more luggage than expected.

Prior to his stepson's return, Madison learned that Baring Brothers, the leading banking house in London, had extended considerable funds to Payne Todd during the young man's trip abroad. The bill came to $6,500 and included a diverse collection of artworks that Todd had purchased for Montpelier. This amount was on top of the $1000 that Madison had sent earlier, having been assured by one of the commissioners that the sum would adequately cover Payne's expenses for the negotiations and some travel abroad.

The wayward son did not return to Montpelier until the fall of 1815, displaying very French manners when he did.

"The artwork was extensive," said Cary. "It took a great deal of effort to ship it from New York to the Madison's rural estate in the foothills of the Blue Ridge Mountains in central Virginia. Lacking a nearby port, the Madisons had to arrange for shipping over land from Fredericksburg. One religious painting measured 16 feet by 8 feet. It was so large it wouldn't fit into a regular cart."

The fourth president and his family were respectable Anglicans who owned copies of the Bible and the Book of Common Prayer. Religious icons, particularly those of immense proportions, had no place in his residence. "I wish I could have seen Madison's face when the servants unpacked the giant painting, a depiction of the Supper at Emmaus, originally designed for the altar in a Dutch church."

"Dolley was almost certainly no help in identifying the other religious works. More than a dozen of them were included in the booty from abroad. Raised a Quaker, whose meeting houses were devoid of decoration of any kind, she had never studied the iconography of Catholic art." Cary noted.

"Of course, she probably recognized the painting of Jesus being lowered from the cross, another painting showing him in life, and the well-known theme of the expulsion of Adam and Eve from paradise, but I bet she was lost in trying to identify some of the other subjects."

"Give me some examples," urged Ham.

"I don't know who gave her the art history lesson, but in an inventory of oil paintings at Montpelier that she made on July 1, 1836, Dolley had assigned titles to most of the works. One painting we know depicts a naked young woman, whose hands are partly covering her exposed breasts. In Dolley's list, it is titled *Magdalen*. Madison had a good knowledge of the subjects from his extensive readings. Payne Todd could have patiently explained to her that a landscape she much admired depicted the Flight into Egypt. In addition to the predominantly gloomy religious art works, there were genre scenes – a popular form in Northern Europe – additional landscapes, and some depicting themes from classical mythology. The painting of Pan cavorting with some Nymphs – probably more nudity – may have struck Dolley as pagan, and a reputed Titian shows up as 'Saint Helena' in one list and 'Mistress of Titian' in another. On the other hand, it's entirely possible that Dolley may have wanted to preserve some of her privacy by keeping personal letters out of the hands of future historians."

"You mean she might have deliberately destroyed correspondences with President Madison?" Ham was surprised, having assumed that the Founders were careful to preserve every suitable word for posterity.

Cary nodded.

"But what about the voluminous correspondence between John and Abigail Adams?" Ham had read some of the books based on their letters.

Cary shrugged. "Abigail seems to have had no qualms about preserving her intimate writings with her husband. Maybe it was one of those frugal Puritanical urges. You know, waste not, want not."

"Where did the Annie Payne materials end up?"

Cary outlined the line of dispersal of the Madison collection. "It began with intermittent sales that Todd made to neighbors in Orange County to get ready cash. After the Madisons' deaths, there were several sales at Montpelier, two sales in Washington, D.C., and an important sale of the Annie Payne materials in 1899 in Philadelphia."

Ham shook his head. Payne Todd had forced his relatives to attend public auctions, where they purchased mementoes of their illustrious relatives. "The family must have despised him."

"To put it mildly. Everyone in Orange County came to hate him. In fact, when I was first performing research down there, one of the old timers shared a ditty that the locals used to recite about Todd."

> *Here lies the body of ol' Payne Todd;*
> *He's not dead; he's drunk, by God.*
> *He's cheated the poor and robbed from the rich;*
> *Now he's gone to hell, the son of a bitch!"*

Their conversation turned to the Madison-Kunkel Collection that was sold in Philadelphia in 1899. Ham asked about the connection to the Madisons and learned that Mary Kunkel was the only child of Annie Payne, who had married a Washington physician named Dr. James Causten shortly after Dolley died. Anna herself died in 1852, followed by Causten only a few years later, and the orphan

Mary Causten was raised by others. She eventually married a man named Kunkel.

The items that did not go off on the block remained with Mary and her descendants, who sold some things and eventually turned the rest of them over to the Greensboro Historical Museum. Why? Because Dolley Payne had been born in Guilford County, near the present site of Greensboro, North Carolina.

⟞⟊⟝

Ham and Cary had their first date two weeks after Ham returned from Greensboro. By Valentine's Day they were splitting their time between Richmond and Williamsburg, seeing each other as often as possible. The sex was frequent and steamy. Just as importantly, they enjoyed sharing a common interest in history and the Madison/Coles families. Cary found herself wondering if their relationship would mature into something long-term. Ham rarely talked about his family or his late wife, and Cary remained hesitant to take him to Hampton to meet Cap'n Johnny.

Then, in May 2000, Ham abruptly broke it off. He did so in a terse and startling note Cary pulled from her mailbox one afternoon while taking a break from her dissertation.

Cary, I am sorry. I cannot continue our relationship.
Be well, Ham

CHAPTER 11

MONTPELIER – MORNING, MAY 25, 2011
John Abbott

At Montpelier, John Abbott called Bob Read, the editor of the Papers of James Madison at the University of Virginia, to invite him to a special meeting at Montpelier. After getting his agreement to meet at 11:00 that morning, he called Will Privale, the nation's leading Madison historian, at his northern university office, and arranged to conference him in with Read. The county sheriff was contacted and arrived within minutes of Read, followed by Hamilton Coles, whom Abbott introduced to the group. Abbott explained that Coles had done a lecture and book signing of his biography on Edward Coles at Montpelier in 2002, and later taken a faculty post at William & Mary in the history department. Abbott noticed that in the nine years since their last meeting, Coles' hair had started to gray, but he still looked fit.

Ham shook hands with the sheriff and the editor before winking at Abbott. Once the men were seated, Abbott picked up the phone and conferenced in the academic historian. Sheriff Leigh took control from there. After thanking Abbott, Coles, the archivist, and Dr. Privale for participating on such short notice, the sheriff asked for access to Abbott's computer and plugged in a portable file.

"What's your email, Professor?" Leigh asked the historian. Then he typed the address into the computer and sent the file.

Privale acknowledged receipt of the document. "I'm all ears," he said.

The sheriff opened a folder and removed the original letter, which had been properly supported on acid free mat board and encased in a clear envelope. He handed it to the editor of the Madison Papers for examination.

"John, the letter is clean for prints," said Leigh to the Montpelier president. Ham was not surprised.

Abbott cleared his throat. "This letter bears a date of 'May 16, 1816, Montpelier,' and is written entirely in French. It's incomplete and contains no formal salutation and no signature. We have translated the brief text.

I am in receipt of your letter of March 15 and can assure you that arrangements are being made to satisfy your wishes on the matter in que... [paper torn off here].

"Can you tell me who wrote this letter, and to whom?" Abbott asked.

Bob Read was silent while reading the manuscript. Then he handed it back to the sheriff and cleared his throat. He asked if everyone concurred with the accuracy of the translation. Everyone in the group nodded. Read then informed Privale that he was examining the original document. No one likes to make an attribution from a copy.

"It seems to be Madison's handwriting," said Read. "This fragment is not connected directly to any of the manuscripts known to the Papers. Offhand, I have no idea to whom he wrote the letter or where he sent it. It bears the month and year date, and Madison's location. He spent most of his summers at Montpelier to avoid the risk of malaria in Washington and was present at the estate during May in 1816. The salutation mentions only 'Monsieur,' a common formal address to half the educated men in Europe that that time."

"The subject is vague," Professor Privale admitted. "Madison states that he has made arrangements to handle the matter 'in question.' As president of the United States, there were many 'matters' in question on any given date." The historian agreed with the editor's identification of the author. On the nature of the "matter in question," he asked for a moment to think.

"Dr. Coles," Dr. Privale said, "I assume you're here in your capacity as a leading expert on Edward Coles." Before Coles could reply, the historian continued. "Gentlemen, I believe you have your answer sitting in the room with you, if I'm not mistaken. Please, Dr. Coles."

"Well, as you all know," said Ham, "in 1816, President Madison asked Edward Coles to serve as a special emissary to Russia. Coles had left Madison's employ, but he was a close cousin to former First Lady Dolley Madison, and almost like a son to Madison himself. Coles made a preliminary trip west in 1815 to scout for land, returning to Virginia to get his affairs in order before settling in the Illinois frontier. He planned to free his slaves on the second journey; in Virginia, one could only free slaves by the terms of a legal will. Coles was hesitant to accept the posting abroad, and it took the president some time to secure his agreement."

"Professor, would you like to explain why Coles was asked to go to Russia?" asked Read.

"There was a diplomatic incident that caused a rupture in U.S.-Russian relations. Namely the trial and conviction of Russian Consul Nicholas Koshkoff in Philadelphia. Koshkoff was accused of raping a twelve-year-old house maid. Russian Minister André de Daschkoff wrote Tsar Alexander I, insisting that the conviction was a violation of the laws of international diplomatic immunity, which was not the case at all. The tsar was furious, of course. He canceled the privileges of the American *chargé d'affaires* in St. Petersburg and barred the agent from appearing at the imperial palace, thereby freezing trade relations between the United States and Russia. Madison then approached Edward Coles, in part because the president trusted the young man's discretion. Coles left for Russia late in the summer of 1816, traveling alone on the Prometheus, a Navy ship of war with a crew of fifty seamen. The Prometheus arrived on September 30 at Kronstadt Island in the Gulf of Finland, about 35 miles from St. Petersburg."

"Please continue," said Read.

"The Russians didn't know quite how to deal with the young envoy. Coles was not an ambassador or *chargé d'affaires* and Tsar Alexander I was away, having left Count Karl Nesselrode to handle his affairs. At one point, Russian officials even applied flames to Coles' papers of introduction, believing they might contain alternate instructions written in invisible ink. After repeated delays, Coles was finally allowed to enter St. Petersburg. Once there he learned that Levett Harris, the American *chargé* who had resigned, would be permitted to serve as liaison between Coles and Count Nesselrode. Coles' appearance in Russia impressed the tsar, who, after reviewing the American report on the Koshkoff incident, agreed to resume diplomatic relations with the United States. Alexander also recalled both Koshkoff and Daschkoff."

"This took some time, if I'm not mistaken," said Privale.

"It did. Diplomacy moved at a snail's pace in imperial Russia," Ham continued. "Coles was forced to spend three months in St. Petersburg during the negotiations. Payne Todd wrote to his cousin, offering advice about people to meet and places to visit in the Russian capital. By his own account, Coles was welcomed warmly by the Russian aristocracy and enjoyed many entertainments there before he dispatched the Prometheus to return to the United States and set out alone for his own grand tour of Europe.

If Coles kept a diary during his European tour, no one has located it.

"I'd have to agree that the letter most likely referred to the Koshkoff incident," Privale said. "This would seem like the likely reason for Coles' extraordinary trip to Russia."

"So, does this seem like the best working hypothesis?" asked Read. One by one, members of the group slowly nodded.

After a few pleasantries, the professor rang off. The editor of the Madison Papers turned to John Abbott and asked about the provenance of the letter fragment.

"Also, I'm wondering why the sheriff's here," Read said. Sheriff Leigh had just left to visit the facilities.

"You don't miss a thing, do you, Bob?"

Abbott swore the editor to secrecy and leaned in. "We had a break-in," he said. "At the mansion. It was last night. The security alarm was activated, summoning Montpelier's onsite staff and officers from the sheriff and fire departments. It's customary for the sheriff himself to appear in cases involving threats to Montpelier or its priceless treasures."

"And the fragment?" Bob asked.

"Left in an envelope on the floor of the rear portico, leaning against one of the triple-hung windows. Contact with the window activated the alarm."

"So, the letter has no provenance." Read said. Abbott half-expected the editor to grab the manuscript, spirit it back to UVA, and record it as an accession in the Alderman Library there.

When Leigh returned, he clearly saw the gleam of potential acquisition in the editor's eyes.

"Bob," said the sheriff. "We've had a series of robberies in the county over the last month. For all we know, the fragment may have been in the possession of some local family here since the contents of Montpelier were dispersed well over a century and a half ago."

"I understand, Sheriff."

"Believe me, the letter will remain with the sheriff's office until every effort's been made to find its rightful owner." Abbott did not mention that the manuscript would soon be on its way to the FBI.

With that, Bob Read rose, thanked Abbott, nodded to the sheriff and Coles, and took his leave, escorted by John Abbott. The meeting was over, leaving Leigh and Coles alone in the conference room. "You think he bought all that shit?" Leigh asked.

"You bet," he said, smiling. They laughed at once.

Although the two Madison specialists couldn't have known it, Ham Coles had another reason for sitting in on the meeting. He had called John Abbott on a secure line late on May 24 to provide a brief on the multiple invasions. First, Ham explained his long involvement with the CIA and his subsequent position at Homeland Security.

"Were you a spook during your graduate work at William & Mary?" asked Abbott out of curiosity.

Ham confirmed his involvement and gave Abbott a heads-up about the impending investigation and his desire to use Montpelier as one of the bases of operation for the team.

"John, I'm in a bit of a bind about one aspect of the investigation. I wonder if you could help me out."

"Ham, we're all in a bind. How may I be of assistance?"

"I need Cary Mallory on the team. It's just the assets she could bring to the investigation."

Abbott agreed about her potential value but knew that she could be ornery.

"You see, Cary and I have a history together."

Abbott's eyebrows shot up. "Go on," he said calmly.

"Cary and I had a thing going for about four months back in 2000 when I was getting my degrees at William & Mary. I haven't seen her since. I didn't do a very respectable job of breaking it off."

"Did she know about your intelligence work?"

"No, not a clue," he stammered. It was hard to share personal information with Abbott, who he barely knew.

"Sounds like this damn thing's risen up to bite you right on the ass, hasn't it?"

"Well said," confessed Ham. "Look, I might need to borrow some of her time. What's the deal with her contract with Montpelier?"

"I don't know, really. I can find out."

"We're meeting this lunch, but maybe it'd be best if I meet with her this afternoon. That way we could get her cooperation with the investigation before we get the ball rolling."

"Okay, great. And look, any monetary loss to Montpelier caused by shifting her workload will be borne by DHS. And tell her she'll be compensated well by the government for her assistance with the investigation."

Abbott explained that Cary's main job was to double-check and update the collections files at Montpelier. Although she had turned over most of her research years before, the collections had grown, and Montpelier wanted her to check new accessions against her notes in search of additional documentation. "Thanks again for all your help," Ham said.

"God speed," was all Abbott could muster. He shook his head, thinking about his own history with volatile women. "And good luck."

⋙⋘

Ham thought things over during his walk to Cary's apartment on the estate. He was carrying sandwiches for a light lunch before the afternoon conference. Mallory was living in a small, restored house not far from the Constitution Center. Her current services were being paid by a grant. Abbott had assured Coles he could arrange an extension.

Ham thought back on their relationship and smiled. He recalled their intimate moments. After a wild weekend at the Homestead resort, they had settled into a steady commute between Richmond and Williamsburg. Cary drove up to Montpelier several times a month to update her research and meet with her advisor at UVA, while Coles settled down to block out everything in the world while he worked on his dissertation on Edward Coles. He dumped Cary long before he sailed through his orals, completed his thesis, successfully defended it, and was offered a chance to publish the dissertation.

Ham was still uncertain about the exact reasons for breaking things off with Cary. He knew he was still traumatized at the time by the loss of his wife and blamed his own involvement in government intelligence for her death. Of course, he never told Cary about his work with the CIA.

His book was in press when the terrorist attack on 9/11 led to the formation of the new Department of Homeland Security. Ham's former job overseeing the protection of national landmarks was reshaped into a special and much larger protection sector within DHS. Provisions of the new Patriot Act and other legislation made anti-terrorist efforts to protect the nation's landmarks a full-time job. No one could forget that the plane that crashed in Pennsylvania was probably headed for the White House, the patriarch of all American historic homes.

Their mutual friends told him that she was devastated by the abruptness of the breakup. Connie Taliaferro had phoned in the middle of the night, drunk, and called Ham every name in the book. "How dare you treat someone who loves you this way?" he asked. Ham never heard another word from Cary Mallory.

Late in 2002, Ham took a position in the history department at William & Mary. He remained there while the new sector within DHS was being established, with its main offices in Washington. His new job called for close coordination with the National Park

Service, and by the fall of 2003 he resigned from the college and moved into a small house in Old Town Alexandria.

Ham's surprise call to Cary in Richmond the night before had barely prepared her for their meeting.

"So, what's going on?" Cary asked, a moment after Ham knocked on her door. She wore slacks and a silk top. Ham thought she had changed very little during the past decade. A different dog, even larger than Amanda, stood by her side. She turned to the dog and introduced her to their guest. "Lizzy, this is Ham Coles, an old friend. Try to like him."

Why the fuck does she always have to get Chesapeake Bay retrievers? Ham smiled inanely at the behemoth. *They're entirely too smart, too strong, too mean, and too protective of their owners.* He reached down and gently patted her head. Lizzy sniffed the bag of sandwiches, grinned, and examined his privates. She licked his hand dutifully and disappeared into the interior of the house, leaving them alone at the front door.

"She looks a lot like Amanda," Ham said.

"Lizzy's her granddaughter." Cary led Ham into the kitchen and they sat down at a table.

"So why don't you tell me why you're at Montpelier."

Ham described the details of the events of May 24. It took about ten minutes to outline the circumstances of the case.

Cary thought for a few minutes. "Then why are you *here?*"

Ham drew a deep breath and admitted his role in American intelligence. "During most of the years since my graduation from college, during graduate school and for the years since 9/11, I've been involved with a special unit of what became the Department of Homeland Security. The unit develops protocols for and coordinates the protection of American National Historic Sites and Landmarks and other national treasures. These priceless symbolic assets are likely targets for terrorist attacks. Americans would be enraged if they were damaged or, God forbid, destroyed. Since 9/11, these threats have been very real."

"So, if we thought the Twin Towers were bad enough, imagine the reaction to the destruction of Independence Hall, Mount Vernon, or the White House?"

"Or Montpelier," added Ham. "Particularly since 9/11, we've gathered a lot of information about cells that want to target our landmarks. We keep files relating to anti-American efforts to discredit our heroes and thereby erode confidence in our government." He had checked and, until the incident last night, there was nothing much in the database about Madison.

"Why didn't you tell me about your other job?" Cary asked. She looked stricken by his lack of trust. Maybe she never really knew him at all.

"I wasn't allowed to."

She shook her head in silence.

Ham shared his sandwiches with Lizzy while he gave Cary additional facts about the invasions and explained more about the evidence left at the scenes. He outlined the scope of the work for the official investigation.

"Tell me more about how I can help you."

CHAPTER 12

MONTPELIER – AFTERNOON, MAY 25, 2011
John Abbott, Julius Stella, Cary

Ham and Cary entered the president's conference room together for the 1:00 pm meeting. Abbott and Sheriff Leigh were present, along with Ned Willis, Montpelier's head of security. Dr. Julius Stella, director of the James Madison Constitution Center at the estate, entered after all were seated. Ham introduced him to everyone. Julius already knew Leigh and smiled in greeting.

Once the new arrivals were seated, Coles slowly rose to his full six-foot-four, nodded at Abbott, thanked everyone for coming, and reached for his briefcase in one fluid motion. He passed folders around to everyone in the room. His expression was grim.

"I am afraid the information that I will share with you today is top secret. You must shred the contents of your folders before we leave this meeting."

"There's a shredder in the office," said Abbott.

"Thanks, John. You remember me from my dissertation research on my ancestor Edward Coles. I believe I sent a copy of my book for the library here."

Abbott acknowledged the gift with a smile and did not let on about the meeting earlier that morning.

"What you may not know is that I was working for federal intelligence at the same time I was attending graduate school at William & Mary."

The museum official feigned surprise and motioned for Coles to continue.

"Of course, my work was much easier before 9/11. To make a long story short, I am the principal coordinator at the Department of Homeland Security for threats to the nation's landmarks." Eying both Abbott and Sheriff Leigh, Coles reiterated the main provisions of the Patriot Act relating to the nation's landmarks and summarized the chain of command for dealing with threats.

"Montpelier's not the only historic property that experienced an incident on May 24."

Abbott's office came equipped with a large erasable whiteboard, which doubled as a screen. The administrator pressed a button and a projector lowered from the ceiling behind the participants. Coles inserted a disc and a slideshow began. Ham narrated as images of historic landmarks appeared on the screen. When he was finished, he asked that the projector be raised, and wrote for several minutes on the conference room board. He then turned to let the group see the list he had compiled. It repeated the names of the properties shown earlier on the screen:

1. American Philosophical Society, Philadelphia
2. Belmont, John Jay Homestead, Katonah, NY
3. Federal Hall National Monument, New York City
4. First National Bank of the U.S., Philadelphia
5. Franklin Court Print Shop, Philadelphia
6. The Grange National Monument, New York City
7. Grove Street Cemetery, New Haven, CT
8. Gunston Hall, Lorton, VA
9. Montpelier, Orange County, VA
10. Mount Vernon, Alexandria, VA

11. Thomas Paine National Monument, New Rochelle, NY
12. U.S.S. Constitution, Charlestown Navy Yard, Boston, MA
13. University of Pennsylvania, Philadelphia

"Four of the thirteen sites are in Philadelphia," Ham said. "Four are in New York. Three are in Virginia. One's located in Boston, and one in New Haven. Seven are either operated by or affiliated with the National Park Service. All of the sites are under the purview of the Northeast Regional Office, known as NERO, of NPS." Ham explained that the investigation would be coordinated through DHS and NERO. Ham turned back to the conference board and made a notation next to each landmark:

American Phil Society	T	left hand
Belmont	J	left arm
Federal Hall	S	13 teeth
First National Bank	W	right leg
Franklin Court	P	head
The Grange	U	left leg
Grove Street Cemetery	B	right hand
Gunston Hall	W	left foot
Montpelier	U	eyes, fragment of letter
Mount Vernon	A	right foot
Thom Paine Monument	P	ears
USS Constitution	C	torso
UPenn	L	right arm

Coles gave the audience time to absorb the information. Slowly, the group made the connection among the sites. There were murmurs of shock, but Ham raised his hand in caution.

"The first alert to reach the National Park Service came in at 9:00 pm on May 24 from the USS Constitution, known as Old Ironsides, at the Charlestown Navy Yard in Boston. In a routine tour of the deck, a naked female torso, carved on the stomach with the letter *C* was discovered propped against the double wheel on the helm. You'll probably recall that the ship is manned by an active Navy crew that serves under a Commander rank officer. The Navy officer of the watch heard nothing and discovered the remains while making his rounds. The airport-style security on land should have prevented anyone from getting aboard. Since the ship has its own watch, there was no alarm.

The second alerts came in at 9:05 and 9:07 pm, when the Park Service got a report from New York about evidence found at two NPS sites in the system. We know that the thirteen teeth found at Federal Hall were placed there before 4:45 pm, obviously by a tourist. The leg at The Grange was found by night security after the alarm went off at 9:03 pm. Federal Hall is the old New York City Hall and was revamped for use by the new U.S. Congress in time for the inauguration of George Washington as the first president in 1789. New York served as the seat of government until Congress moved to Philadelphia. Thirteen teeth, one drilled with the letter *S* in the enamel, were noticed and misidentified as popcorn, late in the afternoon by a National Park Service interpreter during the last tour of the day. The incident was not reported at the time."

Ham explained that Federal Hall was replaced by a new structure in the 1840s, with parts of the old edifice incorporated into the new building. The evidence was scattered near the original stones that were salvaged from the balcony upon which Washington took the oath. "No alarm was engaged. The custodial staff recognized the material as human teeth when they were about to clean the area at 8:50 pm. The Grange was the only permanent American home of Alexander Hamilton and was moved to a new site in New York City decades ago. It's operated by the National Park Service as a part of a complex of historic sites in the NYC area. A leg carved with the letter *U* was found on the dining room table by a security guard within minutes of the sounding of an alarm there at

9:03 pm on the evening of May 24. Nothing was stolen and there was no further evidence of the intruder. The NPS guard made it out before he threw up."

He paused and turned to see the uncredulous expressions on every face in the group.

"Belmont in Katonah, NY, received an arm carved, perhaps appropriately, with the letter *J.* Belmont was the home of diplomat and first Chief Justice of the United States John Jay. The property is operated by the state of New York. The arm was found on the front porch of the house, so no alarm was activated. The discovery was made by state police staff about 10:00 pm in response to a call from my office asking them to check the premises."

"Ham, how did you know to notify the Jay Homestead?" asked Sheriff Leigh.

"The calls coming in to my office from NPS were all sites associated with the Constitution and its principal leaders. I issued instructions for one of my agents to call known NHLs associated with the Constitution. I also asked my NERO security liaison at NPS to contact the Capitol Region Office to see if there had been any intrusions in Washington. Finally, Hamilton and Jay were two of the three authors of the *Federalist* essays that urged ratification of the Constitution. Madison was the third."

"I see," said Sheriff Leigh.

"As you know, the American Philosophical Society was founded by Franklin and is located within the boundaries of the complex known as Independence Hall National Historical Park. A left hand carved with the letter *T* on the palm was placed on top of a wooden cabinet holding John J. Audubon's personal copy of his elephant portfolio, *Birds of America*. The cabinet is in the second-floor conference room at the society. The alarm sounded at 9:04 pm on the evening of May 24. The intruder activated a silent signal and the hand was discovered by National Park police within eight minutes.

There was no sign of the intruder and nothing was stolen from the collections, which are priceless.

Franklin Court complex, also a part of the Independence Hall National Park, is located close to the Delaware River on Market Street, several blocks east of Independence Hall. A head was found on top of the printing press in the shop exhibit there on May 24. It had chestnut brown hair, no eyes, no ears, was missing 13 teeth, and had the letter P carved on the cheek. The alarm went off at 9:05 pm; the National Parks security patrol found no sign of the intruder when it arrived at 9:14 pm. Upon discovering the head, the National Park Service put the rest of the park on red alert.

The intrusion at First National Bank in Philadelphia, built between 1795-98, seems to have taken place at the same time as the other break-ins. Unfortunately, no alarm sounded there. The building is not presently open to the public and Park Service security did not discover the break-in until Park police noticed that the front door was ajar when making rounds, immediately after the red alert sounded at 9:16 pm. The leg, carved near the ankle with the letter *W*, was on the floor in the main lobby of the historic building. Alexander Hamilton was the main voice calling for a national bank, which was founded in 1791.

"My goodness," said Sheriff Leigh.

"An arm was discovered by a student about 10:00 pm on May 24 near the statue of Benjamin Franklin at the University of Pennsylvania," Ham said. "The letter *L* was carved posthumously into the skin inside the elbow. The park that separates the library from College Hall is open to the public, so security there's relatively lax. We learned that an alert security staffer from INHP had called campus police at the university on the chance that the invasions were somehow related to Franklin. And that's it for Philadelphia.

The foot at Mount Vernon, carved on the sole with the letter *A*, was carried into the mansion by a tourist during operating hours on May 24. A guard found it on a chair in the dining room while making his evening rounds. No alarm sounded. Mount Vernon is privately operated by the Mount Vernon Ladies' Association of the Union, but is affiliated with the National Park Service."

"What about security there?" asked Abbott.

"The MVLA has taken immediate steps to beef up its own security," Ham said. "The ladies remain fully in charge, I can assure you.

My office also issued a search alert for properties in Connecticut associated with patriot Roger Sherman, who signed all our original governing documents. Sources put us in touch with Grove Street Cemetery there, located very near the campus of Yale University. The cemetery is the resting place for generations of notables from New Haven. The hand was left resting against the base of the headstone of Roger Sherman and was collected by DHS agents at 11:30 pm. on May 24. The letter *B* was carved into the top of the hand.

Someone broke into Gunston Hall outside Lorton, VA on May 24 and deposited a left foot carved on the top of the arch with the letter *W*. It was found at 10:17 pm lying on the floor beneath a table owned by George Mason in the small back parlor. Gunston Hall is owned by the Commonwealth of Virginia and is equipped with an electronic security system. The intrusion did not set off an alarm. DHS had called the state police to request an investigation at the site."

"Pardon my ignorance," said Sheriff Leigh, "What was Mason's role in the Constitution? As memory serves me, he wasn't a signer."

Coles nodded and motioned to Dr. Julius Stella who stood and cleared his throat. The legal historian was considered among the top three living experts on the U.S. Constitution. The, short, swarthy Italian was a third-generation immigrant who hailed from Pittsburgh. Most people called him "Julie."

First, he confirmed that the sites are all connected with men who were leaders in shaping and obtaining passage of the

Constitution, or were directly connected with the document by name or association.

"Franklin was the great sage at the Convention," he said. "Washington chaired it; Madison kept the most detailed notes and did extensive research prior to the Convention on the history of governments. People listened to his arguments during the deliberations. Madison joined Hamilton and Jay in writing the *Federalist* essays that were so instrumental in getting the states to ratify the Constitution. Franklin founded the University of Pennsylvania. Grove Street Cemetery is the main surviving site associated with Roger Sherman, the great signer. The USS Constitution, our beloved Old Ironsides, of course, bears the name of the foremost governing document of the nation. George Mason refused to sign the Constitution because it did not have a Bill of Rights. Such a bill was prepared and was among the first items of business adopted once the Constitution was ratified. Ten of the proposed twelve amendments were passed." Everyone nodded their thanks to Stella as he sat down.

Ham resumed his brief. "At some time around May 24, someone placed two ears, one carved on the lobe with the letter *P*, at the base of the Thomas Paine National Monument in New Rochelle, NY. The 12-foot marble column was carved by artist and architect John Frazee in 1839. Political reformer Gilbert Vale organized the project. Wilson McDonald added a 4-foot bronze bust of Paine to the top in 1881, and the whole kit and caboodle was moved in 1905 to be near the little cottage that Paine occupied from 1802-1806. A groundskeeper employed by the Huguenot & New Rochelle Historical Association discovered the ears shortly after dawn this morning. They contacted the New York State Police, which was already working on the Jay site, and they contacted us."

"Why Paine?" asked Stella, frowning.

"Why, indeed?" asked Ham. "Paine was famous for his literary contributions to the Revolution, not the Constitution. In fact, he was in France during most of the Constitutional era."

Ham noted that the Thomas Paine House in New Rochelle is an NHL, and that parts of UPenn have landmark status. Then he promised to give the subject additional study.

Turning to a discussion of the remaining sites, he reminded the group that the incident at Montpelier took place on the evening of May 24.

"So far, Montpelier is noteworthy for the presence of a partial letter, in Madison's hand, in addition to the second use of the letter *U* on the wrapping around the carton housing the eyeballs. We also have two body parts marked with the letter *P*. At this point, the significance of the letters on the body parts remains a mystery."

The room was deathly quiet for nearly half a minute. The agent noticed that Dr. Stella was scribbling busily on a piece of paper. Then John Abbott stood, opened a cabinet, and removed a bottle of whiskey, which he held up to offer to the others. When no one accepted the offer, Abbott rang his secretary to ask for a selection of soft drinks and water. He assumed correctly that nobody wanted any food. The soft drinks arrived promptly. Everyone waited until the secretary had closed the door behind her.

Julie Stella rose and scanned the eyes of the group. "I think I have the answer to the letters carved on the body parts," he said. Then he recited the opening words of the U.S. Constitution:

We the People of the United States, to form a more perfect Union. establish Justice, insure domestic Tranquility, provide for the common defense, promote the general Welfare, and secure the Blessings of Liberty to ourselves and our Posterity, do ordain and establish this Constitution of the United States of America.

Ham had been inscribing the words on the board as Stella spoke. The Constitution scholar waited for him to finish before approaching the board to capitalize some of the words.

W-P-U-S-U-J-T-W-B-L-P-C-A

"Why didn't they capitalize *defense?*" asked Leigh.

Dr. Stella shrugged. "I dunno. We'd have to ask the Founders." He stepped back from the whiteboard. "The preamble contains fifteen, not thirteen capitalized words. Gouverneur Morris wrote it. It was the last major part of the Constitution written."

Ham tapped away at his phone, texting his office to call off the encryption gurus and asking them to download a copy of the Constitution. He studied the board and turned to Stella.

"Dr. Stella, in the preamble, the letter *U* appears three times. *W* and *S* appear twice, each time capitalized. Only two *U*'s and one *S* were used on the body parts."

Stella thought for a second. "Ham, the first *W* is for *We*, and the second is for *Welfare*, so both are used. The two *U*'s stand for *United* and *Union*. Both appear. *United States* appears twice in the preamble, but only appears once on the body parts."

"Do these body parts all come from the same person, or are there more victims involved?" asked Cary, speaking for the first time.

"We're fast-tracking the DNA and other analyses, and believe we may be dealing with the remains of one woman, age 22-26, with brown hair and eyes and no major identifying marks."

"So far," he continued, "we know she was three months' pregnant, and the fetus was present in the torso found on the deck of the USS Constitution." He turned to Leigh and confirmed that all the evidence was undergoing detailed analysis at the Armed Forces forensic facility in Dover, Delaware.

At that point, the sheriff and Abbott alternated questions about the bizarre sequence of events. Coles was notified when the first discovery was made within minutes of the first report to the NPS on May 24. Homeland Security had staffed up a special investigative unit and would be the official clearinghouse for developments.

"John, I think we're going to need some assistance with the investigation."

"Anything." Abbott assured him.

"Excellent," Ham said. "There's obvious symbolism in the involvement of 13 historic sites and the discovery of 13 teeth and 13 letters. As for the cause of death, the forensics team is almost certain there was evidence of a slit throat, which was not completely obliterated by the dissection of the body. The dissection was posthumous and performed with precision, using very sharp tools, possibly medical instruments.

The lack of decay and odor suggests that the remains were kept frozen and then refrigerated until shortly before placement at each site. Obviously, the evidence is gruesome. DHS is treating the death as a homicide. The dental work is of mixed quality and suggests some foreign work. Interpol has already been brought in and international DNA data is being gathered. Despite having been frozen, the remains yielded excellent quality DNA."

This brought a murmur from the team.

"The intrusions into the historic sites were extremely well-timed. For unknown reasons, the criminals decided to deposit the remains during operating hours at Mount Vernon and Federal Hall. In both cases, the evidence was left by a visitor on the last tour of the day. The rest of the break-ins were timed at 9:00 pm, or as close to that hour as possible."

"It was a huge operation," said Leigh. "It involved multiple teams, careful planning, a full support network, access to sophisticated equipment, detailed knowledge about security systems, and professional timing. The entire series of invasions was almost elegant and definitely scary." He turned to Ham. "So, can we be clear that this is a terrorist action?"

Ham knew the question would be asked. DHS had discussed the matter in depth at headquarters. There appeared to be one murder victim, who might not even have been an American citizen. No people were injured in the invasions and no property was damaged.

On the other hand, the law was clear in declaring that threats to the nation's landmarks were threats to national security. Most of the body parts had been examined by explosives experts before any further investigation was permitted. The remains were threatening in themselves, each suggesting that a crime had been committed by persons unknown.

There were also varying interpretations about the message being sent to the government. One group of analysts favored the incidents as a collective warning that our national treasures were not secure from attack. The *big* attack was still to come. Another posited that the motive would only be revealed when the U.S. knew the identity of the victim and could work out her connections to individuals and groups known or believed to be terrorists. In other words, they viewed the victim as a clue about another plan yet to be implemented. Everyone concurred that the invasions were expertly executed from start to finish; that there was a large, established network of talent within the U.S. and that the resources of Homeland Security should be employed in solving the mystery.

"In most cases," Ham explained, "threats to the nation's landmarks have been included in larger plans by terrorist groups to destroy property or citizens. Agents in the Middle East, Europe, Meso- and Latin America, and the U.S. would decode mail and voice traffic, or infiltrate cells known to be in place in American cities." Ham's group would be brought into the loop only when specific landmarks might be at risk.

Now the worm had turned. No sooner had Landmarks taken charge of the investigation than some veteran spymasters in the U.S. intelligence network were grousing that the future of the country had been turned over to a bunch of historic preservationists with limited sleuthing ability.

Meanwhile, in Washington, news of the invasions was moving up the chain of command. Ever astute to the political climate in Washington, Briggs Colonna, the youthful and charismatic Director of the National Park Service, got the full backing of the secretary of the interior and asked for an appointment to brief the president of the Unites States. The NPS director waded with determination through various White House middlemen before finally getting connected to the chief of staff.

"Briggs" said the chief. "POTUS has already spoken with the secretary of interior, and I've cleared his calendar for a ten-minute brief at 11:30 pm today. Can you make that?"

"Sure thing," said Colonna. He had barely disconnected before yelling for his deputies to assemble what he called a *POTUS Quality Brief* for his use. The staff had two hours to assemble it and fully prep the director before his appointment in the Oval Office.

Ham had to smile, recalling the results of that briefing. The president himself had called the head of Homeland Security, who tried to explain the difficulties involved in getting the CIA, NSA, FBI and other intelligence agencies to take their lead from "a bunch of tree huggers and historic preservationists."

The DHS secretary was trying to lighten the mood. Bad move.

"Mr. Secretary," growled POTUS, "I'm issuing an executive directive to every worthless intelligence agency to cooperate fully with DHS in this investigation and to help Assistant Deputy Secretary Shaw and Agent Coles without complaint."

The agency head winced in embarrassment and shook his head.

"Listen up and listen up good," the president barked. "No one, no agency, no foreign country, messes with our national treasures."

The cabinet secretary then made the mistake of reminding the president that none of the thirteen landmarks were damaged during the invasions, which, he neglected to add, were so exquisitely executed that they suggested the presence of a dangerously well-organized terrorist group already armed and mobilized on American soil.

"And what's next?" demanded the president. "I can tell you this. No one is going to blow up the National Archives, Independence Hall, the Library of Congress, the Capitol, the White House or any other symbol of our nation on my watch."

Obviously, Briggs Colonna had painted a clear picture of impending historical Armageddon, with the president being sacrificed on the altar of public outrage after attacks on the symbols of the soul of the nation and its people.

⊷⊶

The Montpelier briefing continued.

"What the hell type of security does the Park Service have?" asked Sheriff Leigh. "How could they allow multiple break-ins over a period of minutes without nabbing someone or recording something?"

"You know the Park Service has a deficit in the billions that's growing every year," Abbott said. "The response times to the alarms were well within established national security parameters. Traditional museum security's designed to protect the buildings and their collections from damage or theft. The very notion of blowing up our landmarks is relatively recent."

He mentioned some of the challenges Montpelier had faced when it installed security devices during the extensive renovations to the mansion. Wires needed to be concealed, but preservation standards did not readily support removing original plaster to conceal them. Custom system designs and installations cost a great deal.

Leigh nodded and clenched his jaw.

"Besides, museum security alarms go off when security's penetrated," Abbott said. "That said, I concur that the landmarks under

Park Service stewardship deserve the latest and best security systems. They simply don't have them."

They began to discuss those landmarks and sites that had not been invaded. Coles cited Independence Hall, the National Constitution Center, the National Archives, and the Library of Congress. Abbott added numerous buildings in the capital, along with colleges and universities named for prominent men of the founding era. Other names came from the participants. Ham dutifully recorded them on the board. Predictably, Leigh and Abbott also wanted to know how Montpelier and Madison ranked in the hierarchy of sites.

"First, Madison was the central architect of the Constitution," Ham said. "Second, the break-in at Montpelier has a distinction, an important clue. The eyes were accompanied by the partial letter written in Madison's hand. Finally, the letter accompanying the eyes left here suggests a direct link between the victim and the Madisons, the invasions, and the Constitution."

Sheriff Leigh asked how Homeland Security was organizing its resources. He was accustomed to joint police force investigations from his days on the D.C. Metro Police.

"The main base will be at DHS headquarters in Washington," Ham said.

"There'll be a Park Service task force based at the Northeast Regional offices in Philadelphia, because all of the affected NPS and NHL sites are in that region. The third office will be located at Montpelier."

"Is that all?" asked Leigh.

"We value the staff resources at Montpelier in addition to the likely connection between this site and the other invasions. You've already shown that you can reach out instantly to the scholars of Madison and his legacy. Your Constitution Center has contacts to every known Constitutional historian, and Dr. Stella himself is an acknowledged expert. We'll need his help in identifying additional sites or events that might be targets for terrorist activities. Dr. Stella has already outsmarted some of our best cryptologists at DHS by linking the initials on the body parts with words from the pre-amble to the Constitution."

"You'll have our full cooperation," said John Abbott.

"Same with us," said Dr. Stella.

"Your visiting scholar, Cary Mallory, also comes to the table with strong assets," said Ham. "There may be DNA evidence on objects that came from members of the family. We think we'll need genea-logical expertise to identify the victim and to link her with the sites, if possible. Because of Payne Todd's disorganized dispersal of the Madisons' possessions, Cary has had to authenticate objects said to have been associated with James and Dolley by conducting de-tailed research into the provenance of each artifact and either trac-ing it back to a known sale or to one of the inventories or invoices describing the Madison family possessions. She's a walking ency-clopedia on Madisoniana. She also knows the families descended from leaders of the early Republic, since many of them either gave or sold things to the couple or attended the dispersal sales to buy mementoes of the fourth president and his wife. Finally, she has a good nose for solving puzzles, and we need her gut on this one."

While the sheriff took a break to phone his office, Abbott called his director of facilities and arranged for office space and equip-ment for the task force. Members of the team coming in from the other centers could stay overnight in the furnished rooms in the resi-dences on site that had been converted into dormitories for teachers attending multi-day seminars on the Constitution. The operation here could be kept very secure. Finally, Abbott asked his secretary to set up afternoon tea and sandwiches in the adjacent room.

The team members munched away while reading copies of the eyes-only file Ham had handed each of them when they arrived in the conference room. Then they waited patiently to resume the group meeting.

This time Abbott led off with the information about the location for the task force office and accommodations for visiting members of the team. The museum president told Julius Stella that their top priority was the investigation and asked him and Cary to be in direct contact if they needed additional staff assistance with their regular responsibilities or the special investigation. Privately, Ham had told John that Dr. Stella could name his own additional assistants and the agency would pay the bills.

Since Mallory was not a member of the staff, Abbott was careful to thank her for her cooperation. He informed her that he would notify the granting agency and his curatorial department that she was on special assignment. He would also instruct his staff to provide any additional assistance that she might require. Same deal. Ham knew he would need a lot of her time.

"What about the media?" asked Sheriff Leigh.

"The Patriot Act gives certain powers to Homeland Security that are deemed by some as restrictions on individual rights and freedom of the press. We take threats to the national security very seriously and do not hesitate to take whatever steps are necessary to quell reportage when required."

"Makes sense," said Leigh.

"There was a reporter from the *Enquirer* in Philadelphia who got wind of the arm discovered near the Franklin statue at the university. He was assured by both UPenn and the Philadelphia PD that the appendage was a fake planted by a medical student as a prank." Ham added that the Huguenot Historical Association in New Rochelle was told that the ears were cadaver parts stolen from a medical school and placed there to scare the tourists. Grove Street Cemetery had been read into the DHS anti-terrorism protocols and would remain on alert for any future incidents. The NPS had media security guidelines which were implemented shortly after the first break-in took place on federal park property. None of those incidents had been reported in the news.

"As for the other landmarks: Mount Vernon, Gunston Hall, and Montpelier use security procedures that conform to the Secretary of the Interior protocols. Each also has an established security code and procedures to coordinate with their respective investigative agencies." Ham didn't need to mention that news stories about scattered body parts would guarantee headlines, but not of the type that the cultural facilities desired.

As the others left the briefing, Abbott was reminded of the popular claim among museum professionals that the media would not show up to cover educational and cultural events unless you could promise them a body bag at the door. *How the hell's everyone going to keep a lid on this thing?* he wondered. Lurid headlines suddenly flashed into his tired mind without warning:

Give a Hand (or two) for history!
Victim had Eyes for the Father of the Constitution
Heads up for Franklin!
Follow in the Foot-steps of History!
History worth an Arm and a Leg!

Ham found the Montpelier president shaking with nervous laughter when the agent entered his office to say goodbye. Ham knew the signs of too much shock and stress from his own experiences.

"Sometimes black humor helps a lot, John," said Ham. He leaned across Abbott's desk and poured himself a shot of whiskey, then refilled Abbott's glass.

"What's on your mind?"

Abbott told him about the mock headlines circling through his mind, and Ham laughed before sitting down to sip his whiskey. A moment later he sat up, smiling.

"*Washington Gets New Teeth, finally!*" he said.

It was the end of a long and terrible day.

CHAPTER 13

MONTPELIER – EVENING, MAY 25, 2011
Cary

Ham left Abbott's office at 6:30 pm, feeling calmer but slightly drunk. He knew he needed dinner and a good night's sleep. A helicopter would be picking him up in twelve hours to fly him to Philadelphia for a multi-agency meeting.

The agent strolled past Cary Mallory's residence on the grounds and peered into the kitchen window. He noticed her standing in the kitchen with the window and curtains open. The crisp air was cooling down the way it did in the evenings during springtime in Central Virginia, and the smell of fresh flowers and new grass was irresistible.

Ham walked up the steps and knocked on the door, aware that it was a mistake to do so. He stepped back from the door and admired the simple early 20th century frame house. Cary came to the door barefoot, wearing sweats. She had flour on her nose and Lizzie by her side. Ham stared at her with nervous eyes. The incident reminded him of their first meeting a decade ago.

"Come on in, Ham," she said. "I'm making chicken pot pie."

Cary led Ham into the kitchen and sat him down at the table. She slipped the pie into the oven and offered Ham a drink. She was drinking Jack Daniels, a preference discovered in her youth that had served her well over the years.

Ham scanned the room and realized she was using the standard furnishings provided to Madison scholars in residence. The décor was austere but not shoddy.

"You must miss your beautiful home in Church Hill," he said.

"I do," she admitted. She had turned her back to him to make a tossed salad to go with the pot pie.

"How's business been? I mean, all these years."

"Good. We're still in the black. I still deal with the same pickers, my museum clients, and my regular customers, mostly through email and cell phone. Connie runs the business daily now and I go home on weekends."

Ham realized that her commitment to help solve the murder was going to be a great sacrifice. Without her knowledge, he had asked his finance manager to contact her by phone and to agree to whatever terms she chose. He didn't want to negotiate the financial aspects of her work directly.

Ham saw the usual Virginia salted peanuts on the table and grabbed a handful. Cary brought over plates for the table. She put down food for Lizzie, refreshed her own drink, and sat down across from Ham at the kitchen table.

"Did you expect me for dinner?"

"Well, I knew you'd want to spend some private time with John. Obviously, you've asked him to make a huge commitment to the investigation."

Ham nodded.

"I also know that Virginians are somewhat religious about the cocktail hour, so I assumed you'd do your debriefing or whatever you call it over that bottle in his desk."

"Yes, again," said Ham.

"You could say I did the math. I know no one's eaten since that tepid tea Abbott served and that the nearest restaurant is miles down the road."

"Well, I'm starving," said Ham, salivating from the rich aroma wafting from the oven. His explanation this morning had been

brief. He had hardly given her a chance to mull over the circumstances of their breakup, the revelations about his secret involvement with federal intelligence, and the details of the present
murder investigation. Ham had treated her badly a decade before
and knew she hadn't forgotten it.

"Finally, I know you're a lousy cook," she said, "and I want to
assure you that I expect to be paid top, absolute *top dollar* for my
work with you on the murder."

The oven buzzer went off at that moment. She removed the pot
pie and set it down, pivoting to toss the salad while it cooled. She
pulled handsome Royal Daulton plates and real sterling silverware
from her cabinets and set them down on the table. From a pull-
out drawer, she yanked two linen napkins, produced two antique
Baccarat wine glasses from the cabinet and plopped a bottle of
merlot and a corkscrew on the table. Ham opened the wine and
poured two glasses while she served two slices of the pot pie before
sitting down to pass the salad.

Ham had to admit that everything looked delicious. He ate rav-
enously before going for seconds. Twenty minutes later he found
himself declining a third slice of the pot pie and instead accepting
a bowl of homemade strawberry ice cream, one of Cary's signature
dishes. By then the wine was gone, and Ham passed on the idea of
coffee. He yawned and felt embarrassed as he stood from his seat.
Instinctively, he walked toward the door, and Cary and Lizzie followed him. Cary wanted to be sure he was headed in the right direction to the Constitution dormitories, while the canine wanted
to make sure he left without molesting her owner.

Feeling emboldened by the wine and a great dinner, Ham
leaned in to kiss her on the cheek. Cary and Lizzie accepted the
gesture without comment and soon he was on his way. The hearty
meal had sobered him considerably, leaving him to think about
Cary during the walk to the dorm. He realized now that he had
made a mistake when he broke it off.

CHAPTER 14

PHILADELPHIA – MORNING, MAY 26, 2011
Ray Goodson

The investigative team met in a conference room at the National Park Service Northeast Regional Offices in Philadelphia. The NPS director and the head of the regional office had been read into the case, but both elected to appoint their agency's leading specialist on terrorism to the team. Therefore, Ray Goodson was present, along with forensic, terrorist, and security experts from Homeland Security's network of agencies. Ham was in attendance and welcomed the attendees, introducing them all and motioning to a telephone, where Cary was conferenced in.

Ham led off with a briefing on potential sites targeted for additional acts of terrorism. Ongoing assessments would lead the NPS to adjust the threat level at sites like Independence Hall and Mount Vernon. The team wanted to know if one of the sites targeted to receive a part of the victim would be hit again, or whether the terrorist threat would focus on other buildings.

Goodson gave a summary of the locations already affected, concluding that all of them would remain under a red alert until the threat was removed. "The public will be told the threat is orange," he said. "The security force will be beefed up to meet condition red."

"Will they remain open to the public?" a CIA analyst asked. Ham had just met the man but couldn't recall his name.

"Ladies and gentlemen," said Goodson, "in the eyes of the American public, these landmarks belong to the people and are woven into the very fiber of our society. We can schedule a few days closing for repairs, but none of them except The First Bank was actually closed to the public, and if we shut them all down the media and all the conspiracy theorists will have a field day."

"How much does the public know about the murder now?" asked an FBI agent.

Ham stood up and cleared his throat. "Damn little," he said. "Our media service sweeps show no new print, radio, or television reports of the invasions. There are sites on the web where conspiracy theorists blog regularly about ever-present dangers to our cultural heritage. We have been tracking these as well, and there has been no additional news there about the thirteen properties targeted on May 24." He exhaled for a moment. "I must say that the media protocols within the NPS are superb. Our agency in Washington is accustomed to doing business by leak. We're learning a lot from the Park Service model."

"What's the key?" asked another FBI agent.

"No news is good news," said Goodson, smiling.

"I have a question," said Cary interrupting by phone.

"Go head, Cary," said Ham. "You have our attention."

"Ray, several of us fail to understand why the invasion group included the Tom Paine Monument in New Rochelle. Were the intruders soft on their knowledge of American Constitutional history?"

The NERO security chief looked thoughtful. "Cary, we in the region have met with our historians, cultural resource specialists, interpretive experts, and others to try to arrive at a single answer to your very insightful question. Quite frankly, we don't have a clue."

"Paine's authorship of *Common Sense* had a substantial impact on the revolutionary generation and he made several positive contributions to the American Revolution. He also actively supported the Revolution from France. However, his deist book, *Age of Reason*, had an extremely negative impact in the U.S. Christians reviled him when he returned to the United States in 1802. Only six people attended his funeral in 1809."

He informed the team that a group in one eastern city was raising funds to erect a Thomas Paine statue, but admitted that the invasion group might have misconstrued their efforts. "The literature of the movement shows some atheistic leanings." One other take on the matter assumes that the terrorists wanted us to believe that they were foreigners whose resources on American history are flawed, hence their confusion about Paine's importance to our governing documents."

"That idea won't hold water," said Cary, laughing. 'Few Americans know their own history. We all know that the people who are most knowledgeable about our Constitution are foreigners who immigrate to this country and study to pass the citizenship test."

Everyone chuckled. "I had a senior history student at William & Mary who thought the Whiskey Rebellion was a march on Washington led by prohibitionist Carrie Mott," said Ham. "But that's another story. I'd like to ask Fred Schmidt, DNA forensics expert, to address the group now.

"Thank you, Dr. Coles. The body parts, including the ears, came from one person. The victim has not yet been identified. Also, the father of the fetus also remains unidentified. The victim had been pregnant at least once previously before her death. Her liver showed signs of alcohol abuse, and she manifested physical deterioration from sustained drug use. The examination revealed scars from two bullet wounds and a healed fracture in one arm. Although her bones and teeth suggest an age of 26, her physical age was more than 55."

He flashed an image on the screen, an anthropological facial reconstruction of the victim as she must have appeared before her death.

"One of the surprising results of the DNA analysis so far is the connection between the victim's DNA and the genome associated with the late Tsar Nicholas II and his family, whose bodies were uncovered outside Yekaterinburg, Russia in 1991 and 2007."

"Do you have a link back to 19th century Europe?" asked the CIA liaison. Ham had previously briefed him on a possible Russian connection.

Jim Andersen, the CIA Central American terrorist expert in attendance, related that he had received information from other operatives and officials in Mexico. "Birth records are being searched as we speak," he said. "Fred Schmidt tells me that the father was obviously of Indian heritage, because the DNA showed links to well-known indigenous groups in Mexico. So far, we can find no trace of her in either Mexico or the U.S. since March 2011. If she entered this country voluntarily, there's no record of it. She might have used a false passport."

"Does she maybe have connections to any of the drug cartels?"

"Ham, you know how volatile the drug cartel situation is in Mexico," said Andersen. "Particularly since President Calderon pledged to do away with them when he took office in 2006. In recent years, they've been fighting for control of territory among themselves. Mexico is basically at war with them."

"How's the U.S. involved with the cartels?" asked Cary by phone

"Today, about 90% of the marijuana and non-heroin narcotics entering the U.S. come from Mexico," said Andersen. "Drugs have been entering the country via Mexico for years, with Mexicans acting as delivery boys. But after the killing of the main Colombian drug cartel leaders, the Mexican cartels started to assume direct control of the traffic, buying, delivering into the U.S., and then distributing drugs through a sophisticated system of national networks."

The team already knew that the border leaked like a sieve. Mexico traditionally had a class system, with little opportunity for vertical advancement. Mexico's PRI party, which dominated Mexican politics for more than 70 years before Vincente Fox was elected in 2000, had done little to help the lower classes to advance their income, their education, or their medical treatment. In many places along the vast U.S-Mexican border, the poor could walk across the Rio Grande to seek better paying jobs in the U.S. Many vicious *importers* took what little money these people had and bused them to the border in non-ventilated trucks with no food or water. Many of them died without ever setting foot on American soil. Sure, they were illegal aliens, but the Hispanic population of the nation was still surging. Agribusiness needed cheap labor, and most of the immigrants were willing to work and had good skills in carpentry in addition to agriculture. U.S. businesses justified the illegal hiring by arguing that Americans refused to take low-paying jobs. The welfare mentality, they insisted, had produced two entire generations of people who thought that the government owed them a living without any labor at all.

"Dallas will have a majority Hispanic population within a few years," said Andersen. "Virginia's population, more than 1,600 miles from the Mexican border, is now classified as 7% Hispanic. The established population of registered Mexican aliens is having a tremendous influence in the political arena. National, state, and local elected officials and aspirants court their vote now. Admittedly, not all the immigrants were from Mexico, but it was those illegals that were particularly prevalent in the Southern U.S.

"You know I'll be working with Russian, English, and American specialists on the Russian genealogical issue." Cary said.

"Dover wanted a shot at the DNA analysis of the remains of the last tsar and his family," said Fred Schmidt. "But you might say that that the politics of science got in the way. Let me assure you that we can handle whatever analysis is needed on this victim."

"How should we refine our genealogical search to expedite the investigation?" asked Cary.

"Did the victim have a genealogical connection to one of the framers of the Constitution?" asked Schmidt.

Cary explained that the team had a working hypothesis that a Russo-American connection dated to the years 1814-1816, and came to a head when President Madison sent a special envoy to St. Petersburg, presumably to deal with a diplomatic issue involving the Russian consul in Philadelphia. She explained the circumstances of Edward Coles' voyage on the Prometheus in 1816.

"Our working hypothesis is that Madison's stepson, Payne Todd, caused some sort of incident when he accompanied the American Commission to negotiate the end of the War of 1812," she said.

The DNA scientist had a strong New York accent, which came through clearly in his next remarks.

"Got any proof?" asked Schmidt, his abrasive New York accent emerging suddenly.

Ham shook his head and the teleconference phone remained silent.

"If you think there's some connections to the Madisons themselves, then you need to check for American DNA," said Schmidt. "You need to find samples of hair, teeth, bone, sweat, that we can analyze."

"You got that, Cary?" asked Ham.

"Loud and clear, Coles," she said.

"I'm telling ya, the connection to the Romanovs probably wouldn't have been spotted so fast without all the hoopla about Tsar Nicholas and the long-missing graves," Schmidt said. "The Nicholas analyses took years to complete. Science in DNA has advanced light years since 1991 and 2007." The scientist put his elbows on the table and glared at the team. "How much time ya think we got till these assholes blow up the National Archives or Independence Hall?"

The message got across to everyone in the room.

"There are extant objects that may contain DNA," Cary said. "Take hair as an example. Nutrition in the early 1800s was generally poor, and sometimes a minor tug on one's hair yielded both the fiber and its root. There may be traces of blood. Dolley sewed, like all ladies of her generation. But that doesn't necessarily mean she had a talent for it."

"Could help," said Schmidt.

"Look, it's virtually impossible for Madison to have fathered a child connected to the Romanov family," she said. "Madison never traveled abroad except in his own mind, and Alexander I had such a huge empire that a trip to the U. S. was beneath him."

"Well, send me everything ya can find," said Fred.

As the meeting began to break up, Cary asked to speak again with Ham. He clicked the speaker off to take the call.

"Ham, you need to brief John Abbott about this meeting ASAP. He's something of a nervous Nelly anyway, but this stuff is entirely too bizarre to be believable on face value."

Ham agreed to call Abbott that evening.

CHAPTER 15

MONTPELIER – LATE MORNING, MAY 26, 2011
John Abbott

Abbott was alone when he took the call from Ham Coles, who was en route back to Washington. The agent told him to meet with Cary to get a first-hand update on the earlier investigative meeting held at NERO that morning, then launched into a report on the forensic analysis of body parts, which was now nearly complete. The examination showed that the woman was indeed between 22 and 26 and had no recent major injuries – aside from a slit throat. Evidence showed that she was probably unconscious when the fatal injury was sustained.

Her body showed a pattern of uneven nutrition, suggesting periods of poor diet alternating with normal eating habits. Microscopic analysis of her stomach contents suggested that she probably spent some time before her death in the north Texas region known as the Grand Prairie. The slit throat was the cause of death. The body parts were obviously kept in some sort of freezer since their dispersal to the sites involved a large team and careful timing to place them almost simultaneously in historic sites that were several hundred miles apart. Interpol did not have the prints on file, but some of the dental work appeared to be Mexican, with signs of poor dental hygiene.

A full check of international DNA was in process but would take more time. Meanwhile, the woman's DNA showed a link with the analysis performed on the remains of the family of Nicholas II, the last tsar of Imperial Russia.

It just keeps getting weirder and weirder, Abbott thought wildly.

"Mexican? How did we get to Mexico and from there to Russia?"

Ham persisted, telling Abbott about the organ disease, alcohol and drug abuse, and evidence of a previous pregnancy. "She was more than three months' pregnant," he said.

"Do we need to examine Madison-related DNA?" Abbott asked. He had an image of teams manning backhoes descending on the Madison family cemetery on the estate to dig up the Father of the Constitution and his family.

"Probably," said Ham.

CHAPTER 16

MONTPELIER – AFTERNOON, MAY 27, 2011
Cary

H am had asked Cary to take charge of the search for an expert in royal European-Russian genealogy who could try to shed some light on the odd DNA results from the unidentified victim of what they had decided to call the Constitution Murder. She knew it would be a tall order. She sent off emails to her contacts at the Hermitage Museum in St. Petersburg and the Victoria and Albert in London. Fred Schmidt assured her that he had experts at Dover Air Force Base who could also help analyze whatever data she could gather.

Cary frowned. A person born in 1950 had more than 5,000 grandparents dating back to about 1650, a span of 300 years. Any direct Madison family connection with Russia most likely dated to the period of the Madison presidency, a mere two hundred years ago, but that was still a challenge. All those European aristocrats married each other repeatedly.

Her mind swam with memories of the million little principalities and nations in what are now Poland, Austria, and Germany, each of them producing rosy-cheeked, plump brood mares to form marital mergers with the world's major monarchies. Princess what's-her-name from Hesse, or Württemberg, or wherever, would have changed her name when she married into the Romanovs, assuming a new moniker along with her new Russian Orthodox religion. And they reproduced like rabbits.

While she was waiting to get the names of experts in the Romanov lineage, she sent a note to Ham asking him to get the armed forces DNA laboratory people to contact some of the scientists from the U.S who had worked on unscrambling the DNA sequences from the bodies found in the two graves in Yekaterinburg, the remote site where the remains of Tsar Nicholas II, his wife Alexandra, their children, doctor, and servants were discovered. All the newspapers of the day had carried the story of the mitochondrial DNA link between Prince Philip of England with Tsarina Alexandra – Queen Victoria was the key. Cary wanted to know more about the DNA string tests that showed descent in the male line.

Fortunately, the Internet had become a great friend to people trying to trace their ancestors. After a brief search, she located several sites listing some of the Romanov lines. Allowing for errors online, Cary gathered that there were living descendants of the Romanovs who were arguing over the proper heir to the throne, if, for some reason, the monarchy was ever restored in the homeland. Alexander I had daughters only, but his brothers Nicolas and Constantine had sons. One of the sons of Nicholas I became Alexander II, father of Alexander III, who sired Nicholas II, the ill-fated last Romanov tsar. Of course, the published lines focused on legitimate heirs, not the many offspring of affairs, only some of whom were recognized and bestowed with titles and appropriate means of support. After several hours of online searching she realized she had a headache.

Still, Cary believed that there had probably been some sort of connection between Tsar Alexander I and James Madison. The tsar was a student of the Enlightenment, and had expressed respect for the ideals of liberty associated with the American Revolution. He even had plans to elevate the status of serfs in his vast empire, at least until the French revolutionaries decided to sever royal heads and force other members of the French nobility to flee to save their own necks.

Awaiting return calls from her far-flung contacts, Cary turned to the search for a source for the fragment of the Madison letter found with the eyes in the Montpelier library. Again, instinct told her that there was a connection between the subject of the letter and the papers that Dolley Madison's nieces had removed from her Washington home in 1849. Dolley's brother John Payne even stated that the former president showed him some of the contents of the packet before he entrusted Payne with the task of delivering it to his wife.

Historians had differed in their opinion about whether John Payne had delivered the packet to a grieving Dolley Madison. Cary decided to assume that the delivery had been made, and that at least some of the contents of the packet were included in the nieces' carpet-bag heist from Dolley's sick room on Lafayette Square shortly before her death.

Were they all invoices for gambling debts? Cary wondered. She could see John Payne accepting Madison's invitation to peruse the collection, but wondered if the part-time secretary bothered to study each document in any detail. Payne seems to have waited to hand the packet to Dolley until after Madison's funeral. Then she took it to her room.

But then what?

She turned to a review of the literature and source material that related to Payne Todd's fall from grace. She consulted some notes Ham had made about Edward Coles' 1816 trip to Russia and Europe. Payne Todd had returned home in September 1815. He worked as secretary for his stepfather for a while and wrote to

Coles about his cousin's planned trip to Europe, recommending places to see.

Taking a break to check on emails, Cary found a note from the Hermitage recommending Natalia Kruskov as a Romanov genealogist. Contact information for the researcher was included in the note.

Now we're making progress, Cary thought.

CHAPTER 17

WASHINGTON, D.C. – JULY 1849
National Hotel
Cary
[Note from CT: this narrative is designed to provide contextual information about Dolley Madison's final days.]

ord spread quickly throughout the Federal City. "Mrs. Madison is dying," they said.

Many residents shook their heads sadly, having assumed that the old and great lady, with her jet-black false curls, rouged cheeks, and frayed turbans, would somehow live forever amongst them.

Cabinet ministers, members of Congress, and what passed for the city's elite all paid calls to the little house on Lafayette Square across from the White House, bearing a kind word or small gifts of food. They were received in the parlor by Dolley's niece and companion, Annie Payne, or by one of the Cutts clan, children and grandchildren of Dolley's beloved late sister, Anna Payne Cutts.

Visitors to the little house felt like they were touring a museum of American history. The walls of the parlor were hung with portraits of the early discoverers, complemented by handsome portraits of the first five presidents of the United States, several of them by Gilbert Stuart. There was also a Stuart oil of the ubiquitous

Dolley herself, executed in Washington in 1804 when she was wife of the secretary of state. These artworks were displayed along with a few select European pieces from Montpelier's extensive holdings in Old Masters, most of them purchased for the Madisons in 1813-15 when Payne Todd was abroad.

It was said that Mrs. Madison had known eleven presidents during her lifetime. Certainly, her social standing in the federal city was supreme among the political gentry and the residents. So high was her position, in fact, that it had become customary for each president to pay a call on the widow when he entered office. President James K. Polk and First Lady Sarah had included Mrs. Madison in their White House dinners and receptions. The president often gave his arm to the octogenarian at large receptions for the traditional parade among the guests in the East Room.

Leaders of both political parties paid calls on her birthday, June 20, and pretended to be surprised when she told them, year after year, that she was 74. She always wore mourning garb after Madison's death in 1836, but kept to her turbans until her death.

James Buchanan and Daniel Webster discussed the ailing political diva over dinner one sultry night. "She is at least 80," insisted Buchanan, tucking into his crab imperial.

"I imagine that Mrs. Madison would dispute your mathematical calculations," Webster replied with a grin, mentally calculating that she was probably 81.

"Corcoran says she is 80," said Buchanan. "And he ought to know since he never misses her birthday."

Prominent Washington banker and art collector W.W. Corcoran dutifully called on Dolley Madison at her home to offer his congratulations every June. Guests circulated through the small but elegantly appointed rooms on the first floor, drinking punch and admiring the art displayed throughout the interiors.

Corcoran found Dolley Madison to be down to earth, with a keen wit and bottomless charm. She eschewed the current female trend for pious, demure, behavior and laughed at all his jokes, some of which were slightly off color. When the banker baldly asked her age, people within hearing distance winced. But Dolley Madison lived up to her reputation for tact.

"I am 74, Mr. Corcoran," she responded, smiling sweetly. "How old are you?" They had repeated the exchange every year, with no change in Corcoran's question or Dolley Madison's reply.

Her clothing and the décor in her little house attested to a state of arrested style. She always wore *widow's weeds*, with contours that softened along with her aging figure. Her lustrous deep brown hair had been replaced by false black curls that peeked out from each side of the ubiquitous silk turbans she always sported, decades after they had passed from fashion. The furnishings in the Lafayette Square house dated from the Republican era, although she had added an ottoman to her parlor during the 1840s to acknowledge modern tastes in household accoutrements.

No one in 1849 in Washington really cared how old Dolley Madison had become. She was a legend in the city and was credited with establishing the first semblance of a truly national social etiquette in the fledgling capital, when it was little more than a swamp containing a few pretentious public buildings. Pennsylvania Avenue had been a quagmire during those early days, and some congressmen got lost between their lodgings near Capitol Hill and the President's House, where "Queen Dolley," as she became known, hosted receptions for both political parties and other notable visitors when the government was in session.

Guests called her Wednesday night parties "Mrs. Madison's Drawing Room", referring to the elaborate and high-style décor in the White House public rooms open for receptions. The oval drawing room and its two adjoining parlors were thronged with visitors during these gatherings. Dolley circulated among the guests, offering kind words and making introductions. The state dining room was added to the suite during the eight years of the Madison

Administration, but the East Room remained off limits pending its completion. Abigail Adams, the first presidential wife to occupy the mansion, had used the cavernous hall to dry her laundry.

Madison's predecessor, the widowed Thomas Jefferson, had preferred small, all-male dinner parties in lieu of large coed public receptions. His freeform style of etiquette, called Pell Mell, had offended members of the diplomatic corps stationed in the new American capital. The widower from Monticello had called occasionally on the wife of his secretary of state to serve as hostess for formal dinners during his administration. But Dolley was helpless to impose traditional European rules of protocol on Jefferson, who insisted on strict equality among all his guests.

The national experiment in Republican government required some rules of social conduct, so after Madison took office as president in March 1809, he and his wife made some changes in protocol and revamped the interiors at the executive mansion. Madison placed the task of decorating the main rooms in the hands of Dolley and British-born architect Benjamin Henry Latrobe, who served as superintendent of public buildings in the federal city. Latrobe drew inspiration from the neoclassical interior designs of Britain's Thomas Hope, and dressed up the oval drawing room (the Blue Room) with fancy Grecian-style painted chairs and benches custom-made in Baltimore. The benches were embellished with the arms of the United States. The oval room was set off with brilliant red velvet curtains, large looking glasses, and a handsome patterned Brussels carpet. Plump red velvet cushions adorned the seating furniture.

Mrs. Madison's parlor (the Red Room) was finished in the English neoclassical Sheraton style with mahogany furniture upholstered in bright yellow satin. Windows were framed with silk in the same color. Dolley dressed formally for the weekly receptions. She was frequently attired in the latest French fashions, including her elaborate turbans, often festooned with ostrich feathers. The ornaments bobbed above the crowds, making it easy to find the first lady as she circulated among the guests. Pretty young ladies, imported for the season, played the pianoforte for the attendees, who drank lemonade and heavily-spiked punch while they ate pastries and tiny frozen sweets wrapped in decorative paper.

Madison followed Jefferson's adherence to equality insofar as the receptions were open to everyone without formal invitations, and no strict dress code was in force. Dolley relied on subtler measures to bring some style and decorum to the occasions. She dressed regally, so visitors took pains to look respectable for their appearance in the handsomely-decorated rooms. Backwoods congressmen cleaned their boots and the tailor shops in Georgetown supplied evening wear for others who arrived in the city without the appropriate dress.

Although all were welcome, it was expected that each stranger would have an introduction to the president and his wife. Crude behavior earned frowns from the assembled guests. When the capital was in New York, and then Philadelphia, elected officials often left their families at home, taking rooms in boarding establishments. In Washington, many wives accompanied their husbands, creating a demand for social activities in the sparsely-settled town. Dolley's system of entertaining was popular with these women, who were desperate for social diversions. Besides, everyone wanted to rub elbows with the government officials and diplomats who made up the new elite class in the federal city.

It was Madison's habit to take a secondary role at these affairs. He continued to dress in the old style, with his hair powdered and pulled back into a small queue at the nape of his neck. He also wore pantaloons, buckles, and stockings, even though the more recent fashion favored long pants. The president usually stood in his parlor (the Green Room), letting guests approach him for brief conversations, while Dolley moved among all the rooms with a smile and a meaningful word for everyone.

James Madison's most ardent detractors were often disarmed by the first lady's ability to remember names and her uncanny knack for tracing kinships. She also engaged in matchmaking with considerable zeal. Friends and relatives sent their daughters to Washington for the session of Congress, where Mrs. Madison introduced them to eligible young congressmen, civil servants, and members of the diplomatic corps.

The Washington's and the Adams's had based their style of entertaining on the royal French levée, although the Americans did not follow the European custom of receiving in their bed chambers. Guests at President George Washington's weekly receptions in New York and Philadelphia were all men, who were escorted to a parlor where they formed a semi-circle while they waited for the arrival of the chief executive. The president, dressed elegantly and bearing a ceremonial sword, would enter last, circulate, and speak briefly with each gentleman. Everyone remained until he departed.

Women attended separate receptions hosted by Martha Washington; these gatherings were nearly as formal. As politics grew more partisan during the Washington administration, the first couple tended to extend invitations more freely to the conservative Federalists than to the liberal Republicans.

Receptions were much more relaxed in the Madison residence. There was no receiving line at the weekly drawing room. Dolley Madison passed from group to group, occasionally pausing to take snuff from a silver box. She would sniff, then blow her nose into a large bandanna for the "heavy work" before "polishing off" with a fine linen handkerchief. If nothing else, her habit served as an ice breaker to strangers.

Buchanan and Webster chatted nostalgically about those early years in the capital before moving on to Dolley's heroism during the War of 1812. Neither man had been present in Washington during the war, but the stories had become a part of her legend.

"Did you know she planned to defend the President's House from the British army with a Tunisian saber?" laughed Buchanan.

Webster had heard the stories of her courage when she found herself alone in the mansion when British troops marched on the federal city in late August 1814. Rumors had circulated that British Admiral Sir George Cockburn planned to take her prisoner and hold her for ransom.

The two men discussed the ensuing evacuation of Washington, centering on Mrs. Madison's insistence on remaining in the house until she had packed the cabinet papers, the silver, and, for some reason, the red velvet curtains from the oval parlor. John Pierre Souissat, her doorkeeper, hurriedly delivered her pet macaw to the French ambassador for safe keeping.

Servants urged her to flee, but she waited until the large portrait of George Washington could be taken from its frame and spirited out of the city by two male passersby from New York who were pressed into service. Only then did she enter her own carriage and leave the city. Within hours the British entered the capital and on the night of August 24, 1814, the main public buildings in Washington went up in flames.

Dolley Madison's importance as a social model in Washington was cemented during the months after the British burned the town. She and the president returned to the city and established quarters in Octagon House, an elegant residence on New York Avenue owned by wealthy Virginia planter John Tayloe. She reestablished her weekly drawing rooms and hosted a grand illumination and party to announce Andrew Jackson's victory at the Battle of New Orleans.

The largest reception at the Octagon took place after word reached the federal city in February 1815 that the Treaty of Ghent ending the War of 1812 with Great Britain had been signed on Christmas Eve, 1814. The terms effectively maintained the status quo, but the infant United States had boldly taken on the mighty British lion and survived. People rejoiced.

Buchanan and Webster had looked after Dolley Madison after she returned as a widow to Washington in 1842. They were instrumental in completing the sale of the remainder of James Madison's papers to the Congress in 1848, paid some of her debts, and secured the remaining $20,000 in a trust fund whose income could support Mrs. Madison in her final years. No one wanted Payne Todd to get his hands on any of it; he had already ruined his mother with his endless gambling and drunken sprees.

"Where is Todd?" Buchanan enquired with a scowl.

"Mary Cutts sent me a note yesterday stating that Todd and his creditors were trying to get access to Mrs. Madison to make her sign another will, leaving everything to Todd." Webster made a face of disgust.

Both men knew that Mrs. Madison's will called for the trust to be split equally between her son and her niece and ward, Annie Payne. Annie was devoted to her famous aunt, but she was poor, plump, and plain, with limited prospects for a good marriage. The funds would give her a dowry large enough to secure a decent husband.

"Who is pulling Todd's strings? Is it Ferguson?"

Webster nodded.

Buchanan cursed under his breath. William Ferguson was a formidable adversary, they knew. A successful businessman with a taste for art, he had been loaning money to Todd for years and taking payment in art objects and political memorabilia from the once-rich stores at Montpelier. Dolley had carried only a small portion of the collection with her when she moved from Virginia to Washington, first in 1837 for the season, and then permanently in 1842.

Todd was charged with transporting the remaining Montpelier furnishings to his bizarre Orange County estate, Toddsberthe, but never got around to completing the move. When Dolley had received word in 1844 that the Montpelier slaves were to be auctioned off to pay overdue property taxes, she negotiated a quick sale of the mansion house, its remaining furnishings, and some surrounding acreage to Henry W. Moncure of Richmond.

Now the politicians would have to deal with Todd's latest attempt to get money from his mother. Both men were determined to block him, whatever the cost.

>==++>

July 12-16, 1849

Dolley Madison died quietly on July 12, 1849, with her family and her great friend Eliza Collins Lee by her side. She had written to Eliza in 1793, telling her to "come to me," because James Madison wanted to meet her. Eliza had married Congressman Richard Bland Lee of Virginia. Their home in Fairfax was close enough for her to reach Dolley's bedside before the end.

The federal city began planning for a major tribute to the memory of the beloved former first lady. The newspaper announced that her body would lie in state in St. John's Church, located only a stone's throw away from the Madison house on Lafayette Square. The newspaper published the "Order of Procession" for her funeral, scheduled to take place on July 16.

The president and cabinet would march behind the family, followed by members of Congress, the Supreme Court, and other dignitaries. Burial was to take place in Congressional Cemetery. "Citizens and strangers" were relegated to the rear of the parade. President Zachary Taylor would deliver the eulogy.

As the funeral party moved slowly through the city, people lined the streets to get a view of the casket and the national leaders who followed in its path. Few noticed one dark-haired woman toward the rear of the mourners, who marched beside a boy about 14 years old. Both wore black. The woman was tall and comely, with dark curls, blue eyes and a dignified bearing. She neither smiled nor wept.

CHAPTER 18

CARY TRAVELS–MAY 27-28, 2011
Cary

ary was working from her Montpelier office and decided to look through her files for possible leads on DNA. Ham had cleared her to speak with Natalia Kruskov, who was now briefed on the project needs. He would handle the researcher's contract.

She and Ham were now exploring the avenue of investigation, suspecting that Edward Coles' 1816 trip to Europe also had something to do with Payne Todd's earlier foreign trip in 1813-1815. By all accounts, Todd had done a poor job as secretary to the U.S. delegation to Ghent. John Payne Todd had been a handsome young man, and letters from abroad reported that he was treated like a prince in the foreign capitals he visited.

Cary turned her attention to surviving DNA among the Payne and Todd clans. She had spoken by phone with Fred Schmidt at Dover, who repeated the mantra for historical DNA searches: *blood, sweat, tears, teeth, and hair.* Cary repeated the list silently while examining the files for locations of items believed to have belonged to close members of the family. She had no idea how degraded any surviving evidence might be and decided to leave the answers to the government specialists with their fancy equipment. Finally, she compiled a list for further research:

- Extant miniature portraits of John Todd, Dolley P. Todd and John Payne Todd. Did they contain locks of hair on the reverse of the image?
- Mourning jewelry containing hair. Same question.
- Clothing and accessories said to have belonged to women in Dolley Madison's family. Had it been washed? Sweat marks under arms; stains on fabric?

She called the curator at Independence National Historical Park and asked for information about collateral descendants of John Todd, whose house on the corner of Fourth and Walnut Streets was a part of the INHP complex in downtown Philadelphia. She would need the line of descent from John Todd's brother James.

Cary seemed to recall that Dolley as first lady did some service for the son of her former brother-in-law. After the ugly way that James had treated her when she was first widowed in 1793, Cary would not have blamed Dolley for ignoring James Todd's request for assistance.

After her husband, John Todd died, the young widow, recovering from her own bout with the yellow fever, was stranded in Grey's Ferry outside Philadelphia with only $19. Appeals for assistance from her brother-in-law were initially ignored, and James Todd was equally slow in settling John Todd's estate and that of his own parents. Dolley was sole beneficiary in the will of John Todd, Jr., and was scheduled to receive 2/3 of the possessions of her in-laws, John Todd Sr. and his wife Mary.

The curator at INHP reported that the Todd line of descent was not overly detailed. Admittedly, that family was less well known to historians than Dolley's own kin. In fact, the Park Service had interpreted the house for many years as an example of middle class Philadelphia life during the late 18th century. The focus was not so much on the Todd's as on the lifestyles of people in their socioeconomic position.

⊷╬╬⊷

The Greensboro Museum got an email asking for information about Payne family descendants, including the Cutts line. Kim Field, the curator there, might have something to add to the information that was already in Cary's files. Everyone wanted to know why she needed the information. Cary told them that Montpelier was preparing a special exhibit, "CSI, Montpelier," where visitors would pretend to be forensic analysts. Mentally, she wondered if lightning would strike her dead for the lie.

Cary then called the chief of archaeology at Montpelier, determined to pursue all possible avenues. Amory James had been digging at the site for more than a decade. The resulting collection was large and still growing. James picked up after three rings.

"Got a few questions, Amory," she said. She told the archaeologist that she was curious about fingerprints that might survive on original artifacts. Her interest lay in the artifacts associated with the mansion house, and specifically with items used by James and Dolley there. Cary knew it could easily be a dead end.

"Some of the shards have not been cleaned," said James. "There may be some evidence on the stems of broken glassware or large pieces of ceramic." She asked him to hold off cleaning likely fragments until she checked back in.

Then she phoned Ham to discuss the possibilities. Ham nixed the fingerprint suggestion, but immediately warmed to the cover story about a CSI exhibit at Montpelier, approving it as the official storyline for any in-depth examinations of Madisoniana.

Cary did not give up easily. "Ham, have you thought about digging on the site of Toddsberthe?" There were no visible ruins, but

127

the location of the complex was known by people all over Orange County. Cary knew that Payne Todd had taken many valuable items from Montpelier to his odd home. Given his alcoholism, which usually led to breakage, there was probably a large trash pit on the site. Ham promised to think about it, but reminded Cary that time was of the essence. Each summed up the results of the day and then signed off.

If I'm checking the object lists, I might as well make another pass at locating missing papers, she thought. Perusing the list of artifacts associated with the Madisons, Cary focused on those that might have hidden compartments containing documents. Papers hidden in compartments in desks would have already been located. Quickly, she eliminated case pieces and tables with drawers. China, glassware, jewelry, metals, unlined containers, and small objects were also discarded from the list.

She already knew that all but a few surviving dresses had been restored and most often, relined. *What about upholstered furniture?* She examined the photographs of sofas, couches, and chairs, and could find no likely examples with original fabric.

Textiles? Flat textiles had all been professionally conserved. Maybe not all of them....

Paintings and prints? All the paintings had been relined and the prints reframed with hidden acid-free matting.

Boxes? This category might be promising, since the interiors were sometimes lined with decorative wallpaper or fabric, which could disguise manuscripts tucked beneath. After an hour of searching through the files, she selected three collections for further examination and put in a call to Ham. He picked up almost immediately.

"Hi. I need to make a road trip," she said.

"Where to?" Ham asked.

"Washington, Richmond, and Greensboro."

After a call to Abbott, she went to her apartment and packed for a two-day trip. It was not yet noon when she managed to reach

Nancy Sayre, the curator at one of the Smithsonian museums, who agreed to see her at 2:00 pm. Before leaving her apartment, she emailed her potential DNA list to Fred Schmidt.

The box at the Smithsonian was in storage. Tradition held that it had contained the state papers that Dolley Madison had saved from the White House before the British burned it in 1814. Legend had swelled the story to include the Declaration of Independence and the Constitution, but the document box had contained the cabinet and state papers of Madison's administration. The size nearly matched a modern storage carton for files, except this example had brass handles, a lock and handsome leather covering.

Nancy opened the box carefully while fully gloved, to protect the surfaces from skin oils and dirt. Cary peered in, using a microscope and pin light. After examining the interior surfaces for any lumps or breaks and finding none, she withdrew. Cary thanked the curator and left the museum. She returned to her car and headed down I-95 toward Richmond.

The number for the curator at the Virginia Historical Society in Virginia's capital city was stored on her cell phone. Cary reached Harper Wade before closing time and was pleased when she agreed to see her in the morning. Upon arriving in Richmond, Cary grabbed carry-out from the Church Hill grocery and retired to her house for the night. Connie was still there, and they enjoyed a leisurely meal.

The box at the Richmond museum was an old jewelry box of mahogany that had an excellent provenance associating it with the last major sale of the Madisons' possessions, the Kunkel auction in 1899 in Philadelphia. The donors to the museum had also donated the original bill of sale, the newspaper notice of the auction, and a sheet from the auction catalogue.

⊷⊷

Dr. Harper Wade had been curator at the history society for decades. Before Cary arrived the next morning, Wade had retrieved the article from storage and showed it to Cary in a basement workroom. After removing the documents relating to the provenance, she and Cary saw that the container was unlined. No luck. Soon, Cary was on her way to Greensboro.

Among the Madison objects in the Greensboro museum was a large trunk, obviously from the mid-19th century. It was lined with cream wallpaper printed with deep brown maple leaves that may have originally been black. The interior was stained and some of the paper was starting to separate from the walls and bottom of the domed trunk. Kim Field, the curator of the Madison collection at the museum, had worked with Cary for years. The two women had become good friends, so the Virginian was greeted warmly. Field took Cary into the museum storage area. Both curators donned protective gloves and peered inside the open trunk, examination tools at the ready.

Cary saw it first. There was a small, slightly raised rectangle beneath the paper along one side of the right interior wall, near the top.

"Kim," she called. "Look at this!"

They examined the outline and determined that there was an area at the top of the protrusion where the wallpaper glue had completely separated from the side wall of the trunk itself. Kim retrieved tweezers, a slim surgical knife, and a brighter light to take a closer look at the opening. She gently inserted the very thin blade and expanded the opening to a size slightly wider than the rectangle without tearing the wallpaper.

Then she reached in with the tweezers and, inch by inch, extracted the document from the hidden pocket.

"Got it!" she announced.

Cary was ready with an acid-free mat. Kim carefully laid the artifact on the supporting surface and they huddled over the exciting discovery.

It was one folded page of writing that consisted of a report from Edward Coles to President Madison in December 1816. Coles had written the letter from St. Petersburg, before the young envoy left for his tour of Europe.

Mr. Madison,
President, U.S.
Washington, D.C.

Sir,

I am pleased to report that the matter has been settled to the satisfaction of all parties. The agents here have agreed to match the funds you offer to help support the first phase of the plan until the next phase can be implemented. The beneficiary in question will remain at the palace of the Dowager, who welcomes the opportunity to assist.

They have also agreed to your proposal that I be appointed agent for the funds. I will place them with a reputable bank in London when I arrive there on my way back to the United States.

With profound respect, etc. etc.
Edwd Coles

Kim eyed Cary sternly. "What in God's name is *this* all about?"

It sure ain't about any trade agreement, Cary thought. She explained about the packet of debts long missing from Dolley's estate and urged Kim to examine the trunk further to see if other documents had been hidden under the wallpaper lining. As soon as Kim turned her back, Cary entered a special code into her cell, pressed *send*, and pocketed the machine.

The curator's search came up empty. The two women turned their attention to a cream-colored silk bodice, said to have been part of Dolley's wedding gown at her marriage to James Madison. Kim told her that the piece had never been conserved, since it was a fragment not suitable for display. In addition, the shape of the top suggested some later alterations, quite common during the Civil War, when the blockade of Confederate states made fine imported fabrics unavailable. Women had rummaged through trunks and created new fashions from old ones. There were stains under the arms. Cary asked if Kim would allow some testing on the fabric prior to the proposed loan exhibition. The Greensboro curator frowned but promised to give the request her consideration.

Suddenly, Kim's cell phone rang. She carefully removed her gloves and answered the call, listened for a few seconds, and frowned.

"You want me to do *what*?" Kim asked into the phone. Cary froze and looked at her. She couldn't hear the voice on the other end, but she heard the strident tone of the speaker. Finally, Kim disconnected the call and turned to face Cary again.

"You're not going to believe this," she said, seeming confused and exasperated.

Oh, I think I can guess what's getting ready to happen, Cary thought. She was shocked at the speed with which DHS had already removed, examined, and returned objects from several other museums in the DNA search.

The museum director entered the storage room, accompanied by a burly, middle-aged man who looked like a bouncer. The stranger's natural expression was south of a scowl and north of a sneer. Cary knew William Searle, the museum director, from previous visits. He did not look happy either.

He nodded curtly to Cary and turned to Kim. "This is agent Smith of the Department of Homeland Security. He'll be removing certain Madison materials for examination by the federal government."

"What?" Kim asked, her jaw slack.

"I've signed the appropriate papers," Searle said. "Please assist him in packing the items."

With that, the museum director turned on his heels and strode out of the room. Before he closed the door, he turned and announced, "Fuckin' Patriot Act," as he closed the door.

As if by magic, a museum preparator appeared with a dolly, soft packing materials, and acid-free folders. The young man kept his eyes focused on the floor, avoiding all eye contact.

"Do you people have any training in handling works of art and fragile historical materials?" Kim asked. Her cheeks had gone flush. When Agent Smith ignored her, and moved toward the trunk, Kim shoved protective gloves in his face. The preparator had already donned his from a box on a nearby table.

The trunk, the extracted document, the bodice, and one of Dolley's turbans were carefully packed for transport. Kim forced the agent to sign a loan form before she would release the items. The man silently inked the form on the appropriate line. Within ten minutes, the materials were packed in an air-cooled, cushioned van, and on their way north. Cary, Kim, and the preparator had done all the work. Smith seemed content to watch the proceedings.

"I hope he knows how to drive in addition to his obvious skills in throwing his weight around," said Kim. She was trembling with rage over the violation of her turf, the lack of adherence to established protocols for moving museum collections, and, Cary surmised, a deep distrust of the agent who has absconded with parts of the collections under her care.

Finally, Kim calmed down enough to thank the preparator, who fled as soon as he could. She then turned to Cary.

"Care you tell me what this is about?" she asked.

Cary shook her head.

"Are you in danger?" Kim asked.

Cary felt a keen sense of guilt over her silence, along with a flush of affection for her long-time friend and colleague. She leaned forward and hugged Kim, assuring her that there was no danger to her or to the artifacts.

"From what little I know," she assured her, "the stuff will be back before you even calm down."

"Kim smiled. "Fat chance of that."

Cary declined an offer to have dinner and stay the night, and was back in Richmond by 9:00 pm. She called Connie on the way to say she was coming home, and arrived to find a nice dinner, a big bottle of bourbon, and an inquisitive house sitter firmly ensconced at her kitchen table. She relaxed and swigged from her bourbon, mulling over the past two days.

"What is it?" asked Connie.

"Sorry, Con. Can't say anything about what's going on."

A solid pout appeared on Connie's face, which faded once they had their second cocktails in hand. Connie filled Cary in on correspondences and other business, local gossip, deaths and marriages, and the state of his ever-volatile love life.

CHAPTER 19

MONTPELIER – MAY 29 - JUNE 1, 2011
Cary

Cary headed back to Montpelier after a good night's sleep. She found a message to call Ham on her office desk there when she arrived. The DHS agent brought her up to date on the analysis of the trunk, which had not yielded additional papers. They were checking for DNA on the bodice.

"What do you think of the report from Edward Coles?" he asked.

"You and I both think Coles was referring to something Payne Todd did in Russia," she said. "but the language is sufficiently vague. We may still need the family DNA and additional genealogical confirmation to pin it down." She wanted to check her emails before saying anything else, so she told him she'd call him back.

Natalia had emailed her to say that she had found a Romanov descendent who might be of service in unscrambling some of the royal genealogy. Cary phoned her immediately.

"Princess Sasha Troubetzskoy, a maiden lady," said Natalia, chuckling. "She's known as something of a character among Russian royals. She's a bastard tracker."

"She's a *what?*"

"She traces the genealogy of descendants born to the Romanov royals," said Natalia, "*including* the illegitimate ones. She's been working on this stuff for more than thirty years."

Cary was informed that the princess, who enjoyed excellent health, lived outside Nice, France, in a family villa. After writing down the address and phone number for the woman, Mallory asked Natalia to plan a trip to the U.S. and said she'd have DHS make travel arrangements for them both.

"Where to?"

"Probably Philadelphia," said Cary, assuming that Ham would want several additional experts on hand for their meeting. She suspected that a confab could be arranged in record time and she was right.

———✦✦———

Three days later, Cary took Amtrak from Union Station in Washington to 30th Street Station in Philadelphia for the meeting with the Romanov descendant and Natalia. After clearing building security, she was escorted to a small conference room on the 3rd floor of the NERO regional office. Ham emerged from behind the door and smiled. She was not surprised to see him there.

"Her name is Sasha Troubetzskoy," he said. He turned to walk down a long hallway and she followed him. "She's connected to the Romanovs through Nicholas I. She's a monarchist, but not in line for the succession."

"Is she a bastard, too?" Cary asked, smiling.

"You'll have to ask her," he said, laughing. "I didn't have the nerve."

Cary entered the room and introduced herself to an elderly, aristocratic woman with white hair, piercing black eyes, and a firm but pleasant mouth. The princess smiled and inclined her head but did not extend her hand. Natalia, who was already in the office, greeted Cary with the warmth of an old friend. Fred Schmidt stood stiffly behind her.

Ham began the session with thanks for their cooperation and assurances of confidentiality for any information that they might share in the investigation, which he described as a possible terrorist threat to national security. The princess sniffed and tried to look suitably impressed. Ham laid out several scenarios and confided that the team was inclined to trace a Madison-Romanov connection to Edward Coles' diplomatic voyage to St. Petersburg in 1816.

Coles also noted their suspicions about Payne Todd's possible involvement in some scandal that took place during his assignment as secretary to the American delegation to negotiate an end to the 1812 war, or his European tour that followed the treaty.

"The child was named Maria, after the Dowager Empress of Russia, the widow of Tsar Paul I," said the princess. "Empress Maria raised her, you know."

Mouths gaped all around the table.

"She was the natural daughter of Tsar Alexander I's sister, Natasha."

Bingo! Ham looked at Cary, who smiled.

The old woman saw them nod. "In her journal, the Empress recorded that the pregnancy was kept a secret from the court, and that Natasha was sent to complete her term under the watchful eye of her mother at Pavlovsk Palace outside the city. After the birth, Tsar Alexander I, little Maria's uncle, wrote to President Madison about the child and asked that joint arrangements be made for her support and upbringing. The tsar offered to provide funds and suggested that the American leader do the same. Madison was told that the Dowager Empress Maria was extremely fond of her namesake, wished to provide financial assistance, and would raise the child in her own household. Clearly, the royal family would not bestow titles on the girl or outwardly acknowledge her as the daughter of a grand duchess, whom Alexander had rapidly married off to a Prussian prince when the infant was less than a year old."

"We know that Madison wrote a letter in May 1816," said Cary, "presumably to the tsar or his emissary."

Princess Troubetzskoy nodded. "It is my understanding that President Madison said that he was sending an envoy to discuss the arrangements under the pretext of settling a misunderstanding between the U.S. and Russia about the activities of the Russian consul in Philadelphia." She chuckled. "He sent the agent on a ship of war. The tsar was away and no one in St. Petersburg knew quite what to make of the gesture. The Troubetzskoy's dined on the story for years."

Cary and Ham exchanged sidelong glances, both aware that they were correct.

"What happened to little Maria after the Empress died in 1828?"

"She remained with the Empress's servants for a few years before she was sent to the United States for education and further upbringing. The agent – Coles was his name – was placed in charge of the funds set aside for her use. I believe she arrived in Philadelphia in 1832 at the age of 17."

" Please continue," said Cary, smiling warmly.

"Maria was educated in Baltimore. She married a respectable gentleman in that city and was left a widow with a young son eight years later. She then moved to Washington and used funds set aside by Coles, along with her inheritance from her late husband, to purchase a property near the Navy Yard, where she operated a boarding house. In 1852, she returned to Europe with her son Alex and a negro servant, traveling as a widow named Mary Nicholas. The journey took her to the Ruhr region to live with her mother. By that time, the Russian-born grand duchess lived apart from her husband, so she was free to reunite with her long-lost daughter."

Princess Troubetzskoy paused and exhaled, before continuing when she saw the room's attention trained on her. "Maria never remarried and died in Brussels in 1860. Her mother outlived her and died in 1867. Natasha had arranged a marriage for her grandson Alex to a Georgian noblewoman of the Bagrationi of Muhrani line, direct descendants of the last king of Georgia. The Russian Empire had absorbed Georgia in 1801, deporting the royal family. Many of the line ended up in Russia and others took up residence in other parts of Europe."

"So, Alex's father was Maria's first husband?" asked Ham.

"We always assumed he was the man from Baltimore," Princess Troubetzskoy said. "Maria later remarried, of course. It was to a ship captain named Nicholas, who was abroad when she left Washington for Germany."

Ham waved for her to continue.

"Maria's mother Natasha was a Russian grand duchess, so her illegitimate daughter Maria carried the Romanov blood line. The grandson Alex also had the bloodlines and, having married into the Bagrationi-Muhrani family, produced another son. This child also produced a son. He already carried Romanov blood from his matrilineal ancestors."

"Did he have a daughter named Marie?" asked Cary.

The elderly woman shook her head. He married an Italian noblewoman and they did have a daughter, but they named her Angela. The child was born in Italy in the 1950s and married a minor noble. She does not claim to be the legal heir to the Romanov throne, but there are several claims to the title among other descendants of Tsar Nicholas I. "One claims there are no direct males in the Romanov line who qualify. Under the edict issued by Tsar Paul I, a female could only claim the title after all male descendants were dead."

"Where did our victim come from?" Ham asked.

Princess Troubetzskoy frowned. "Every family has its black sheep, my dears. And there was a pattern that appeared among some of the descendants of Maria, the bastard daughter."

"What kind of pattern?" Ham asked, He was leaning forward and nodding in anticipation.

"Sometimes alcohol, sometimes drugs. Maybe promiscuity or unsuitable behavior. The signs have varied widely from generation to generation" The old woman shook her head sadly. "Family tradition holds that Alex, the grandson of Grand Duchess Natasha Pavlova, was highly eccentric if not insane. His family had to separate him from his family and keep him in semi-isolation, lest he do them harm.

There are multiple descendants of Nicholas I, and several of them displayed strange traits. I believe that Angela is your best route to Mexico and a birth in the 1985-time frame."

"Is Angela eccentric?" Cary asked. She wondered if the gene showed up dominant in every generation.

"Hardly. She may have had a liaison in Europe or perhaps in Mexico, but royals have been doing that for centuries. No, she is well-educated and dignified, a model of propriety. There is a chance that a child was conceived when Angela was in the process of obtaining her divorce during the mid-1980s."

"Did you know about the existence of our victim?" Ham asked. He could admit that he was intrigued by the old woman's peculiar interest in genealogy.

Princess Troubetzskoy chuckled. "Not specifically, but I plan to follow up. One never knows when another offspring will appear in our lineage!"

Fred Schmidt asked the princess about towns in Mexico frequented by Russian aristocrats after World War II. "Well, Acapulco has waned in popularity, to be supplanted by San Miguel de Allende, the well-known artist colony located in Guanajuato.

Several members of Russian nobility have homes in the resort city, and quite a few have visited there during the period under investigation."

Cary made a mental note to meet privately with the princess after the meeting and arrange to introduce her to her old college roommate, VE Shane. VE has strong contacts among Mexican aristocrats and government officials and might be able to team up with the Princess on the investigation there.

After the session broke up, she discussed the possibility of such a trip to the princess, suggesting gently that a visit to San Miguel might yield some more definitive results. The notion seemed to appeal to the elderly lady, who promised to share any additional information she might gather. Cary told her about VE Shane, assuring the aristocrat that the Texan would be contacting her soon.

CHAPTER 20

PHILADELPHIA – JUNE 1, 2011
Cary

Ham arranged for the princess to have a private tour of cultural sites in Philadelphia. After she had gone, Natalia, Cary, Ham, and Fred Schmidt met to hear the results of the frantic behind-the-scenes testing and research of fragile museum artifacts that took place over the previous week. From what Cary could surmise, several of them had been spirited away from major museums in the dead of night, taken to Dover for analysis, and quietly returned to their owners. She herself had been present when items were hauled out of the Greensboro Museum only days before.

Natalia Kruskov, the Russian genealogist, was still wading through the bulky records of what she called the House of Holstein-Gottorp-Romanov. She assured Cary that she had enough facts to offer a plausible brief to the team. The Hermitage Museum curator had recommended her as "the only person on earth who can keep all those Germanic principalities straight."

Natalia had received the DNA results in time to prepare a draft lineage chart concerning the young victim. She also had gotten an email from Cary two days before explaining the wording of the 1816 report to Madison from Edward Coles. Cary imagined that

Madam Kruskov's final report would exceed 400 pages and would read like a chapter from the *Iliad*, with someone "begetting" someone else for dozens of generations.

Cary had already shared her information about descendants of the Payne and Todd families. Schmidt came with a briefcase and a laptop and led off with a PowerPoint presentation. He explained that the DNA lab analyzed four samples of hair, three of which came from miniature portraits of Dolley. They belonged to John Todd, John Payne Todd, and a lock of hair said to belong to Dolley that was handed down in the Cutts line. They also examined blood stains from a pincushion at Montpelier and perspiration stains from one of Dolley's turbans. The DNA from the bodice in the Greensboro Museum was too debased for detailed analysis. Images of the objects came up on the screen as he spoke

Within minutes, Schmidt had lapsed into DNA-speak. The group listened patiently to dense jargon about mitochondrial DNA, STR DNA and haplogroups, all of it illustrated with dots and dashes that looked like some arcane military code. Ham interrupted the briefing and asked the scientist to cut to the chase.

"There's just a few things we need to know," he said. "Was the victim related to John Payne Todd?'

Schmidt nodded.

"Was the victim related to Dolley Payne Madison?"

"Yes."

"Were there links to Russian royalty?"

"Yes."

"When does it show up?"

"Well, it's hard to say. The hard evidence on hand for examination was early and very late, with large holes in the middle. Details about generations in between Dolley Payne and the victim have not yet been traced. Additional research might yield the identities of living descendants or evidence of additional historic descendants who could be tested for DNA linkages."

"Was there anything peculiar," Ham asked. "A marker or markers that helped in the identification?"

"Maybe."

At this point, Schmidt gave a gentlemanly bow to Natalia and asked her to show the lines *tentatively* connecting Russian royalty to the victim. Natalia put up another PowerPoint showing a lineage chart.

Name	DNA Marker	Dominant
Dolley P.T. Madison b.1768	Yes	No
Anna Payne Cutts	Yes	No
Attorney John Todd	No	No
John Payne Todd b.1792	Yes	Yes
Maria Todd, b.1815 Russia	?	No
Alex McGehee, b.1836, Baltimore	Yes	Yes family
Nicholai McGehee Bagrationi-Muhrani b. 1861	?	?
Son, b. 1889	?	?
Selena, B-M b. 1920	Yes	No
Angela Bagrationi, b. 1950	Yes	No
Unidentified victim, b. 1985?	Yes	Yes

"In most instances, we do not have any DNA evidence," she said. "The Payne gene shows up in Dolley, Anna Payne Cutts, JP Todd and, per family tradition, Alex McGehee. Then we go along until Selena and her daughter Angela, who both had their DNA tested after the bodies of Nicholas II and his family were uncovered. Both women have the Payne and Romanov combination in recessive form. Our victim and John Payne Todd have the same genetic mutation. The Payne gene and the Romanov gene show up dominant in our victim."

"So, what do we *think* happened?" Cary asked.

"We believe that Payne Todd impregnated Grand Duchess Natalia, also known as Natasha Pavlovna, a younger sister of Tsar Alexander I, during Todd's visit to St. Petersburg in 1814. A child seems to have been born in 1815 and placed in the care of the dowager empress, Maria Feodorovna, born in 1759 and deceased 1828. Natasha was one of eleven children born to Maria – nee Princess Sophie Dorothea of Württemberg – and Tsar Paul I. Tsars Alexander I and Nicholas I were two of the empress's sons. Maria always accused Alexander I of murdering her husband. The child's mother was seven years younger than Payne Todd."

"Now we're getting somewhere," Ham said.

"After the birth, Alexander I arranged a quick marriage between Natasha and a younger son of Frederick William III of Prussia," said Natasha. "The couple wed in the Winter Palace at St. Petersburg in 1816. The tsar stated publicly that the union would strengthen the bonds created under the terms of the Congress of Vienna. Natalia moved to Berlin, gave the prince several children – two girls and a boy – but never rose to become queen or queen consort of Prussia. The couple did not get along very well. Natasha considered her status to be well above that of a lesser Prussian prince and lived apart from her husband for much of their later marriage. She eventually left the court, settled in the Ruhr area of Germany, and lived quietly until her death in 1867."

"Why do you think the child was raised by Maria and not by her birth mother?" Cary asked.

Natalia smiled. "Natasha's marriage was something of an expediency. The power was in Russia. Tsar Alexander was less interested in a strong alliance than in getting his disgraced sister off his hands. As dowager empress, Maria had considerable influence in the royal court. Few people challenged her. She was imperious and generally got her way. Empress Maria resided at Pavlovsk Palace, several miles outside St. Petersburg, kept her own court, and lived in great refinement and elegance. By comparison, her son Alexander I was Spartan in his tastes. Empress Maria was a patron of the arts and gained a reputation, at least within royal circles, for her watercolors. She kept Pavlovsk Palace as a monument to the memory of her late husband, Tsar Paul I, and upon her death it was kept up by her descendants as a sort of museum to 18th century taste. After The 1917 Revolution, the new government kept the site, which was restored at great expense after World War II."

Natalia ran through several slides of the palace, grounds, and interiors. She paused and changed the slide to the image of a painting of a young girl in Pavlovsk Park, the classic landscape garden at the palace designed by Britain's Charles Cameron. It showed the little girl standing in the flower garden behind the palace, near a statue of the Three Graces. Natalia explained that Empress Maria would have been able to see the statue from her private apartments. The genealogist showed a close-up of the watercolor, which revealed a title and date in German.

"It reads, 'My beloved secret granddaughter and namesake Maria, Pavlovsk, 1825.'" The child appeared to be about ten years old.

"When did Empress Maria die?" Ham asked.

"1828. The estate stayed in the Romanov family until the Revolution. Before the Germans occupied the site during World War II, the curatorial staff there carefully packed and moved a great deal of the collection, which was returned when the property was restored after the bombing."

The murder team learned that the Germans set the palace on fire when they abandoned Pavlovsk during the liberation, but much of its original collection survived. "Some of the old tapestries are in the collections of the J. Paul Getty Museum in your country." Natalia turned off the projector in anticipation of more questions.

"What happened to her granddaughter?" Cary asked, with Ham and others leaning forward with curiosity.

"The child was never legitimized," she said. "At least according to the records. But she was accorded a respectful status among the family due to the affection of her grandmother, the dowager empress. You must understand that Payne Todd, although the son of the U.S. president, was deemed unsuitable as a mate for Grand Duchess Natasha Pavlovna. After all, he was a mere commoner."

"Sorry guys," said Fred, clearing his throat. "But the genetic variation helps us at this point." He turned back on the projector and brought up an image showing a string of numbered DNA that was supposed to mean something. It was clear that he had gone through his presentation with Natalia before starting.

"Dolley Madison had a genetic mutation that passed down to her descendants," Fred said. "We now know enough to analyze dominant and recessive mutations. Her sister Cutts had it as a recessive gene, but Payne Todd did inherit it in the dominant mode. Little Maria, the bastard child, had it as a recessive gene, and it continued, sometimes recessive, and other times dominant, until around 1985, because it showed up as dominant in our victim."

"The victim is the 7th great-granddaughter of Dolley Madison."

"What do we know about the marker?" asked Ham.

"Well, the human genome and genealogical DNA are new frontiers, but we know that when it goes dominant, it produces some behavioral disorders."

"As in?" asked Ham.

"We know that Dolley Payne's father had some sort of problem," said Cary. "We know that one of Dolley's brothers came to a bad end, and that her surviving brother John Payne battled alcoholism for decades."

"We did not have any DNA from many generations of the Coles or Payne families to include in the analysis," confessed Fred.

"Princess Troubetzskoy told us it manifests itself with several variations in behavior."

"What about the Todd's?" asked Ham. "Logically, if John Todd did not have the marker, neither did his brother James."

"John Todd was clean," said Fred.

"That makes sense," said Cary. "Dolley's brother-in-law, James Todd, was an SOB, drinking, and refusing to take responsibility for his newly-widowed sister-in-law in 1793. He later embezzled funds from the First Bank of the U.S., but the line seems to have remained relatively clear of problems among most of his descendants, at least the few I know about."

"I repeat my question," Ham said. He was not about to give up.

"There's enough DNA information about the Romanovs," said Fred. We could isolate mitochondrial and STR DNA for the Dolley Payne anomaly and trace records from Russia through France to Germany and Italy and Spain. The victim is almost certainly a relative of one of the modern dynastic claimants to the Romanov throne."

"My question about personality characteristics is still on the table," Ham said.

"Ham," said Fred, "we simply don't know enough at this juncture. The possessor of the dominant form of the gene can be charming, with the morals of a flea, and yet still be highly susceptible to alcohol, drugs, gambling, sexual promiscuity, and other forms of deviant social behavior. Tends to blame someone else for his or her own faults."

"Ouch," said Cary.

"Are any of them psychopaths?" Ham asked. He wondered how it could get much worse.

"Can't be sure," said Fred. "No sense of right and wrong. Compulsive behavior taken to a higher degree. Rage. Voices urging criminal behavior. Murder is possible. Many of these types are legally crazy."

"So, who was our victim?" Ham asked.

"She was like Payne Todd in her amoral approach to responsibility to society," said Cary. "She was an addict. She was promiscuous. She resisted authority. She probably played the game for family affection only to get her immediate desires. The presence of scars from old bullet wounds might suggest a tendency towards violence."

"The genetic mutation could produce all of the above results. Cary, do you think Payne Todd was a murderer?"

Cary mused over the question for a few seconds. "No, my sense tells me that he was more pathetic than dangerous. I suspect that he was more likely to become a victim of murder than commit the act on someone else."

"Okay, folks," declared Ham, "Time for a wrap up."

He walked to a work board and laid out the clues and facts as they were known.

Tie to DPTM and PT	DNA and mutation
Tie to Romanovs	Natasha, sister of Alexander I and Nicholas I and later Bagrationi line
Victim's Parents	Conjecture, Maybe Angela?
Victim	Still unknown

The group meeting broke up, with the attendants filing slowly out of the room. Ham turned to pack up the projector. When he turned around he saw Cary silently waiting for him.

"Have you got major assets at work on this in Mexico?" she asked.

"Some," he said, frowning. "I'm having some difficulty within DHS, due to a collateral issue. But I think I can get it straightened out fast, which would free up more investigators to handle work both in Mexico and the United States."

"Well, Natalia will continue to work on details about the generations between Natasha and the victim. Also, I have a contact in Texas who's very knowledgeable about San Miquel, expats in Mexico, and probably even drug cartels."

"Can your contact be discreet?"

Cary nodded with a smile.

CHAPTER 21

MEET VIRGINIA SHANE
VE Shane

Cary had taken Amtrak from Philadelphia to Union Station, and then driven the hundred miles back to Montpelier. The long trip gave her time to mull over the revelations about the ancestors of the victim and DNS links.

Cary rang a number in Dallas. The call went through with ease. Virginia Eliza Shane, debutante, billionaire executive, society maven, and globetrotter extraordinaire, answered quickly. She had recognized Cary's number and screamed into her cell phone.

"Mallory! God*damn*, how's it goin'?"

Virginia and Cary had roomed together at Sweet Briar back in the day and kept their friendship alive over the decades. The Texas connection between their mothers had no doubt led the school to place them together for freshman year. Cary was a bridesmaid in at least three of VE's weddings, or was it four?

They spent their summers together during undergraduate school. VE learned about the mysteries and stubborn independence of the Chesapeake Bay culture, while Cary got to know the true meaning of *Texas rich*. The Shanes made the Montagues look like pikers.

VE always loved Cap'n Johnny like a father, and Cary felt the same way about John P. "Paw" Shane, one of the biggest Texan legends who ever walked the small face of the earth. Paw was VE's grandfather, and got himself a degree in engineering from MIT before moving west to work in the oil fields. He made money in the East, North, and West Texas fields, then continued from a base in Fort Worth, advising government oil companies around the globe. Paw also picked up some additional oil shares and a great deal of cash and real estate along the way. The elder Shane lived long enough for Cary to get to know him before he died at the age of 98. John P. Junior, known as Little Paw, VE's father, was carrying on the tradition ably but much more quietly.

Cary had visited the sprawling Shane mansion in Fort Worth, the Shane villa outside Cancun, and a smattering of the Shane houses and condos in major cities here and abroad. Neither she nor VE had ever stayed at the Shane compound in Saudi Arabia.

"You won't like it a damned bit, girls," said Little Paw, "You can't drink or drive over there. They don't much cotton to women at all." Paw junior didn't much like it over there either, and sometimes complained that his father should have asked for more money rather than real estate, before giving away a lot of free advice about the value of the vast oil assets in the Middle East. That was long before 1950. By now the rest was history.

Fortunately, engineers tended to be well-organized people, so Paw sought excellent legal and financial advice. This thankfully protected the trust he set up for VE from the slings and arrows of worthless and philandering relatives, ex-husbands, eager venture capitalists, and other low-lifers. VE was raised to be an entrepreneur, but a cautious one.

"Lil' *darlin'*," said Paw before he died, "I truly believe there's no way in hell you can spend all this money, but if you got half the brains I think you do, you can build on it a bit."

She did exactly that. VE was the only grandchild and had traveled frequently with Paw over the years. She had learned her way around the obscenely rich and the dangerously poor who worked in the fields, as well as the political majordomos in multiple countries. Fortunately, she was almost as wily as the oil baron and just as much fun to be around. VE told Cary on more than one occasion, "It's easy, *darlin'* Plus, I got big tits!"

And she did. Big brains, big red hair, big jewels, and big tits. She was blessed with the ability to throw big parties, and the big charitable contributions she gathered were huge assets for a woman who also had really *big* money. VE had some extremely good advisors, which Paw had helped her recruit. She was accustomed to handling many of her financial affairs herself and looked after the high-tech side of the family businesses.

Cary also knew about VE's prenuptial agreements. Little Paw had confided this to Cary after just the second of VE's marriages. By then VE had assured Cary that she could be a perpetual bridesmaid without any fear of financial damage to her fortune.

Cary tried to remember how many children had come from VE's marriages while listening to her buoyant voice. *It was two, all from the investment guru from Boston,* she recalled. They played catch-up per both the female and southern traditions before getting down to brass tacks.

No, VE did not have a new flame.

No, Cary did not have a new flame.

Yes, Cary was seeing Ham Coles, but not romantically.

"Tell me *more!*" cawed VE. It was her who initially promoted the idea of the match.

"It's a business deal," Cary said. She heard the defensiveness in her voice.

"So, what's the drill?"

Cary loved her down-to-earth buddy. She outlined some of the issues involved in tracking down the identity of the victim in the

153

Constitution murder, mentioned San Miguel as a possible birth-place for the girl, and posed questions about the drug cartels working across the border around Nuevo Laredo. She asked VE about any contacts she might have who were familiar with San Miguel during the 1980s. Finally, she asked about the network that the drug cartels were using throughout Texas for distribution.

"I'll get right on it," said VE. They hung up a moment later, Cary still holding the phone for a moment. VE was all business when she had a friend in need.

Natalia had sent a memo prepared by Princess Sasha that filled in some of the gaps about the descendants between Payne Todd and the victim. The Russian noblewoman agreed with Natalia's proposed line of descent. There were few facts, except that some of the offspring had been sheltered from public view, probably because of the genetic flaw. The princess had found no additional information about the victim's biological father. Cary was hoping that DHS or VE could shed light on that part of the mystery. Ham checked in and they discussed the memo from Natalia. Then she had a nightcap and went to bed for a much-needed evening of sleep. She returned to Richmond the following morning. It took VE less than 48 hours to get back to Cary with the results of her investigation, calling the next afternoon while Cary filed through evidence she had pulled from the museum.

"Well, *darling*," she cooed. "There's some nasty buggers involved in this little caper."

Cary opened her laptop and started typing.

"My main source in San Miguel is getting on toward ninety, but she's still sharp as a tack. She remembers a Russian noblewoman spending some time in San Miguel during the mid-'80s. Said she used the name 'Sophia,' but lots of expats use aliases in the close upper-class society of the art colony."

"How'd your friend know she was a Russian noblewoman? "

"The jewels, *darling*, the jewels. My source is from Dallas and the women in this town can recognize real bling when they see it."

"Anything on the lover?"

"Word is she was seen with an artist from Acapulco who spent a part of each year in San Miguel."

"Name?"

"Don't know for sure."

"What *do* we know?"

"Sophia seems to have been introduced to San Miguel through some of the early Mexican muralists who may have known some of her relatives in Spain or Italy. As you may recall, some of the muralists were major communists. One David Sequiras spent some time in Spain fighting the Fascists, but also worked as a teacher at the Instituto de las Bellas Artes in San Miguel."

"The Bellas Artes School?"

"Yeah, *darling*. "It's still there. It was the creation of Peruvian artist Felipe Cossio del Pomar and the American Stirling Dickinson. They started it back in the '30s. The school became popular with Americans after World War II who could study under the G.I. Bill as a companion to the school. In 1942 Pomar purchased a ranch owned by the famous early 20th century bullfighter Pepe Ortiz, which was located on a hill overlooking the town of San Miguel. This became Rancho de Bellas Artes, a colony for artists and writers, including Sequiras and others."

Cary knew the tale was leading somewhere, but she wondered where.

"Okay, so Pomar leaves in 1944, and an Italian family named Campanellas takes over the ranch. Did I tell you it was originally the hacienda for a silk factory?"

"Uh huh."

"Anyway, the hacienda fell into decay, and in 1956 a former Mexican military officer bought it from the mortgage holder. The family still owns it. They converted it into a small resort called Rancho Hotel Atascadero."

"And?"

"And the family has the complete booking records for everyone who has stayed in the hotel since 1957."

"No hint about the artist father? I mean, if in fact the father was an artist?"

"Nope. Per my Dallas source the family's extremely discreet. Seems Sophia may have taken art lessons in the town at one point. My source was unable to get any other information, except that the Russian noblewoman made two trips to San Miguel during the mid-1980s, probably staying at the hotel both times."

"Okay, that's helpful. Can you return to the hotel in search of surviving records? Also, I need you to contact Princess Troubetzskoy to see if you can link up in San Miguel to track additional leads." Cary gave VE the contact information for the Russian noblewoman and promised to get back with whatever additional information she could gather.

"Do you want me to research the Mexican drug cartels? I'm much better at mining information about rich ex-pats than delving into the underbelly of the drug world."

"If you think that'll help."

"To be honest, the Shane empire has to keep track of the drug traffic as a matter of course. I can tell you San Miguel's not a hotbed of activity for the Mexican drug cartels. You need to look a little closer to the U.S. border. That's where the real action is."

They hung up with promises to get together soon.

Cary immediately started to call Ham but then disconnected. She could wait and brief him when she had more information.

CHAPTER 22

WASHINGTON NAVY YARD – FEBRUARY 1852
Cary [being somewhat creative about details]

The man in the bed was sixty years old and suffering from pleurisy. His grey hair was matted and filthy, with patches of flaking red scalp visible through the dirt. His bloated body had sallow skin and multiple bruises caused by rupturing blood veins beneath the surface. He gasped and tried to turn on his side to ease his breathing. The decrepit mattress sagged under his prodigious weight, hindering the motion.

"*Sam!*" he gasped, trying to call his servant. But there was no answer.

Dim light shone through the curtains covering the one window in the tiny room. The air was cold and damp. Opening his eyes, Payne Todd saw that it was daylight. The walls were covered with a sunny floral wallpaper. White curtains framed the window, which was closed to keep out the winter chill. The floor was covered by a blue rag rug, much repaired.

He coughed and called out again.

This brought a response. The woman who entered the chamber was tall and plump, with raven hair and startling blue eyes. She wore a plain day dress of brown wool without crinolines, the material hanging limply around her legs. Wool stockings helped to keep her feet warm. A shawl covered her shoulders.

She just turned 37 but looked older, in part because she rarely smiled. Her lips were compressed into a thin line as she scowled at the pathetic figure on the bed. Sam, a towering black man with biceps like a blacksmith, followed close behind her. Finally, a thin, disheveled teenage boy entered the sick room. He glared with hatred at the bedridden invalid.

"Maria," he croaked. "Come to me, my daughter."

Maria stood firm and motioned for her son to approach the bed. Sam remained silent, standing just inside the doorway into the hall.

"Take the pillow," Maria commanded, and the boy obeyed.

"Put it over his ugly face."

The child had no problem carrying out his task. Payne Todd struggled weakly but the pleurisy, his bulk, and the debilitation caused by years of self-abuse left him helpless to save himself. His muffled groans fell on deaf ears.

The boy smiled cruelly and held the pillow firmly on Todd's face until he was motionless. The trio waited to make sure the man was dead. When the odor of excrement and urine started to fill the room, they turned quietly and left John Payne Todd to his maker.

They had to make haste. Todd's creditors had a habit of showing up at the boarding house at all hours. Maria had already packed most of their belongings, which included a secret stash of jewels bequeathed to her by her grandmother, Dowager Empress Maria of Russia. Maria instructed Sam and her son to change their clothes for travel, attended to her own wardrobe, and was soon ready to leave the home near the Navy Yard that she had occupied since arriving in the federal city in 1843.

The house had just recently been sold. It had operated successfully as a boarding establishment. Maria double-checked to make sure she had the cash from the sale and the carefully amassed savings she had hidden from her father. She also tucked away the papers from her mother, who had arranged for Maria and the child to join her at her home in the Ruhr. They would travel as the widow Mary Nicholas and her son Alex. Sam would accompany them as a servant.

Maria did not remember her mother, Grand Duchess Natasha Pavlovna, who had left St. Petersburg for Prussia when the child was less a year old. Her grandmother, Empress Maria Feodorovna of Russia, had given her a miniature portrait of Natasha before the empress died. Maria was only thirteen at the time.

She had moved into the home of one of the late empress' faithful servants, where she remained for four more years. In 1832, in accordance with arrangements made in her infancy by her uncle, Tsar Alexander I, and her step-grandfather, President James Madison, she sailed for the United States. Madison had retired to his Virginia estate before Maria arrived in Philadelphia, and he died without her ever meeting him.

She had seen her grandmother Dolley on drives around the city of Washington after Maria opened her boarding house there in 1843. The widow Madison lived in penury during those final years, Maria recalled, but she enjoyed universal respect and admiration. Maria had joined the huge funeral procession that walked behind her casket to the grave.

Her "uncle" Edward Coles had attended to Maria's education at a Catholic school in Baltimore. Coles called her his cousin – there were hundreds in the large Coles family – and gave her hand in marriage in 1835 to Millard McGehee, a successful Baltimore import merchant, when Maria was 20. She was widowed eight years later when Alex was a year old. Using her inheritance from her husband, and supplemented by funds from Coles, she purchased the property near the Navy Yard.

Operating a boarding house was a respectable occupation for a widow. Coles had told her that her great-grandmother Mary Payne

Coles had run such an establishment in Philadelphia decades before. After settling in the federal city, Maria made the mistake of looking up her father, only to fall victim to his constant demands for money to pay his debts. A quiet marriage to a naval officer named Nicholas in 1848 had been happy, but he spent most of his time at sea. By the time he received her letter, the boat for Germany and the Ruhr would have sailed.

Alex's education had been left to his mother, who had benefited initially from royal tutors hired by the empress, and later from instruction by the nuns in Baltimore. Maria thought privately that it was probably a waste of time to try to educate Alex, who was a sly and violent child. He was accustomed to lashing out in rage, lying, and stealing from his mother and her boarders. Perhaps her mother would know what to do about his behavior. At times, Maria wished that he was dead.

The trio that emerged from the boarding house had been transformed into a respectable lady and child with a well-dressed servant. Maria wore a handsome traveling dress of dark blue silk trimmed with black fringe, tightly corseted at the waist, with a wide bell-shaped shirt over crinolines. The ensemble included a fine black Merino wool coat, gloved hands, and a fashionable bonnet festooned with artificial flowers. Maria's heavy coat was also trimmed with fur at cuffs and collar. Alex was attired in long pants and short coat, with an overcoat of Merino wool. They traveled by hired conveyance to Baltimore, where they spent the night in an elegant hotel before boarding a ship destined for Europe and their new life.

Payne Todd's creditors found his body and arranged for burial in the Congressional Cemetery in Washington. Then they systematically sold off the rest of Todd's possessions, inherited from Dolley Madison. Later the same year, they held an auction in Orange, Virginia, at Toddsberthe, the bizarre, unfinished collection of buildings that Dolley's only son had erected as a planned retirement home for his mother. She never saw it. Madison and Payne family relatives had to bid on mementoes at both auctions. The Madison descendants were so disgusted at the loss of Montpelier and the public dispersal of other cherished family heirlooms that they burned the private family papers acquired at the sale in Orange.

CHAPTER 23

WASHINGTON, D.C. – JUNE 2, 2011
Various contributors from DHS

The day after his return to Washington, Ham got a call from Assistant Deputy Secretary Shaw's office asking for an update. Shaw had requested copies of everything relating to the Constitution murder investigation.

What now? he wondered, as the DHS executive motioned him into his spacious office. Ham knew this was going to be a terse meeting, and that they needed to show some progress at this point.

Shaw held a unique role within the government. The nation's most significant landmarks were overseen by a sector within DHS with the exhausting title of the National Monuments and Icons Sector of DHS's Office of National Infrastructure Protection. Failing all attempts to assign an intelligible acronym to the unit, everyone finally ended up calling it "Landmarks." As head of the larger NIP office, Shaw was the main representative from DHS to the Department of the Interior, whose security office coordinated issues relating to the safety of these unique assets.

Shaw's executive assistant was also in the room when Ham was ushered in. He saw the focus in their eyes and paused.

"Ham, what do you know about Operation Fast and Furious?"

Coles thought for a moment. "Mr. Secretary, I recall it was an operation run by the ATF and overseen by the Justice Department. The plan was to arrange for weapons to be sold by U.S. gun shops to straw buyers, who would turn them over to smugglers, where they eventually would end up in the hands of the Mexican drug cartels. Ostensibly, the ATF would track the smuggling and arrest cartel leaders. The plan to track the weapons failed, with the result that the guns that were *walked* into Mexico led to more violence from the Mexican drug groups."

Shaw nodded, as if to say so far so good. "Someone blew the whistle on the operation a few months ago, didn't they?" Ham asked.

"Damn right! Shaw said. "One of our people, Border Patrol Officer Brian Terry, was murdered by a Mexican drug cartel last year. Seems that weapons found at the murder scene were among the ones that had *walked* from American gun shops across the border as a part of the ATF operation. One of their agents, John Dodson, revealed the whole sordid story to CBS News last February and March."

Ham could see the possible connection to the Constitution murder case. If one of the Mexican cartels had killed the female murder victim, and if the story hit the media, it would only fuel the flames of outrage against the Mexican government's failing war with the cartels and ineffective U.S. efforts to support it.

"So, what's next?" asked Ham.

Shaw frowned and shrugged. "The only thing that everyone agrees about is that the ATF fucked up big time. Of course, the Bureau's tried to cover up the operation for months. ATF never answered the inquiry about the operation from a member of Congress. Even worse, the elected official got an answer from the Justice Department denying that any such operation ever existed."

Shaw's disgust was obvious. "Apparently, the operation began in 2009, escalated early in 2010, and was cancelled earlier this year.

The whole thing took place on the president's watch and I'd bet my granny's false teeth that the opposition in Congress is going to try to make this into some sort of Watergate. After all, the election is next year." Shaw noted that the House Oversight and Government Reform Committee was convening formal hearings about Fast and Furious.

Their conversation turned to trying to figure out who knew what and when. They concurred that the president would not have supported Ham's continued leadership of the investigation into the Constitution murder if he believed he could be held responsible for the separate ATF action.

"Maybe POTUS thinks you're an idiot," said Shaw, somewhat tongue in cheek. "Maybe he thinks you'll never figure out the identity of the victim, much less any potential ties to the Mexican drug lords."

"Does his office know we're making progress on the identity of the body? Do they know we're leaning toward a connection to the Mexican gangs?"

Shaw nodded. "Well, first he read me the riot act. But I got a follow-up call from his chief of staff asking for immediate notice about important advances in the investigation. We notified the COS first thing that morning."

"No word?" asked Ham.

Shaw shook his head. Both men looked at their watches. It was nearly mid-afternoon.

A moment later their cell phones rang at the same time.

CHAPTER 24

PHILADELPHIA – AFTERNOON, JUNE 2, 2011
Ray Goodson

The two school buses from Read High School in Centerville, Delaware, had arrived before lunch. Seventy-two juniors, accompanied by teachers and chaperones, were studying United States history, so a trip to the National Constitution Center had become an annual event since the facility opened in 2002. Besides, the school was named for George Read, a signer of both the Declaration of Independence and the Constitution.

The tour began in the circular theater on the ground floor, where visitors learned the story of the formation of the union in a compelling dramatization by a professional actor. The main exhibits upstairs were a mixture of graphics, animated films, stage sets, interactives, and displays of historical materials, all revealing the meaning of the Constitution to American life. The students participated in a mock citizen naturalization ceremony, explored the functions of the three branches of government, and examined the Bill of Rights and other amendments to the central document.

Most of the tour was self-guided, but the group assembled outside the Hall of Statuary before entering the replica of the original assembly room within Independence Hall. It was here that deliberations had taken place in secrecy during the summer of 1787. The modern tableau was set up with anthropomorphically correct, life-sized bronze statues of the delegates who attended the Constitutional Convention. At first the students merely gaped at the figures, who seemed frozen in mid-movement. Then the teens began to wander among them, closely examining their features. Benjamin Franklin was seated with his gnarled hand on a cane. Earlier visitors had touched the hand repeatedly, giving the dark patina of the bronze a brilliant gold shine. One student comment-ed that the famous scientist and patriot had been the sage of the proceedings.

Across the room, the teenagers recognized George Washington, looking every inch the leader. Beside him, and a full head shorter, was little James Madison. Washington had chaired the convention and Madison had been the prime mover in debates about a new form of national government. None of the statues were labeled, but there were museum interpreters scattered around the room who could identify them, the states they represented, and the role each had played in the deliberations.

The educators also invited visitors who were American citizens to sign large books laid out on tables placed around the room. Each contained a replica of the Constitution with room at the bottom for modern signatures. By adding their names, American citizens could affirm their belief in the government of the nation. Non-citizens were invited to add their signatures as a sign of sup-port for the values that the Constitution embraces.

Hans Lawson, the football team's quarterback, asked one of the educators, "Where's Thomas Jefferson?"

An interpreter told him that Jefferson had been in France dur-ing the convention.

"Where's John Hancock?" asked another student.

"Wrong document, dude!" said Andy Williams, the class clown.

"Did anyone sign all our important documents?" asked Alicia Rosen, the Brainiac of the class. Normally she was hesitant to ask questions because they were a sign that she didn't know everything. The interpreter led her to the statue of Roger Sherman of Connecticut, explaining that the humble-looking delegate was the only person to sign all four of the nation's organizational documents – the Articles of Assembly, the Declaration of Independence, the Articles of Confederation, and the Constitution.

Davie Ballard, one of the smallest boys in the junior class, had wandered close to James Madison, surprised by the Virginian's diminutive size. The Father of the Constitution and George Washington were standing behind one of the tables holding copies of the Constitution. Just as Davie leaned over to grab a feather pen to become a signer, he felt a strong burst of air pressure. Then it all went black.

The blast was deafening. The table disintegrated into thousands of tiny flying splinters that penetrated everything they touched. Scorched fragments of paper from the Constitution book fluttered down like confetti. The bomb released a barrage of nails and other metal projectiles that ripped Davie Ballard apart, pieces of his body splattering against the wall on the far side of the large assembly hall. Students, teachers and educators screamed. Others moaned from injuries. Many lay silent, their awkward positions on the floor mute testimony to the ravages of the incendiary device. Those who could, ran or limped toward the main exhibit hall behind them.

Ham and Bill Shaw were winding up their meeting when their cell phones buzzed at the same time. It was the report on the explosion. Quickly, Shaw arranged to have a helicopter meet Ham on the roof of DHS. On his way out the door, Coles asked Shaw to check on the status of the Constitution Center. The agent couldn't remember whether the modern edifice was on the list of landmarks under their jurisdiction.

By the time Ham got to Independence National Historical Park, the entire area was cordoned off. Ham was met on the grass and rushed into the Constitution Center, which smelled of blood, burnt flesh, and fire. Goodson stood with Ham outside the statuary hall until security issued the all-clear to enter. The NPS security chief looked ten years older. He was covered in blood and debris, having assisted in triage of the victims after the blast. Goodson used the time to explain the sequence of events.

"We're officially in hell," he added.

As Ham entered the smoldering blast area, he saw that the walls, roof, and floors of the chamber had withstood the bomb. The figures of Washington and Madison were unrecognizable, suggesting that the temperature from the explosive was extremely hot. Many of the statues father away from the blast had survived with little or no damage. The injured had been removed, but many of the dead remained. The walls and floor were still awash in blood and other body fluids. The damage was largely confined to the assembly hall exhibit. Park Service and Constitution Center staff wandered by with their cell phones, reporting on the condition of original collections, structural damage, and the status of the HVAC and electrical systems.

The power had been turned off. Automatic generators controlled the investigation scene and all areas where artifacts were on display. NPS staff had erected flood lights to illuminate the bomb scene, where forensic technicians were gathering every speck of evidence they could find. The place was a mess. Ham's deputy had appeared and reported on the body count. Her face was grim. "Nineteen dead, twenty-five injured, four of them in critical condition. The total roll call of dead and wounded is thirty-six students, four NCC educators, two teachers, and a middle-aged couple from Missouri." The assistant reported that the governor of Pennsylvania and the President were standing by for ongoing briefings.

"And the media?" Ham asked. He dreaded the report, which came promptly from Bonnie Allison, a senior NPS public affairs officer.

"We have briefed the press about our protocols," Bonnie said. "They call for attention to human health and safety first, followed by assessments of physical damage to structures and collections. Our office has informed the media that no person or group has contacted us to claim responsibility for the attack, and we have asked all news agencies to call us on our emergency number if someone notifies them."

"Does the press know it was a bomb?" Ham asked.

Bonnie gave a wry smile.

"As they say, if it looks like a duck and quacks like a duck. The explosion was heard nearly a mile away. TV reports on bombings in the Middle East have made our audiences very sophisticated in identifying IEDs."

Ham shook his head dolefully.

"The bomb was taped under the table near the statues of Madison and Washington. It was activated by a timer. The juniors who would never graduate from high school and the rest of the dead and injured seemed to be victims of bad luck. Bomb techs were working to identify the device and its materials."

Probably Semtex, thought Ham. Goodson was wondering aloud how the terrorists had managed to install the bomb without being detected. Four incidents in Independence National Park in less than two weeks had to be a new record. A bad one. Ham felt a stab of sympathy for the beleaguered NPS official.

As if divining his thoughts, Goodson used a lull in the reports to fill Ham in on the reaction within the Department of the Interior and the NPS.

"I'm surprised you couldn't hear the roar from C Street when your helicopter left D.C," said Goodson with a grimace. Apparently, the wrath of the secretary of the interior was surpassed only by the fury of NPS Director Briggs Colonna, who dressed down everyone in his inner circle and continued his tirade as he marched down the main hall of the NPS headquarters. The harangue did not abate until after he had washed his face with cool water in the executive washroom.

"Liz Rodgers has her tits in the wringer," said Goodson. "She told me DNPS has promised that her next posting will be at the Great National Sand Dunes in Colorado, where her main job will be to count the desert mice."

"And you?" Ham asked. He knew Goodson's ass was in the old gar hole.

"I'm going to be dipped in bronze and put somewhere where pigeons will poop on my head from dawn until dusk."

"Drug tests for staff?"

"Required by all agencies who occupy NPS land. NCC does it anyway monthly."

"Security cameras?"

"Under review," said Goodson. "In fact, let's look.

They descended to the main security office where they were met by Julia Sheridan, one of the DHS agents reviewing security tapes from NCC.

"Sir," said the IT expert, "we have a progression of security gaps from the loading dock to the statuary hall and back that began at 5:00 AM and finally ended at 6:24 AM."

He explained that the gaps, about 30 seconds each, were controlled off site. The cameras in the statuary hall were blocked for two minutes.

"No alarms?" Ham asked.

Sheridan shook her head.

"So, we add cyber terrorism to the list of complaints," Ham said.

"Sir, it was pretty slick," Sheridan said. The agent chanced a glance at Goodson. Her cheeks flushed.

"We helped NCC design their system. In addition to the exterior contact alarms and the interior cameras and contact pads, we have a wall of monitors that rotate images from cameras. The security desk there is staffed 24/7 by guards who watch for problems."

"Let me guess," said Goodson. "The monitors showed nothing: no people; no snow; nothing."

Sheridan confirmed that the guards had no way of knowing that individual monitors were deactivated. Each screen showed a picture with no unusual activity. She added somewhat lamely that the alarms from touchpads were also silent for the entire episode.

"Bill Shaw has called a meeting in his office for this evening." said Ham. "I'll call in a report tonight. If I survive it."

CHAPTER 25

WASHINGTON, D.C. – EVENING, JUNE 2, 2011
Cary

Shaw opened the briefing with the announcement. "I have heard from the White House."

"And?" asked Ham. He discerned from Shaw's expression indicated that the conversation had not been pleasant.

"POTUS is en route as we speak to visit hospitals in Philadelphia. Then he'll give his personal condolences to the families of the children and others who did not survive the blast. He will be accompanied by the governor of Pennsylvania."

"Any other instructions?" Ham asked. He was curious about Operation Fast and Furious but didn't know if the other agents had been fully apprised of the operation. He saw a few fresh faces in the room.

The Secretary motioned for Ham to wait before introducing two new analysts. Shaw introduced the first as Billy Johnson, a cyber-sleuth expert. He wore loose jeans and a faded Phish T-shirt. The other was Ben Manheim, a specialist in Russian Federation relations. Jim Andersen, the CIA Mexico expert, and Cary were also present, sitting forward with elbows on the table.

"Assessments of growing terrorist operations in Mexico have led to a consensus that the most likely attack against the U.S. will be cyber terrorism," Billy Johnson said. Ham noted that he was energetic and articulate, and imagined that he graduated from MIT when he was sixteen, only to earn a gazillion dollars in Silicon Valley. "They're sometimes accompanied or followed by more conventional methods of attack."

"Such as dismemberments and bombings?" Shaw asked.

"That's what we saw happen today," Billy said, nodding. "And it probably played a part in the bypass of security systems when the thirteen landmarks were hit on May 24."

"So, first they screw with the security and then they can send in their well-trained drug squads to slice and dice or blow things up at their leisure?" Ham asked. He saw a few others around the room nodding.

"Any more on the first victim?" Shaw asked, turning to Andersen.

Andersen turned on the projector, revealing a map of Texas and northern Mexico. He used a pointer to show pertinent areas of the ongoing investigation.

"We know she came in to the U.S. through Nuevo Laredo in March of this year. She did not use a legal passport or any known alias identities. A surveillance camera near the border captured her picture, which they matched to the forensic reconstruction made at Dover."

Ham recalled an earlier brief stating that the drug cartels had dug a tunnel under the border near Nuevo Laredo. "Jim, what was the name of the main gang in control of the area?"

"We're confident that the Zeta cartel brought her across the border," Andersen said. "Either under duress or with her acquiescence. She seems to have formed a close relationship with one of the leaders prior to the crossing."

He flashed another grainy image of the victim seated with a known Zeta leader in a cafe in Nuevo Laredo. Then he posted another map showing the territory of the Zeta cartel, an area extending from the Yucatan Peninsula all the way up to the U.S. border along the eastern coast of Mexico. Andersen explained that identification of the Zeta connection suggested that the victim entered their distribution pipeline and went north toward San Antonio and Austin. He then returned to the first map and pointed to an area west of Dallas.

"We have infiltrated a Zeta cell in Grand Prairie, a suburb west of Dallas. It appears that the victim was taken to an old ranch there and kept until her murder. The area is a suburb midway between Dallas and Fort Worth. Interstates 20 to the south and 30 to the north cross through it on an east-west axis. The closest city is Arlington. The city is growing at a rate of 38% per decade and now has a large Hispanic population; about 42.7% of its 175,000 residents. There is no significant Russian-born element in the city itself, but the area around Dallas, particularly to the north, has quite a few immigrants. RussianTX.com is an online newsletter with more than 2,500 subscribers. The crime rate in Grand Prairie is above the national average but it's not terrible."

"So, what happened to her?" Shaw asked. He tapped his pencil on the desk.

"Our sources report that the murder victim was selected carefully," Andersen said. "She was kept drugged for a week or more and then murdered. Apparently, equipment and facilities for dismemberment and freezing were available at the ranch."

"Any links to the Texas Russian community?" Cary asked.

"No. We think the arrangements with the Zetas were made by revolutionaries from the Russian Federation, or even Georgia."

"What's the point?" Shaw asked.

"Maybe Sochi," Ben Manheim said. He rose to address the group.

"Who in God's name is Sochi?" Ham asked, his frustrations starting to boil over.

"Not *who*," said Ben, "*Where?*" He walked to the computer and turned clicked the presentation to a map of the Caucasus Mountains of Russia and the surrounding area near the Black Sea. Ben pointed to a dot on the map in the southeast part of the country.

"That's Sochi," he said. He clicked the presentation and the logo of the International Olympics Committee appeared.

The room fell silent. Cary's arm fell to the table and she shook her head. "But we haven't even had London yet. Russia isn't until 2014."

If Assistant Deputy Secretary Shaw was surprised that a specialist in American antiques was familiar with international sports, he didn't show it. In fact, many of his stereotypes were crumbling like stale biscuits.

"This theory throws a much broader light on the situation," said Shaw. "The deputy secretary of the interior told me today that the Park Service fears it's getting pushed to the sidelines. He cautioned us to remember that it's our landmarks that seem to have been selected as the grand stage upon which to perform acts of terrorism."

Everyone's minds turned to the larger issue of threats to the Olympic Games. The murders of members of the Israeli Olympic team during the 1972 Munich Games was still a recurring nightmare in international security circles. *Was it eleven dead, or more?* Ham struggled to remember the details.

"Ben, give us your take on this," Shaw demanded, getting the attention of the room.

"Mr. Secretary, we're even less certain about *who* than we are about *where*," Ben said. He clicked the presentation again and a new slide appeared.

"One obvious goal might be to cancel the Sochi Games in advance. Another might be to disrupt them when they take place."

"How can they cancel them now?" asked Billy. "The Russians are more than doubling the communications systems in Sochi.

The Games themselves will pull almost as much juice as the entire city has at this point. Billions are being invested."

Cary was an armchair Olympics freak. Although not an avid sports fan, she inevitably followed the Games from the opening ceremony to the conclusion.

"Aren't they building a special island for hotels?" she asked.

She looked at Ben, who flashed a glare to the room that implied that everyone should remain quiet until he completed his brief.

"There are many, many groups that would be giddy with delight if the president of Russia ended up with egg on his face," said Ben. "We have the Georgians, who are still pissed off that Imperial Russia dissolved their kingdom back in 1801 and kicked their rulers out of the country. Then Russia has recognized the two breakaway governments of Abkhazia and Ossetia, which are located within Georgia. Georgia and much of the rest of the civilized world consider these regions to be a part of its independent nation. Abkhazia is very close to Sochi and was a Muslim region for centuries, although the official party line today calls it Christian."

"Georgia has a movement to restore its monarchy," Shaw said, interrupting despite Ben's ire. "They've issued complaints against Russia for acts of terrorism. Of course, there was that train bombing that the Russians blame on Georgian insurgents. Suffice to say the two governments are not in love with each other. Georgia complains that the present U.S. administration has not been overly helpful."

"We believe that the victim was descended from former rulers of Georgia," added Cary. "Through the Bagrationi line."

Ben waited patiently, irritation evident on his face.

"Let's not forget that Georgia put in a bid to host the games," Ben said. "It was a long shot. Second place went to Salzburg in Austria. Nevertheless, the government in Georgia has written to urge the Russians and the IOC to cancel plans for the games in Sochi due to increasing unrest in the region. Typically, Russia ignores all expressions of concern about security, and the IOC has taken its usual stand of staying out of the dispute, only reaffirming that the safety of the athletes is of the highest concern."

"Isn't Sochi near an important UNESCO World Heritage site?" asked Cary. She was referring to the global UNESCO agreement, and the 800-plus historical and natural sites that had been added to the world priority list for preservation. Jefferson's Capitol in Virginia was the first U.S. site added to the list, and that was in the recent past. *Small wonder,* she thought, *since the Taj Mahal, Jerusalem, the pyramids at Giza, and a few other monuments far outclass Mr. Jefferson's genius in both age and originality.*

"You win the trip to Disneyland," declared Ben. He pulled up an image of the large natural site in the West Caucasus Mountains. He explained that the head of Greenpeace in Russia had already demanded that the Russian site for the Games be changed due to damage that might be caused by new construction in the largely pristine rural ecosystem. The site had already caused a stir among preservationists. "The Russian Federation has agreed to remove a part of the protected acreage from UNESCO and turn it over for development associated with the games."

Cary had mental images of massive bulldozers ripping up ancient habitats, new roads running through virgin forests, birds losing their nesting grounds, and other desecrations to the ecosystem. Russian leaders would talk the talk and walk the walk, but the money from new development would be irresistible. In some respects, the new Russia could out-capitalize the capitalists. She heard Ben confirm her suspicions with a description of the light rail system being installed in the region. It was apparently the first Olympic Games hosted by Russia since the fall of the Soviet Union.

"Anything else pertinent?" asked Shaw, clearly looking for a wrap-up.

"Mr. Secretary, we believe that the Romanov connection has celebrity value only," said Ben. "The dynasts fight among themselves, but seem to be content to go through channels in asserting their position for restoration of the monarchy."

"Are they still living off the jewels they smuggled out in their clothes?" asked Billy. He was obviously not into reading court circulars.

"They marry well and have a long tradition of rock-solid off-shore investments," said Ben, who told Secretary Shaw that the brief was concluded.

Everyone spoke at once. Were the landmark attacks a trial run or a distraction? What are the next steps? Who will be in charge? What will DDHS think? What will the White House think?

Shaw raised his hands for silence in the room.

"First, we're assigning additional assets to the Russian Federation sector," he said. "The Mexican operation will continue. Expect reports very soon. Second, both DHS and the White House want this thing cleared up on our side of the water before anyone or anything else gets blown up. Third, POTUS has asked the IOC and the Federation to allow us to send appropriate representatives to the region to meet with their colleagues and to perform an independent assessment of potential damage to the World Heritage Site."

He turned to look at Cary. "Ms. Mallory, you've done an admirable job locating DNA materials and documents that have firmly established the Madison-Romanov link to the murder victim, and further, your recommendation for a Russian genealogical consultant was first-rate."

Shaw reached over and patted her hand. *Oh, shit, here it comes,* thought Cary. She tried not to cringe.

Shaw smiled. "You'll be appointed as a representative of the visiting U.S. delegation to Russia. Further, my dear, we understand that your contacts at the Hermitage are outstanding and that every professional courtesy will be extended to you."

How the hell do you know that? she wondered.

178

"And we understand that one of your friends and colleagues happens to have strong connections to UNESCO and ICOMOS officials in Russia and other parts of Europe as a highly-respected expert in architecture, especially classical architecture."

Holy Moley! They know about Calvert Rolfe! Cary wanted to protest that natural habitats were not Cal's forte, but she remained silent.

"We have taken the liberty of vetting Mr. Rolfe and believe it's safe to read him into the operation. Ham will handle the brief, but we want you to be present."

"When will all of this happen?" Cary asked shakily. She was thinking of her shop, of her contract with Montpelier, and of getting sliced and diced by terrorists thousands of miles from home.

"We'll fly you and Mr. Coles to Richmond tonight and you'll brief Mr. Rolfe first thing in the morning. You leave for Russia at 2:00 PM tomorrow from RIC."

"Mr. Secretary, I am not a snow bunny," Cary protested. She didn't even buy Sierra Club calendars that showed beautiful snowy mountain scenes.

"Ah, Ms. Mallory, good fortune is on your side. Sochi is a subtropical climate by Russian standards. The clothes you're wearing now will be appropriate for Sochi's 80-degree temperatures."

With that, the team was dismissed. Ham walked with her toward the helipad on the roof of DHS headquarters.

"You okay?" he asked, feigning nonchalance. He assured her that he knew absolutely nothing about what the brief would contain or what actions the secretary had arranged.

"Are you going?" she asked, glaring at him.

Ham nodded, and then raised his hands. "Look, we're both already on the team and we've been read in on the details. Obviously, research indicates that your and Rolfe's contacts will smooth our entry and access to information. Aside from that, I'm as surprised as you are."

"Full payment of fees?"

"My guess is you just got a considerable raise. Hazard duty and all that."

The helicopter was on the pad, rotors starting to turn. They ducked and strode forward to reach the helicopter, and Ham held her hand to help her board. They remained silent for the duration of the short hop to the Richmond airport. A government car met them on the tarmac and took them directly to Church Hill.

CHAPTER 26

CHURCH HILL, RICHMOND – LATE EVENING, JUNE 2, 2011
Connie

I opened the door, two drinks in hand, and gave the first one to Ham. "Boy, have you had a shitty day. It's all over the news. Every channel."

Ham smiled and swigged his bourbon. I had forgotten to add water, but he didn't seem to notice. Cary accepted hers with equal gratitude and surmised that someone had given me a briefing prior to their arrival. Ham dropped his bag inside the front door, probably not daring to assume that he might be invited to occupy the guest room for the night.

We all gathered in the kitchen, where I had prepared a simple dinner of fried chicken, potato salad, and bread. Cary and Ham each downed two drinks before grabbing a plate.

"Darling, I understand that I'm to man the old fort here till you return from parts unknown." I clutched my fourth cocktail in hand, trying not to chug it down.

Cary hugged me as a sign of appreciation. Ham extended his hand in obvious gratitude. I responded with a firm, hetero shake. I took another sip and sat down, exhaling.

"Suffice to say, my dears, it was a shock to receive that phone call. But fear not; your faithful friend Connie is here for you and will run the shop till hell freezes over if need be."

"Who called?" Cary asked, her brow furrowed.

"A very nice man named Frank," I said. "He calmly explained that you and Ham are on a Great Adventure, and that I will be paid an outrageously generous fee to comply and ask no questions. Dear Frank also seems to know every transgression of my life since childhood."

"Including?" asked Cary.

I laughed and took another swig.

"Well, sweet cheeks, they have the names of all my lovers, their ages, my underwear size, the results of all my drug tests, and a pretty accurate assessment of deviant proclivities that I have never confided to anyone, including *toi*."

Cary started to ask for details before Ham kneed her under the table. "Well, thank you," she said.

I suppressed a sudden urge to cry and exhaled again. I looked Ham and then Cary in the eyes. "Per instructions, I have booked Ham at the 2300 Club up the street, but given the late hour, I've taken the liberty of setting up the guest room in case you two want to stay close. I understand you need to go out very early and catch a midday flight." Cary grabbed my hand. "We're both scared, my darling, and you've done everything we could ever ask for. Ham can stay here. Thank you so much."

"Yeah, thanks," said Ham.

They ate dinner and I went upstairs to my apartment, stopping on the landing to listen in.

"Well, what do you think?' asked Cary, as she fixed nightcaps for them both. As in many extremely stressful situations, the alcohol didn't seem to have much effect.

I could see that Ham didn't look good. I also saw that Cary noticed the same. His shoulders had slumped and his skin was pallid. His hands shook when he tried to lift his glass. Cary thought she heard a moan. She froze and watched him.

"The first thing I saw in the statue gallery was a Nike tennis shoe," Ham said. "It was covered in blood. There was a foot still in it. Then, parts of bodies riddled with metal shrapnel, brain matter, pieces of clothing, even an eyeball stuck against a wall."

Cary sighed and looked at him with worry. Ham grasped her hand.

"It was so awful, Cary. I felt so helpless, so incompetent that we hadn't figured it in advance." She rose and stepped to the kitchen counter to grab some tissue.

"Figured what out?" she asked.

"They were counting on the story of the Romanov connection getting out, of the attacks on our landmarks making headlines. The silence ticked them off so much they decided to make a splash so big that it couldn't be hidden from the media."

Ham dried his eyes and took a sip of his bourbon.

"You heard the briefing on the publicity. The anchors of all major networks broadcast the evening news from INHP. One of them even wore a safari jacket, like he was embedded with the troops in some godforsaken outpost somewhere in the Middle East desert. Everyone has embraced a slightly different political theory. It's the fault of the Democrats. The Republicans are to blame because they cut the NPS budget so much that the agency cannot adequately protect American treasures. Radical Islam is the culprit. Anti-American terrorists have made a symbolic attack against our Constitution."

"Thank God no group has actually taken credit for the massacre," Cary observed.

"The editorial think-pieces will be out in the morning," Ham said, sounding rueful. "By tomorrow afternoon the entire country will be hopelessly confused but uniformly enraged. The pundits sure do like to make up the news instead of waiting to report it."

"Let's go to bed," sighed Cary, moving toward the stairs. Ham followed her to the guest room. He was too tired to be disappointed. It had been a miserable fucking day.

183

CHAPTER 27

MONUMENT AVENUE, RICHMOND – MORNING, JUNE 3, 2011
Calvert Rolfe

C ary was packed and dressed when Ham entered the kitchen at 7:30 AM. He felt drained but knew he could sleep on the long flight to Russia.

"Got your passport?" Ham asked. He poured himself a cup of coffee.

"Yup. What about a visa?" asked Cary. She had been to St. Petersburg and Moscow but had never traveled outside the two major cities.

"All of that will be on the plane," Ham assured her.

They ate quickly and drove in Cary's hatchback to Monument Avenue, where Calvert Rolfe had a spacious mansion designed in the 1920s by the famous architect William Lawrence Bottomley. Rolfe had restored the house and revived the gardens during his three decades in residence on Richmond's most famous street. Cary got onto the boulevard near its lower end, so Ham could admire the equestrian statues of famous Confederate generals that anchored the street median. She filled Ham in on Rolfe's career, his many publications, and his eccentricities.

"Cal is a bachelor from old Albemarle County money," she said. "He has a very impressive collection of Americana, some rather good paintings and prints, a superb architectural library, and one 13-inch black-and-white TV set that he bought second-hand about twenty years ago. I also know he can operate a computer because his office is fully wired. But I'd suspect he keeps it hidden in a secret room."

Ham learned that gardening was Rolfe's passion, and that his urban oasis had been featured in *Better Homes and Gardens, Southern Living,* and other major publications devoted to the art of landscape design and growing things well. He had traveled extensively and seen most of the world's major landmarks, particularly those erected in the style of the Italian Renaissance. Rolfe obtained his degree in Architectural History from the well-known graduate program at UVA. He had retired from a Richmond restoration architecture firm when he realized that his pension would more than meet his need for what he called "walking around money."

They parked on a side street and stared at the mansion for a moment before getting out. Rolfe met them at the door, dipped his head in the general direction of Cary's cheek, shook hands with Ham, and escorted them into the rear garden where they sat beneath a gazebo entwined with roses. Ham realized that Cary's description had not done justice to the garden. It was magical in every respect. Their host had put out a tray with iced lemonade and cookies. *Now this is genteel southern,* thought Ham, as their host filled their glasses.

Cal Rolfe was in his sixties and lean, with a full head of stylishly long hair graying at the sides. Ham noted that he was another Virginia preppy: khaki pants, button-down striped short-sleeve shirt, and wingtips without socks. A yellow gold signet ring, probably bearing the ancient crest of the Rolfe's, adorned one pinky. His watch was pedestrian and seemed to be waterproof. Cal was a man comfortable in his skin, with no need for a Rolex or other visible signs of wealth. The man exuded formality and spoke distinctly, with a hint of Britain beneath his soft southern drawl. Cary had informed Ham that Rolfe's late mother had been born across the pond.

Cary looked at Ham while Ham nodded back at her, indicating for her to speak first.

"Cal, I want to introduce Hamilton Coles, of the Edward Coles family of Virginia," she said. "I'm working with him on a very special but highly classified project that involves the Department of Homeland Security. We need your help."

"*Ahhh* yes," drawled Rolfe. He crunched a cookie as a spoke. "I know all the surviving Coles houses in the Commonwealth. I even have your book in my library. Thought I recognized the name. St. Louis Coles branch, isn't it? Harvard before William & Mary faculty in history?"

Ham nodded. "Our briefing has to be kept confidential. For national security issues, of course."

Rolfe gave him a smile and a look suggesting that he was, and had long been, a confidante of presidents and kings, corporate CEOs of Fortune 100 companies, and the odd governor or two.

"Let's hear it," he said. Ham gave a summary of the invasions, laid out the connections to the Constitution, and described the task force. Then he mentioned the NCC bombing and revealed the possible connection to former Russian Federation radicals and the 2014 Sochi Winter Games.

Cal looked wide-eyed at Cary and leaned forward. "Any connections that might nail that bloody bastard Payne Todd after all these years? God, what an awful creature he was. Such a shame since Dolley was such a fun gal." This last word came out as *gel*, as in *gelding*. Cal turned to Ham. "You might as well spill the beans on the invasion sites. No, wait. Let me guess. Mount Vernon, Montpelier, perhaps Gunston Hall, Federal Hall, although it dates from the 1840s, the Grange although it's been moved, John Jay Homestead, one or two sites at Independence Park, something connected to Roger Sherman. He paused for a moment before his eyes brightened. "Of course, Old Ironsides in Boston. How am I doing?"

Cary laughed. "Very well, of course. It was APS, Franklin Court, and First Bank of the U.S. at INHP. Add Franklin's statue at the University of Pennsylvania, Sherman's grave in New Haven, and Tom Paine's monument in New Rochelle."

"Paine? That monument's also been moved, and that dreadful bust on the top is very late. Dear me, why on earth attack *that* place?"

Cary shrugged. Cal saw that they had not slept well of late.

"Independence Hall is still standing, I presume?" Rolfe asked, turning to Ham. "Too bad about the NCC, although it is a thoroughly contemporary building. All those innocent students."

"Indeed," said Ham.

"Studio EIS in Brooklyn did them. Pronounced like *ice*, but the acronym stands for Elliot and Ivan Schwartz, brothers who advanced from plaster statues for museum exhibits to anthropomorphic recreations of historical figures, accurate in terms of size, body shape, clothing, and even facial features. Brilliant work at NCC, absolutely first rate. How did the gallery and statues fare in the explosion?"

Ham described the severe damage to the Madison and Washington reproductions, but assured him that the room itself was still structurally sound.

Cal nodded sadly. "Those children, how evil are the ways of men today."

Ham cleared his throat and launched into his explanation of the IOC mission to Russia. "We want to know if you'll join the commission," he said.

"Presumably we're representing U.S. concerns about preservation of the UNESCO site near Sochi," Cal said. "Do I have that right?"

Cary and Ham nodded.

"I assume you need some doors opened, correct?" They nodded again.

"Are we expected to perform any wet work?"

"*Cal!*" exclaimed Cary. "I didn't know you read spy novels."

Rolfe chuckled. "My dear, I read everything. I just don't display all the books in my library."

Then he frowned. "I say, Coles, you realize that I'm not a specialist in natural UNESCO sites. Buildings are my bread and butter."

"But you do know your way around the Russian UNESCO crowd?"

"Oh my, yes. In fact, I have a good friend, an architect with a dacha in Sochi. Perhaps he would invite us to stay in his guest house. Lovely place."

"That sounds great," said Ham.

Cal got up and walked inside dutifully. He returned a moment later with his address book, a tome of some heft. "Let me just take a look."

Ham informed him that etiquette would require visits to St. Petersburg and Moscow and a formal meeting with IOC and Russian preservation liaisons in both cities. Then they would move on to Sochi to meet with the experts from the local host committee and the Caucasus UNESCO site. Since Cary and Cal were preservationists, they would be able to get in deeper with their colleagues.

"Anyone particularly green on the Commission?" asked Cal. He was obviously thinking of the need for expertise on natural habitats.

"We have Dr. Ellen Harriett," said Cary.

Rolfe's eyebrows raised, as if in a toast. Harriet was a retired director of the National Park Service, an acknowledged world expert on natural habitats, and conversant with all the most vocal groups trying to save the planet, or at least some piece of it. She had also served as an official in the international UNESCO organization.

Rolfe nodded in appreciation. "An excellent choice. Level-headed. What about extremists? Is that something we should be concerned about?"

Ham explained that the Russian Greenpeace chief had written to demand that the Olympics be moved to preserve the Western Caucasus UNESCO site. "I don't think we need to worry about that."

"So, comrades. How long is this going to take?" asked Cal.

"Per the White House, the whole trip will last six days," said Ham. "Including travel."

"Cal, can you make a few calls and dig up the scuttlebutt on international reaction to the development plans for the Olympics in the affected area?" asked Cary.

Rolfe nodded.

"I have a great many emails from colleagues who are outraged by the strong potential for destruction of the habitat. Shameful."

"Cal, do you know anyone from Russian Greenpeace?" asked Ham.

Rolfe's countenance assumed a truly aristocratic demeanor.

"Good Lord, I hope not. Bunch of looneys, throwing themselves around: no relevant knowledge of the issues. Amateurs who have no idea how to work things out."

Ham made a mental note to let DHS handle that aspect of the trip. Rolfe agreed to participate in the mission and signed a confidentiality agreement that Ham had prepared in advance. Ham exhaled as he signed his name, and Rolfe turned to him slack-jawed.

"Yes?" asked Rolfe.

"We need to know if you can you fly out today at 2:00 PM," said Cary.

"Oh my," said Rolfe. He stood for a moment and looked at them. "Yes. I can. But I need you to leave now and give me time to make some calls, send some emails, and pack a few essentials."

Ham and Cary rose at once. Ham said that a government car would pick him up at 1:15 pm to get to the airport.

"What about hotels and food?" asked Rolfe. "I trust I shall not be thrust into mufti and forced to rough it like some Boy Scout."

"Cal, presidential commissions travel extremely well," Ham said, laughing.

Rolfe looked relieved. He assured them that he had enough cash on hand and credit cards for the journey.

"Pretty sure I have enough bourbon too," he added.

Ham asked to use the men's room, and they entered the house. Cal and Cary talked about some of Rolfe's recent antique acquisitions. Later, as they pulled away from the curb, Ham gave Cary a sardonic look. "Now this is going to be a real adventure," he said. "Does he really know everyone?"

"You have no idea," she said, nodding. "All those years of not watching television have paid off for old Cal. He moves in exalted circles."

The rest of the morning was spent in Church Hill. Ham checked on the arrangements and Cary made email contact with colleagues at the Hermitage Museum.

Soon, they were on their way to RIC.

They were driven onto the tarmac at the commercial field, where a sleek jet awaited them. The pilot took their passports and handled the check-in. Within minutes they were airborne.

After meeting the other members of the commission on the flight, the Richmond contingent settled down in their leather seats. Once they reached cruising altitude a steward appeared with a plate of shrimp, a wine list, and menus.

Cal smiled with obvious pleasure. "I'd say, this is starting off rather well, old man."

Ham gave Cal a briefing book, which the historian read on the plane after finishing his shrimp and a glass of merlot. Cary and Ham caught up on their sleep and were alert enough before landing to answer Rolfe's questions before the flight landed in Moscow.

CHAPTER 28

MOSCOW, RUSSIA – JUNE 4, 2011
Various members of the team

A representative from the American Embassy met the jet at the Moscow airport and took the group to the National Hotel, a five-star lodging near Red Square. They settled into a suite with adjoining single rooms for Cary, Cal, Billy, and Ben Manheim. Ham gave everyone three hours to nap and bathe before launching into a briefing in the sitting room.

"We flew in with only a part of the official presidential delegation," said Ham, who began passing out bios on the other participants. They would be joined by two elected officials with their attendants, plus Dr. Ellen Harriett from the Nature Conservancy. Billy and Ben had cover identities in place. The U.S. senator and representative were both very pro-ecology, which would strengthen the credentials of the visiting delegation.

"I had hoped we could convene at the end of each day for a debriefing, but it will be necessary for us to split up. Fortunately, Cary and Cal have already checked with their contacts in St. Petersburg to test the grapevine among the museum and preservation crowds, respectively. They're now free to set up their own meetings with professionals in Moscow and establish introductions to experts near Sochi."

"So, we're off to a rousing start," said Billy.

"Our presence is required this evening at a dinner hosted at the embassy by the American ambassador," said Ham. "Our elected officials will handle the toasts, endless assurances of the warm accord between the U.S. and the Russian Federation, etc., etc. Billy and Ben will have some time to interact with members of the embassy staff with detailed information about communications and development plans for the Olympics. The dinner will also include senior Russian officials representing the conservation of natural environments and ICOMOS. Dr. Harriett is on a first-name basis with most of them. Finally, we'll meet tomorrow morning for a full briefing from the Russian and IOC officials on plans for the 2014 games."

"How many of the new people have been read into the operation?" Cary asked.

Ham nodded. "NPS and DHS have the full brief. No one else knows anything."

"You're all dismissed," said Ham. As the cultural experts were leaving to make phone calls, Ham slipped a note to Cary. It read: *Natalia has additional information on Bagrationi genealogy.* There was a St. Petersburg phone number.

Cary strode to her room and closed the door. She dialed quickly and sat down in a cold leather chair. Natalia picked up on the second ring and thanked Cary for calling so quickly.

"What's new?" Cary asked.

"It appears that historical genealogy and modern terrorism are coming together through the Bagrationi line," said the Russian scholar. "Can you hold one moment?" asked Cary. She sprinted next door in time to divert Billy, Ham, and Ben.

"Quickly, I need you all to listen in on this call."

They returned with Cary. Cal joined them as well. Cary put the phone on speaker and introduced everyone in the room to Natalia. She reminded both men of the lineage from tsarist Russia to the presumed mother of the murder victim.

"Please, begin your brief," Cary said to Natalia.

"The state of Georgia's relations with the Russian Federation and the U.S. seem to be the key here," she said.

"Natalia, this is my bailiwick," Ben said. "Do you mind if I fill in the general political context before you zoom in on the gene pool?"

"Of course."

Ben Manheim was a short, barrel-chested man in his late 50s with sparkling green eyes, a head as shiny as a bowling ball, and a warm smile. It was obvious that he was extremely intelligent and well informed about his subject area.

"Okay, so we have the Russian Federation and we have a bevy of former SSRs that are now independent. Georgia is one of them. It is bounded on the north by Russia, on the west by the Black Sea, on the south by Turkey and Armenia and on the southeast by Azerbaijan. The Georgian capital is Tbilisi. It had independent kingdoms for centuries and peaked in the 11th and 12th centuries. It was annexed by Russia in 1801, and, after a brief period of independence after the 1917 Russian Revolution, eventually became an SSR. It regained its independence in 1991, and after great unrest – recall the Rose Revolution of 2003 – Georgia has made moves toward democratic reforms. The trouble lies in the situation in nearby Abkhazia and South Ossetia, which are two so-called independent regions within the state of Georgia. They have been recognized by the Russian Federation and a few other nations, but most free-world countries still consider them to be part of Georgia. The Russian Federation provides military and financial support for the rogue governments. The government in exile is based in Tbilisi."

The group learned that the awarding of the 2014 Winter Olympics to Sochi was a double insult to Georgia, which had put in a bid for the games. Although located within the boundaries of Russia, Sochi is very near Abkhazia, which would undoubtedly benefit from the billions in construction that would accompany preparations for the global event. "Sochi will also host the 2014 Paralympics, the Formula I Grand Prix from 2014 until at least 2020, and is among the host sites for the 2018 FIFA World Cup," continued Ben. "Before Georgia was dissolved in 1801, it had its own autonomy, its own royal family, and its own identity. The Bagrationi were responsible for the unification of several kingdoms into one royal house. There are some fairly radical modern monarchists in Georgia, who can see the advantage of embarrassing the Russian Federation and weakening its ties to the U.S. and other nations."

"Thank you, Ben," Natalia said. "Remember, we believe that our victim is also a descendent of the royal Bagrationi. It is possible that radical Georgians are feeding arms to the Zetas, and have a further, or even a separate, goal of disrupting the Sochi games."

"Just what kind of scenarios exist for disrupting Sochi in 2014?" Cary asked.

"I vote for cyber-terrorism," said Billy. "We've already seen that the Zetas have some sophisticated technologies at their command that allow them to hack into major U.S. government security systems; witness them bypassing NPS security with the body parts and later planting the bomb at the National Constitution Center."

"Okay, let's follow this line of thought some more," Cary said.

"Billy here again," said the agent. "Sochi is undergoing a massive communications infrastructure upgrade to prepare for 2014. The media will pull a lot of current, as will new light rail systems, resort facilities, lighting for events, and new security systems. Overall, these improvements alone are estimated to cost several billion."

"The present hydraulic power system is located on a river between Georgia and Abkhazia with joint administration," Ben said. "Would it help to paint a picture of the needs in that area?"

Everyone agreed. Ben noted that Sochi, with a population of about 315,000, is less than fifty miles west of Abkhazia, whose entire population is somewhere in the range of 150,000-190,000 people.

"Black Sea tourism is the big draw for the Russian Federation, Georgia, and Abkhazia," said Manheim. "Estimates vary, but Russia and private industry are investing about $50 billion in the games. The average Georgian earns about $200 per year; Abkhazia is a poor country, heavily reliant on Russia for its economic and military support."

"Tell me about the Western Caucasus situation and its World Heritage site," asked Cary.

"The mountains run along the north, separating Georgia and its two renegade regions from Russia. The importance of the WHS is its unspoiled natural habitat." He explained that Greenpeace and other environmental groups were protesting Russia's decision to cede significant lands in the WHS for private development.

Cary was reminded of some previous government efforts to allow strip mining in U.S. national parks. In addition to cooperative agreements on fuels, trade finances, and other subjects, Cary learned that Russia and China had announced an accord on nanotechnology.

"Does anyone know who will actually make the communications upgrades in the Sochi area?" Cary asked. She thought it was unlikely that the natives in Abkhazia were all computer scientists.

"Okay, I think we need Ben and Billy to work this angle with their contacts," Ham said. "Cal and Cary, see if you can get some scuttlebutt from your colleagues as well."

Everyone nodded.

"Natalia, do you have any names of radical Georgian monarchists?"

"The modern monarchist tradition traces to the Bagrationi, or Bagration, who ruled from the Middle Ages until taken over by the Russian Empire in 1801. The current movement concentrates on the idea of a constitutional monarchy, like England. In 1800, there were two principal Georgian kingdoms, the Kartli-Kakheti and the Imereti. The first was deposed in 1801, the second in 1810.

"She then outlined several attempts to restore the Georgian monarchy, all failures.

Cary felt a headache coming on as Natalia spoke. She made the mistake of looking over at Cal, who rolled his eyes wildly. She stifled a giggle.

Cary was relieved to see that the genealogist was winding up her presentation. "As with the Romanovs, there are competing claims to the Georgian throne. For example, the descendant of the last reigning king, George XII, is Prince Nugzar Bagration-Grunzinsky."

Please, God, let it end with a name I can spell, prayed Cary.

"The good news is that the two competing houses were united by the 2009 marriage of Prince David Bagrationi-Mukhraneli with Nugzar's eldest daughter, Anna Bagration-Gruzinsky. The royal couple is expecting a child, who will be the general heir of George XII of Georgia. I do not want you to become confused about claims to the Georgian throne as opposed to the Russian throne.

I should mention the House Rules that Tsar Paul I issued in 1797, called for a strict order of succession to the Russian throne, always through the ruler's eldest son, until the male line was extinct. Only then could a female be put forward for the title. The Rules ordered that eligibility to the Russian throne required that each claimant be married to an equal, a member of an active ruling royal house. Marriage outside the stricture was ruled *morganatic.*"

"So, what does *that* mean?" asked Billy.

"Well, at least one current claimant to the Russian throne is the descendant of a marriage between the Romanov and Bagrationi lines, and since the Georgian kingdom was abolished in 1801, some earlier monarchs have ruled that the Bagrationi are not equal to the House of Romanov, so marriage between the two is morganatic."

"Let's cut to the chase," said Ben "There are claimants to both thrones, although most of them have social rather than military clout. A strong movement to return the monarchy to Georgia would serve the purpose of weakening any efforts by the Russian Federation to bring Georgia back into the fold and would further strengthen widespread opinion that Abkhazia and South Ossetia are rogue claimants to independence."

"One more tidbit," said Natalia. "In 2007, the Patriarch of the Georgian Orthodox Church gave a sermon describing the return of monarchy as a 'desirable dream' for Georgia."

"Right!" said Ben. "And this sermon gave several dissident groups within Georgia the excuse to launch a 'Georgia without a President' campaign. The bottom line is this: Georgia needs to get its country on a level political and economic course before serious efforts to reinstate the monarchy stand a chance of succeeding."

"Would it be safe to conclude that unnamed forces ostensibly acting on behalf of a monarchy restoration movement might be supplying funds to Mexican gangs with the intent of disrupting the 2014 Olympics and further destabilizing Georgia's economic and political progress?" asked Ham.

There was some mumbling among the experts, but Ben and Billy finally agreed that this scenario was not too far-fetched.

"So, who else is being funded?" Ham asked. "Would it also be safe to conclude that Sochi is an attractive target because its massive infrastructure upgrades and other strategic and logistical needs will require an equally large and sophisticated workforce from outside the region, and quite possibly outside Russia itself?"

The murmurs were more positive from the assembled group. Even Cal mumbled, "damn right," despite appearing dazed by the wealth of information.

"We don't have a snowball's chance in hell of diverting a major incident in Sochi," Ham said, frowning. "That is, unless we can track the source through Mexico fast, before the major workforce is in place and construction underway."

He instructed them all to look for threads leading to Mexico. With that, the meeting was adjourned.

CHAPTER 29

RUSSIA – JUNE 5-8, 2011
Cary and Cal

Cary and Cal suffered through the diplomatic dinner at the American Embassy, contacted their colleagues in St. Petersburg and Moscow, and weathered through the briefing on Sochi with patience. They felt like window dressing, only because they were. Valuable information about potential weaknesses in the Russian Federation's plans for infrastructure upgrades would come from other agents in place. American landmarks were very low on the terrorist priority list, it seemed.

They had set up meetings in Moscow first with representatives from ICOMOS, then Russian preservationists, and finally, museum curators. Everyone was welcoming, polite, and vaguely informative. After only one day, Cal and Cary were certain that the arrangements to build a new resort on the Black Sea would be worked out on very high levels, Greenpeace be damned.

"They would be better off trying to save some whales," Rolfe observed.

Over a quiet dinner at the home of one of the high-level bureaucrats in the ministry of culture in Moscow, they learned that inside efforts to curb the destruction of lands within the World

Heritage Site were in vain. It seemed there were few major historic buildings. The World Heritage Site was a natural habitat after all. The Russian legal system lacked the necessary laws or a powerful National Park Service like that which existed in the U.S.

In St. Petersburg, Cal went off in one direction and Cary in another. At the Hermitage, the curators showed Cary some of the collections from the era of Tsar Alexander I. Cary had used her work on the Madisons as the entrée. The same courtesies were extended to Cal and to Cary at the palaces occupied by Tsar Alexander I and his family in and near the city. At Pavlovsk Palace, Cary expressed interest in how the Russians had preserved the collections after the death of Dowager Empress Maria in 1828. The American was given a detailed briefing on the steps that were taken to protect these holdings until the palace and grounds went on view to tourists. The little painting of the *Secret Grandchild* was hung on a wall near a window that would have given the empress a view into the garden. Cary admired it and was allowed to cross the room to examine it in more detail. She said nothing about the tiny inscription.

Cal landed an invitation for himself and Cary to spend one night with Vladimir Popov, a noted Russian architect, at his dacha in Sochi. Ham was included and joined them the day they arrived. The visit was comfortable, the accommodations outstanding, and the food was exceptional, particularly the varieties of fresh seafood available. When their host announced at dinner that they were drinking wine from Georgia, Cal inquired about the in the former SSR.

"Wine is the most stable thing about Georgia," said Popov. "The country lurches in every direction; one way toward a democratic republic, and another toward dictatorship, with an occasional lurch backward toward monarchy."

"Joining NATO will help," offered Cal, passing his glass for more wine. He knew that the wine was also helping.

"Georgia will eventually decide to participate in the Russian games," said Popov. "They'll posture for a year or two and then take a vote to attend."

"Well, the city's amazing so far," said Cary. Cal had to agree. It had progressed extensively since his last visit.

"By 2014, you will not be able to recognize Sochi," said Popov wistfully. He didn't believe that too many historical buildings would be lost. "We do not have a long and distinguished architectural history here."

"What about the museums?" asked Cary.

"Unfortunately, the same is true for our museums. The damage will be done to the natural habitat, to the water quality of the Black Sea, and to the air we breathe. That said, I am satisfied with the architectural design standards in place. To be honest, I've been given a seat on the review board so it's hard to argue."

"That helps," said Cal with a snicker.

"Yes. Our McDonald's and Burger Kings will blend seamlessly into the environment," he joked, but it was clear that he dreaded the impact that the Games would have on this pleasant semi-tropical seaside city.

"What about the conservation standards to protect the areas of the World Heritage Site that will be turned over for development?"

"Since they turned over the land to others, capitalistic concerns have dominated the decision-making process."

⚖

The next morning the Americans were preparing to return to Moscow, and then on to the U.S. Ham shook hands with his host on the curb in front of his house before grabbing Cary's bag to put in the trunk of the taxi. Ham and Cary turned suddenly at the sound of Cal shouting behind them.

"Everyone, pose for a record of our delightful sojourn on the Black Sea!"

Rolfe had his digital camera centered and took the shot before anyone could blink.

The flight back to Moscow was uneventful and the Constitution murder team reassembled again in Ham's hotel suite. Cary and Cal reported that they had no additional information about Russian interests who might be traced to the Constitution murder case.

"Our colleagues are concerned about protection of the WHS natural habitat," Ham. "But they do not think that there is much anyone can do about it except demand on-site observers to keep them from killing every plant and animal within the area involved with the games."

Ham thanked them and turned to Billy.

"Our sources gathered enough worrisome information to warrant a demand that the communication system plans and their execution for the Games involve some strong outside advisors to keep the Russians honest," said Billy. "There is ample evidence that the Chinese are planning to get heavily into the action. Assignment of outside watchdog specialists will reduce the risk of any dangers."

"I recommend that the Russians bring in the British and another country with Games experience to make sure that security in Sochi will be tight," said Ben. "The Brits are well into their plans for the London Games for 2012, and we trust them to make sure Russia stays on the straight and narrow. If I'm being honest, maintaining security during the games will likely be a nightmare."

Ham thanked everyone for their assistance and walked out of the room to write his report. He knew it would be incorporated into the official findings of the presidential commission.

The flight back to the United States seemed shorter than their initial journey overseas. A few members of the commission napped while others played cards. Cary was drifting in and out of sleep when she felt a tap on her shoulder. It was Cal, who eyed her with concern and motioned for her to follow him to the back of the plane.

"Why in God's name were we included in this frivolous taxpayer junket?" he asked. Cary could see that he was piqued. "The whole trip was a complete red herring." She watched as he continued for minutes, insisting that Ellen Harriet was really the only member of the commission with the qualifications to exert influence on efforts to prevent massive development within the WHS lands. "And for all the good it'll do, she might as well have offered her opinions in a conference call from a telephone booth."

Cary nodded and stared absently out a window to the clouds. Nothing he said was wrong.

CHAPTER 30

SAN MIGUEL DE ALLENDE, MEXICO – JUNE 8-12, 2011
Cary and Sasha

Princess Sasha Troubetzskoy and VE Shane sipped cocktails on the elegant tiled patio at the Rancho Hotel Atascadero in San Miguel de Allende. The view of the city below them was enchanting as the two women watched the sun set slowly behind the hills. VE never missed the cocktail hour, long considered something of a sacred ritual at the Shane compound. Apparently, the Troubetzskoys were no sluggards either when it came to enjoying evening libations.

"After the servants left we no longer had elegant five-course dinners," said Sasha, sounding aggrieved. "We had to learn to fend for ourselves."

VE raised an eyebrow, imagining a table full of inebriated nobles wearing white ties and tiaras, staggering off to their bedrooms after the evening meal. The princess interpreted the gesture as a signal to continue.

"Well, we always had sherry," she said. "But the glasses are tiny, of course, and there was no one to refill them. Anyway, it's so déclassé to drink too much sherry, even very good sherry."

Princess Sasha continued, sip by sip. VE slowly learned that the meals deteriorated without a full kitchen staff, the quality of the wine cellar soon followed suit, and finally, a delightful American heiress visiting in the south of France had suggested that the Russian spinster resort to two large martinis before dinner.

"She assured me the food tasted less mediocre afterward. Besides, the wine even tastes better with dinner."

Princess Sasha smiled as she sipped her cocktail. It was a concoction VE had suggested. "What is this delightful libation called again?" she asked.

"It's called a Tequila Sunrise," said VE. She had chosen to stick to bourbon, whatever the country or time of day. She did not need to warn the Russian aristocrat of its potency. Like most Russians, Sasha could hold her liquor.

The princess confided with dignity that she had never entered a public bar, having been assured by her mother that single women in such establishments were prey for white slavers. VE was only too happy to tell her all about her own, somewhat happier, experiences in these nefarious dens of iniquity.

Neither woman had bothered to dress for the evening meal, electing instead to order room service in one of their suites. They each donned a sweater to ward off the chill starting to creep in from the surrounding mountains. VE thought back to their *debut* in the ex-patriot community in San Miguel several days earlier and smiled.

The first night they had made reservations to dine in the city's five-star restaurant, a popular spot for many of the wealthy Europeans and Americans who frequent the beautiful town. The food was said to be outstanding and the service impeccable. They had dressed carefully, intent on making quite an entrance. VE had walked to Princess Troubetzskoy's suite to escort her to the waiting taxi, fearful at the elderly Russian might get lost in the confusion of hallways in the sprawling estate. She needn't have worried.

Sasha swept from the room regally gowned in what VE recognized was a vintage but timelessly stylish Elsa Schiaparelli. Her ensemble included at least ten pounds of diamonds, which flashed with considerable fire from her ears, neck, breast, and wrists. Her purse was covered in pearls. VE had seen a similar evening bag from the estate of Marjorie Merriweather Post, reputed to be valued at more than $250,000.

As the only granddaughter of Paw and Maw Shane, VE had inherited part of her grandmother's respectable collection of jewels, but had to admit that her bling was positively dreary when compared to the sparkling antique array worn by the princess. She felt more competitive in the long and elegant Vera Lang evening dress that was custom-made for some charity gala or another that she had chaired in Dallas, but conceded that her $5,000 Judith Leiber bag was minor league.

The two ladies glided through the main hotel reception lobby, carriage erect, bosoms high, bangles reflecting like a meteor shower in the large looking glasses hung on every wall. The concierge bowed as they passed. Several guests stood, as if in the presence of royalty.

They are *in the presence of royalty,* VE mused, feeling regal herself. *This is fun.*

The princess was far too well-bred for her emotions to appear on her face, but VE did catch sight of tiny dimples, showing perhaps amusement, or maybe even condescension, on either side of her subtly rouged mouth.

At the restaurant, all conversation ceased as they entered the dining room. The *maitre d',* a veteran of a galaxy of five-star restaurants abroad, nearly swooned at the blinding vision of so many important gemstones. He recovered gallantly and executed a professional bow over the elderly hand.

"*Buenas noches, senoras,*" he crooned, momentarily forgetting the French accent he had so carefully cultivated over the years. He waved off a nearby waiter with a sniff and escorted the two ladies to the main table in the center of the room, where they were guaranteed to be seen by everyone, or at least by everyone who mattered. He seated them with a flourish, bowed again, and disappeared.

An assistant appeared within seconds with menus, followed shortly by a waiter opening a bottle of Veuve Clicquot champagne, vintage '98, compliments of the house. Every diner around them seemed to be staring. However, both women ignored them, instead smiling and chatting politely as they cautiously sipped champagne.

VE quietly informed the princess that her good friend, the American heiress to a mammoth high-tech fortune, would be hosting a party the following evening. Princess Troubetzskoy seemed to recognize the name and smiled before announcing that *her* dear friend, a well-known old-line prince in exile, would honor them at his mansion the evening thereafter. VE knew he had escaped with not only his life but a considerable fortune, and returned Sasha's smile with great satisfaction. VE could already tell that they would get along like a house on fire. She mentioned this to the princess and watched as she pretended not to understand the meaning.

The following morning, Princess Sasha visited the head office at the hotel to make discreet inquiries about the two visits made during the mid-1980s by the Russian noblewoman. Leaning forward, she touched his arm softly with her hand. The manager had already heard of the dinner the evening before and was not surprised to see one finger on said hand weighted down by an emerald ring of at least ten carats.

"It is our greatest pleasure to have you with us princessa," he assured her.

"I am interested in learning about the visits of a certain noblewoman during the 1980s, more than twenty years ago. Would you have recollection of this?" She mentioned the name of the princess and added that she was a close cousin.

"Unfortunately, the grand duchess was in a near-fatal automobile accident," the princess said. "She has significant memory loss because of a head injury. Learning of my plan to visit San Miguel, she asked me to check on her daughter and the child's father. As you know, the girl was raised here."

The proprietor's ears alerted to the title. However, he nevertheless continued to play dumb, raising his shoulders in a shrug. "Child? Father?" he asked.

"Child." The princess smiled in return, carefully extracting an envelope from her purse and placing it on the table before them. "Father."

As if ordained by heaven, a secretary interrupted and announced that there was a telephone call for the princess. "*Me?*" asked Sasha, feigning amazement. She politely excused herself to take the call in the next room.

The proprietor picked up the envelope. He peeked inside at the contents upon seeing that it was not sealed. Inside he saw a stack of very crisp, very genuine bills inside, all bearing the portrait of the ubiquitous Benjamin Franklin. The envelope was gone by the time his noble guest had reassumed her seat.

When questioned further, the princess shook her head sadly, admitting that her cousin could not remember the name of the family entrusted with the care of the child. The owner clucked his teeth in great sympathy.

"And the name of the father?" he asked.

"Gone from her damaged mind," The princess said. She wondered if she should shed a tear or two, but restrained herself admirably.

"Gracious lady," said the owner, "it will be our privilege to assist you in this grave matter."

He asked her to keep his name and the name of the hotel out of any report she might give to the family.

"My lips are sealed," she pronounced, with the dignity befitting a person of her exalted station.

Within twenty minutes, Sasha was rapping on the door to VE's suite. A moment later she entered the sitting room wearing a wide, toothy smile. "As you say in the States, I've hit pay dirt."

They sat down, and Sasha extracted two sheets of paper from her purse.

"Forget about the father," she said resolutely. "His name was Antonio Guerrero, a minor talent but a great lover, at least per my source." The artist had been seen with the grand duchess during her first visit to the hotel, but was absent during her second stay, which would have encompassed the completion of the pregnancy and the birth of the child.

"Is he still alive?" asked VE.

Sasha shook her head. "Murdered by a jealous husband years ago. Anyway, he apparently knew little if anything about the child. The mother made all the arrangements."

"Who raised her?"

The princess handed over the second paper, which had a name, address, and phone number.

"Let's go," said VE, reaching for her purse and a map of San Miguel.

⚍┼┼⚎

The two-story home of José and Francesca Ramirez was located on a narrow side street, its front courtyard shielded behind a stuccoed brick wall with an iron gate. The residence seemed to be in excellent repair. There was an intercom button, which the princess promptly pushed.

Speaking in perfect, Castilian Spanish, the princess gave her name, five or six additional titles, and a brief explanation of the reason for so rudely paying a call with neither an invitation nor an appointment. She described the grand duchess's accident and the need to locate the daughter to check on her well-being. The message ended with assurances that the grand duchess wished to make additional special arrangements for the child, since it was unlikely that her mother would fully recover.

VE could not tell which words did the magic trick – it may have just been the highbrow Spanish dialect – but someone pushed a button and the gate swung open soundlessly. By the time they reached the tall, heavily-carved wooden entry door, it was opened by a tiny woman in full domestic uniform. She bowed and led them into a cavernous foyer with twenty-foot ceilings and a black-and-white onyx tile floor. Several pieces of what VE recognized as Spanish Colonial antique furniture were arranged along the walls, which were hung with oil portraits of long-dead Ramirez dons and doñas.

They followed the maid and were escorted into a sunny sitting room furnished with European Louis XVI furniture. The maid asked if they wanted refreshments. Princess Sasha did not understand her dialect, which led VE to respond graciously in the negative.

In a matter of minutes, a handsome middle-aged lady, obviously Francesca Ramirez, entered the room and extended her hand, first to Princess Troubetzskoy, and then to VE. The Texan thanked Doña Francesca for agreeing to see them and complimented her on her lovely home.

Doña Francesca swept her arm toward two cushioned fauteuils covered in silk damask. She paused as the ladies sat down before sitting opposite them. She wore an expression that combined curiosity and expectation, with eyes wide and slack jaw.

"Please," she said. "Let us converse in English. Don José will be joining us soon." She reached to an end table and rang a small bell, summoning the maid. She glanced at her diamond-studded gold wristwatch and saw that it was 11:25 AM. She ordered sherry and coffee, thinking that it was not too early for one and not too late for the other. VE and Princess Sasha took note that her Spanish was more refined than the standard Mexican vernacular. Obviously, Doña Francesca came from good stock. The maid entered a moment later with a tray bearing a silver coffee service, French antique cups and saucers, silver spoons, and a bottle of top-shelf Spanish sherry. There were several footed crystal sherry glasses arranged around the bottle. The napkins were Irish linen trimmed with lace, demurely embroidered with the letter *R*. VE also saw a small Sèvres plate covered with *pan dulce.*

Don José entered the room once they were all settled and sipping from their drinks. He bowed over the hand of each lady and offered a formal welcome. He walked to a small marble-topped drinks table in the corner and splashed a generous four fingers of 12-year old scotch into a cut crystal old-fashioned glass.

Don José was tall and slender, with dark hair and a goatee. His looks were Spanish, without revealing a hint of Indio blood. Like his wife, he spoke well in English and was obviously the product of formal schooling, possibly on the Continent. Princess Sasha told the story of her beloved cousin with admirable passion, and was just getting to the part about the brain damage and memory loss when Don José made a low polite cough. She paused and stared at him.

"Princess Troubetzskoy, we know the lady and we have heard nothing about an accident or memory loss."

Sasha found herself momentarily speechless.

"In fact," he continued. "I can report to you the contents of a phone conversation held less than ten minutes ago with the banker who handles the other noblewoman's finances."

The princess froze, her face turning flush. VE's eyes wandered to the garden outside the large bay window.

"The banker told me that he knows of you," Don José said. "He explained your formidable reputation as the 'Great Romanov Family Historian.'

"I see," the princess mumbled.

"I must say, my dear Princess, you are certainly worthy of your title. I am at a loss to understand how you have tracked us down after more than twenty years. Furthermore, we were led to believe that our child's mother was a descendent of Georgian, not Imperial Romanov Russian nobility." He rose and started to refill his guests' now-empty sherry glasses.

He paused once more and looked down at VE Shane. "Something a little stronger, perhaps?"

"Yeah, you got any Jack Daniels?" VE asked.

He nodded and turned toward the drinks table. He returned a moment later with an ample serving.

"Some of that scotch please," said the princess. This too he returned with a moment later, setting her glass down gracefully. He sat down next to his wife. Their faces grew gravely serious.

"The child is named Carlotta Franz," he said. "Her mother thought it would be appropriate to name her for Carlotta, the wife of Emperor Maximillian, a former ruler of Mexico. We have not seen nor heard from Carlotta for six years. She ran away when she was eighteen."

He touched his wife's hand gently and swallowed. His eyes turned cloudy as he explained that the girl's mother was fully aware of the situation. As for funds, Carlotta had come into a trust upon her 18th birthday and had dealt directly with her mother's financial representatives ever since.

"Oddly enough, her banker told me this morning that he has not heard from her for more than two months. When she left San Miguel, we told our friends that she had died in an automobile accident. Perhaps you have something you want to tell us about Carlotta?"

Doña Francesca rose, walked to a desk, and extracted a photo of a young woman. She showed it to VE, who nodded in recognition. Cary had forwarded an image of the facial reconstruction when she brought Shane into the investigation.

"I don't know how to tell you all this," VE said, "but a woman whose DNA and photograph matched a description of Carlotta was recently found murdered. This crime was part of a much larger, highly-classified investigation that has reached the top levels of the U.S. government."

Doña Ramirez removed a handkerchief and dotted her eyes. Her husband looked equally distressed.

"Was our Carlotta a Romanov?"

Princess Troubetzskoy nodded and explained the dual royal lineage from the tsars of Russia and the ruling house of Bagrationi in Georgia.

"We know she had trouble with drugs and was said to have been involved of late with one of the cartels," said VE. "But we desperately need to develop a clearer picture of her activities, her character, and her associates."

Doña Francesca sighed and spoke first. "Do you know what a 'bad seed' is?"

VE nodded, followed by Princess Sasha.

"Carlotta was a bad seed," said Doña Francesca. "Rotten to the core from an early age. We loved her, lavished affection on her. We spared no expense keeping her identity private. She played with the children of the best people, using our surname. We sent her to outstanding schools in Europe. Nothing worked. She lied, she stole from us, our servants, and from her acquaintances. She began to run around with drug users. Once she was on her own, we heard she was involved in even worse crimes. Major robberies, drug trafficking, perhaps even murder."

"We know she had at least one child. Did you know about it?"

They shook their heads.

"What about drugs?"

"She started on drugs early, but we were able to keep it quiet," said Don José. "We are not without influence here and elsewhere in Mexico. After she left, we learned that she had involved herself with the drug cartels. The last report said she was among the

Zetas, who have a broad territory with a heavy presence near the border in Nuevo Laredo."

VE nodded. She had heard the same thing from their sources.

Princess Sasha leaned forward. "You say that her natural mother knows about your problems with the child?"

"Yes," said Don José. "By the time Carlotta was twelve, she was a criminal. We had to reach out to her biological mother for help."

"What did she do?" Sasha asked.

"She told us Carlotta had inherited what she called the *bad seed*, a horrible trait that runs through the bloodlines. We were told that Carlotta's great-great-great grandfather had it, that he was violent against his own family, and was insane."

Doña Francesca began to weep openly. Her husband patted her shoulder, shaking his head.

The princess sat back and exhaled, sensing the closure she had come for. However, she felt great dissatisfaction at the same time.

"It is not your fault," she said. "Do you want me to tell you about the trait?"

"Yes," said Don José.

Sasha told the terrible tale, leaving out the name of the father who introduced the tainted strain into the royal family in 1814. "I will send you the lineage. Again, there is absolutely nothing you could have done. It was the bad seed. She was a bad seed."

Neither of the women asked the Ramirez's if they had any children of their own. Obviously, they had pinned so many of their hopes on the little foundling offered to them, as if by a miracle, by one of the most famous families in the world. Neither did they tell them that their adopted daughter had become pregnant with another child who perished with her. Don José explained that the population in San Miguel knew that Carlotta was adopted, but they had no idea of any royal connections. When informed of the invitations to the two parties, one that evening and one the next, he suggested a new cover story.

"We know both of your hosts quite well," he said. He turned to his wife and asked her to call both hosts to inform them that Señora Shane is the granddaughter of an old friend in Texas. "Ms. Shane, I knew your famous grandfather and visited with him at one of your family ranches. He is not easily forgotten."

Don José asked about European cities that VE and Princess Troubetzskoy might have visited during the past decade or so and found several matches close in time. They worked out a story whereby VE – between husbands at the time – had met the princess during a house party on the yacht of a well-known Saudi prince, who spent a part of each season in Monte Carlo. In this story, they had become great friends and later kept in contact, traveling together when their schedules coincided. It was fortuitous that they could meet again in San Miguel to continue their happy relationship.

VE would take the lead on mentioning her grandfather's ties to the Ramirezes and tell her hostess, quite discreetly, that she had visited with Don José and Francesca that day, learning with sadness of the death of their daughter Carlotta. Doña Francesca rang again for the maid and ordered an early luncheon for four on the patio. Over a delicious repast of cold avocado soup, *arroz con pollo* and flan, they perfected their narratives.

"Don José, shall we dazzle the guests tonight with diamonds?" asked VE, partly in jest. Don José and his wife could not have failed to notice that both women wore spectacular rings that were appropriate for day wear, but nonetheless of staggering value.

"By all means, ladies, everyone here likes to show off their finery," Don José said. Doña Francesca filled them in on the usual attire for evenings in San Miguel and assured them that everyone visited the prince in full medals and regalia, whether they've earned them or not.

That evening, at the home of VE's friend Lisa Walter, the two visitors told their story, each finding an opening to drop in the sad story about Carlotta. Lisa was a close friend of VE's mother, having attended the private Hockaday School in Dallas. Fortunately, Lisa liked to mix politics and pleasure, so they got to meet some high officials in the Mexican government, including a senior executive in the country's anti-drug department. Princess Sasha left it to the American to pursue these leads, relying instead on her expertise in genealogy to enlighten some of the other guests about prominent relatives and ancestors that few of them even knew they had.

⚓

On the following evening, the exiled Prussian prince, weighted down with medals, introduced the princess and VE to several young aristocrats who had known Carlotta as a child in a boarding school that catered to wealthy royals and millionaires. They learned that the Ramirezes ranked among the latter category. The prince was not surprised that Don José had known VE's grandfather. Princess Sasha, whose surname was always closely linked to the Romanovs, spent most of the evening holding court with the other nobles, stationed beneath a monumental portrait of King Frederick William III of Prussia.

Now, on the final night of their journey to San Miguel, they ate dinner in VE's suite and sat down to compare notes about their findings. They had not disclosed that Carlotta Franz was murdered, or that she was part of a massive U.S. criminal investigation. They were candid about the illegitimacy, hinting that the Ramirez family was of sufficient stature to adopt well. Besides, illegitimacy was a subject almost commonplace among the ex-patriots. The grand duchess was never mentioned by name or title; the women merely mentioned that the child came from rarified bloodlines. *Truer words were never spoken*, thought VE.

VE led off with an update on her follow-up meeting with local law enforcement and a lunch with the anti-drug official, Reynaldo Mendoza. Reynaldo confirmed the foster parents' description of

Carlotta as a bad seed, citing a lengthy history of misdeeds and crimes.VE was even invited to examine the files at the city's police department. Access would be easy, said the agent. The Mexican officials knew of the vast size of the Shane real estate holdings and business interests on both sides of the border. The family owned nearly half a billion acres.

Some of the Shane holdings were in chaparral country with vast expanses of scrub brush. It was useless for farming, but generously dotted with oil mules. In arid sections of Texas and Mexico, cattle required large areas for free-range grazing. Flat land and desolation were perfect settings for convoys and even small planes to deliver goods and people secretly across the border. The Shanes had a long history of assisting police and drug officials from both countries. A direct request from VE, one of the two heirs to the entire Shane Empire, was almost guaranteed to open some doors.

The princess pitched in briefly, noting that a few old-timers from her circle had confided to her that the girl was constantly in trouble, causing disturbances, running away from school and from home, and hanging out with undesirables. Her adopted parents had used their wealth and social status to cover up her transgressions. Carlotta caused terrible pain to her family in San Miguel, said one famous gambler and philanderer, who whispered to Sasha that he suspected the girl had she not died in a car crash and would have turned out to be "no good at all."

VE added that, according to one homicide detective, Carlotta had murdered a rival for the affections of a boy Franz wanted for herself.

"When we found the body of her victim, its eyes had been gouged out," Reynaldo said in disgust, then shook his head because there had not been enough evidence to pursue the investigation. Shane thought about Carlotta's detached eyeballs on the floor of James Madison's library but stayed silent.

Reynaldo also offered some interesting information about Carlotta and drugs. In summary, she was an addict before she turned fourteen and was believed to deal narcotics on a small scale. "She did not have lasting relationships with any men," he said. "She seemed to use them as much as they used her."

The Mexican drug agent flirted with VE a little at lunch, trying to draw out her real reasons for asking questions about the adopted daughter of a friend of her grandfather.

"Señor," VE demurred, "our family was unhappy to learn about the American operation called 'Fast and Furious.'"

"Why, Señora? Do you know anything about it?" he asked. His eyes were locked on her now. VE knew she had gotten his attention.

"What we know is that the United States government backed a clandestine operation on American soil," VE said. "Much of it very near or perhaps even on our own property, which allowed guns to be sold to straw buyers, who, in turn, appear to have sold them to drug runners in Mexico. I learned about the operation earlier this year from a colleague."

"You knew nothing about this operation before then?" Reynaldo asked.

VE shook her head firmly. "The answer is no. My family checked into the operation and discovered that some of the illegal sales had taken place on property owned by the Shanes, and rented to gun dealers. But it's clear that Operation Fast and Furious was an embarrassment to everyone."

"Yes, of course," said Reynaldo.

"The Shanes are Americans, Señor Mendoza. But we are also neighbors to Mexico." She paused for effect. "And my granddaddy didn't raise no fools. So please tell me what you know about the activities of Carlotta Franz in Northern Mexico and the U.S. during the past six months. Specifically, I need to know whether Franz came into the U.S. or left it by crossing on Shane land."

Mendoza left with the very clear impression that the Shanes were not satisfied with the information they had received from the U.S. government. It took nearly a full day to get information from northern Mexico about Carlotta's activities there. Agent Mendoza called on VE at the hotel to let her know his findings. He started his report with a summary of the growth of the Mexican drug cartels after the top Colombia leaders were slain.

VE cut him off. "We do our homework," she said. "What have you learned?"

"The Mexican government is at war with the drug cartels," admitted Reynaldo, "and the Mexican government is losing."

VE began to speak but Reynaldo raised his hand before she could interrupt. He pulled out a folder containing a grainy color photo of a man and a woman. He identified the female as Carlotta Franz.

"And the man?" asked VE.

"We do not know him," he said. "He is not a regular in our world."

VE squinted into the photo. It was a terrible image, but she could tell that the man was tall with dark hair. He looked to be around 45. She stared at the image for a full minute, her brain replaying her conversation with Cary about the DHS briefing on the activities of Carlotta Franz during the months before her death.

"What alias did she use to cross the border?" she asked.

"None that we can find."

VE nodded. This jibed with the DHS story. "When did she cross?"

"We do not know."

"Do you know whether she was with the Zetas?"

Reynaldo shrugged. "She was with the Zetas in Northern Mexico during February of this year. She was seen in the company of one of the leaders, with whom we believe she was involved."

"Are you telling me that this man in the photo is not a Zeta?"

"We do not believe this man is a Zeta. We do not know who he is."

"Does the DHS have a copy of this photo?" VE asked. She figured it was worth a shot.

"No." Mendoza's eyes flickered, but he remained silent. He knew she would not have asked this question if she had seen the photo as part of a DHS brief.

"Señor Mendoza, was this photo taken at immigration? Either in the U.S. or Mexico?"

Reynaldo shook his head. "It was taken by a camera outside a bank in Laredo."

"Not Nuevo Laredo?"

"No, Señora Shane. Laredo, Texas. This woman had just withdrawn $10,000. We know this because all transactions of this amount or larger must be reported by the U.S. banks."

VE nodded.

"A woman named Carlotta Franz arranged a wire transfer from a bank in Switzerland to the bank in Laredo. There were no photos of Franz or the mystery man on any of the border cameras." He paused and considered her blue eyes.

"Do you recognize this man, Señora?"

"I can tell you that he looks somewhat familiar," she said. "But I cannot name him based on this poor-quality photograph." *He is not Mexican*, VE thought. She knew this for a fact.

"We believe that he is an American." With that, Reynaldo pushed the photograph across the table to VE. The gesture was clear. *Take it. Find out who he is. Tell us.*

"It's time to share, Señora Shane. You may be assured of our discretion. We know that she was in Laredo on March 9 of this year." He added that there was a date stamp on the camera photo.

"She was traced to a ranch outside Grand Prairie, Texas."

"The ranch is a cell for the Zetas?"

"She died there."

"Of a heroin overdose?"

VE shook her head. "Her throat was cut."

They stopped. If Reynaldo knew about the Constitution murders he did not say so. At the same time, he sensed that she was withholding something from him.

"You have been most helpful," said VE, rising to indicate that the meeting was at an end. They exchanged cards. She had written another number on hers in ink, and he had done the same.

⊷⊶

The princess listened with keen attention to VE's summary of the meeting, later that evening in her hotel room.

"My dear, tell me again please. What is this Operation Fast and Furious?"

"It was an ill-conceived operation by the ATF, the full details of which have not yet been publicly revealed." She filled in a few details to Princess Troubetzskoy's stunned amazement.

"VE, are you telling me that this ATF, this tobacco and gun agency of the United States, set up an operation to deliberately sell arms to buyers obviously working on behalf of the drug gangs in Mexico?" she asked.

"Yes."

"And while they had planned to follow these buyers – straw men? – to track their resale to the drug cartels, they somehow neglected to do so?"

"Right."

"And that some of these weapons ended up being used by said drug cartels to commit murder on others, including an American agent?"

VE nodded.

"And, your agency, the ATF, is supposedly helping the Mexican government fight these drug cartels?

"That was the idea."

"Did these gun sales take place on American soil?"

She nodded.

"Virginia, some of my friends have told me that your family owns a great deal of land. Were any of these sales on your property?"

VE thought about the vast ranches and the little towns that the Shanes helped to build on their own, so that the families working there could have easier access to groceries, churches, auto repairs, even movies. Some of those sales took place on land leased from the Shanes, although certainly the transactions were not condoned by them. "I'm afraid so," she admitted.

With a firm nod, Princess Sasha seemed to accept this bizarre story.

"Never trust the government," she said. "We Romanovs, of all people, ought to know."

CHAPTER 31

JOE POOL LAKE, TEXAS – JUNE 13, 2011
VE

V E made the trip to the ranch near Midlothian, Texas by helicopter, having hitched a ride on one of the regular flights that toured Shane land holdings every day. She looked down over Joe Pool Lake, completed in 1985 as a reservoir after decades of delays. As she did, she saw that the area was continuing to develop as a resort fed by its proximity to Dallas and Fort Worth, a metropolitan area of more than four million people.

Paw would have loved to see this, she thought. The helicopter set down smoothly on a pad at Shane #15, as the property was called on the large map at headquarters in downtown Fort Worth. Shane #15 was small by family property standards, only about 2,000 acres, with partial frontage on the south side of the lake. It was used for raising Charolais cattle and as a semi-retreat for fishing. Paw Shane had started breeding *Chars* not long after their introduction into the southern U.S. during the 1940s. They were good beef cattle without too much fat. Executives in the far-flung Shane Empire brought clients for fishing weekends at the ranch, combining recreation with good liquor and barbequed beef to keep business going.

Juan Hernandez met the helicopter on the pad and escorted VE into the office, which occupied one end of a large barn on the property. He had worked cattle for the family since graduating high school. VE knew that as a kid, the steer he entered at the State Fair of Texas had won first prize. She wondered if Juan knew that Paw Shane, a member of the Chaparral Club, had purchased the steer at the Fair. Club members pledged each year to buy the livestock from the young Texans who brought them to the annual fair for auction.

"I need somebody who knows their way around Grand Prairie," she confided, once they were settled into their plush office chairs. The Dallas suburb abutted the northern end of Joe Pool Lake, extending along the western shore nearly to the southern tip. It had become a popular residential area for Mexican immigrants to the U.S.

"We have several men who live there," he said.

"Good." VE handed him a cell phone and told him to stand by for instructions within the next few days. Juan did not ask for details.

CHAPTER 32

DALLAS, TX – JUNE 15, 2011
VE

V E's condo in Dallas was in the Mansion Residences on Turtle Creek Boulevard, one of the most prestigious addresses in the city. With three bedrooms and more than 4,000 square feet, the unit was affiliated with the historic Mansion Hotel and Restaurant, a Rosewood Properties development by Caroline Hunt, one of the daughters of late oil baron H.L. Hunt.

The centerpiece of the hotel development was the restored mansion of Shepard King, a Dallas cotton baron during the early 20th century. VE liked the location and the facilities because she could order in from the restaurant, entertain easily in the spacious interiors, and leave all maintenance and arrangements to the talented on-site staff.

During her recent visit to San Miguel, VE had asked Lisa Walter for assistance in gathering information about the state of computer technology in Mexico. Lisa's late husband had established the largest IT firm in Texas, and one of the most advanced in the world. She had phoned VE the night before to tell her to expect a visit from Ned Donaldson, head of security for the tech giant.

VE sat down across from Ned in her condo library after his arrival. Ned had prepared a confidential report, which lay on the table between them. VE knew him from the society circuit. His wife was active in TACA, Chrystal Charity, Susan G. Komen, and several other leading charities in the city. She knew that she could count on his discretion. After all, she reasoned, he's a spy of sorts.

"The IT expertise seems to be coming in from China," Ned said. "It seems they're sending agents to train members of the cartels."

"Who's funding the training?" asked VE.

"Same folks that're behind the weapons and quasi-military training. You got your Russians, your Middle Eastern crazies like Hezbollah, some nuts from former SSRs. It's a mixed bag. Plus, the cartels can fund a lot of training themselves."

VE nodded. It made sense to her, since advanced computer technology was a critical asset in operating the vast distribution networks used by the drug lords.

"It also helps when they can hack into the security systems that we're using to try to stop the flood of narcotics into the U.S.," Ned added.

VE knew she could trust him with the information about the Constitution murders, so she filled him in on the details, holding nothing back. Ned listened in quiet shock and shook his head. VE got up and walked to the kitchen to get them something to drink. She returned with a glass of soda for him, which he took with a polite nod.

"Honest to God, VE, I'm tempted to say some group just wants to show off. I mean, there's no real financial benefit from the infiltrations at the thirteen historic sites. The victim herself doesn't have any value beyond name recognition, and that's just through long-dead relatives. Carlotta Franz wouldn't make a very good victim in terms of media sympathy."

"Do you think the attack on the Constitution Center could've been the culmination of the earlier invasions?"

Ned frowned. "It almost seems like a completely different operation. But we've seen these types of variations before with terrorist groups. Look at the differences in scope and sophistication between the attacks on the World Trade Center and the thwarted van bomb attack in Manhattan a few years back. One was really big; the other was kind of rinky-dink."

"Okay," said VE. "Let's run with the showing-off idea for a minute or two. Who benefits from the invasions at the thirteen historic sites?"

"Well, it certainly throws a negative light on security at our nation's landmarks," he said.

"And spotlights the importance of the DHS branch that oversees their protection," VE said.

"But word of the incidents at the thirteen sites didn't get out."

"Not until after the kids got blown up at the National Constitution Center."

"Then, they *are* related," they said simultaneously.

"So, what's next?" Ned asked, clearly engaged now.

"I don't think it's Sochi," VE said. She had been in contact with Cary and both women thought Sochi was a diversion as far as the Constitution murders were concerned. They agreed that there were far bigger and more valid concerns about security and communications at the site of the 2014 Olympic Games, not only because of Sochi's isolation, but because of the ongoing political unrest in the region.

VE and Ned tossed around ideas until the maid appeared, telling them that lunch was served in the dining room. Once they were seated in front of Southwestern salads and sweet tea, they continued talking. VE wondered aloud if maybe someone had declared the American version of a Holy War on the National Park Service? Could someone be trying to embarrass the DHS?

Although word of some of the invasions at the thirteen historic sites had leaked, the press did not know the identity of the victim.

Nor did they know that all the body parts came from one person. Of the original thirteen incidents, only four – UPenn, Gunston Hall, John Jay Homestead, and Grove Street Cemetery – had been reported on the news. So far, reporters were speculating about possible connections between these incidents and the bombing at INHP, but the Constitution connection had not been clearly worked out among the members of the Fourth Estate.

There was considerable shouting from the media about the need for better protection of our national treasures, but Congress had so far not moved to earmark additional financing for major security upgrades at NPS sites. UPenn and Grove Street were open areas, meaning that they were accessible to the public. Gunston and John Jay were state landmarks, meaning they were not associated with the Park Service in the public mind.

After lunch, VE walked Ned to the front door of the condo and thanked him warmly for his assistance. "Keep me posted," he said. She promised to let him know how the investigation was advancing.

⇥┼┼⇤

The afternoon was spent playing catch-up on various feelers that VE had put out over the past several days. She had waited for information to come in from Cary before she forwarded it to Juan Hernandez at Shane #15. Some of the same material had gone to a laboratory owned by one of the many Shane companies for analysis. The Texas heiress was anxious to get the results.

Finally, she received a text shortly before 5:00 pm. VE noted the source and saw that there was an attachment. She walked to her office and plugged the phone into her computer, downloaded the file and pulled it up on the LCD screen.

Holy shit!

VE froze. Her hands trembled as she dialed a number on her cell phone. *Pick up. Goddammit, please pick up!*

CHAPTER 33

CHURCH HILL, RICHMOND –
EVENING, JUNE 15, 2011
Connie

Cary returned from Russia in one piece, but faced a detailed list of to-dos for her antique business. I urged her to spend a week at home in Church Hill getting things settled before returning to Montpelier.

I had given her a concise report on purchases, opportunities, and client needs, and gently reminded her that money didn't grow on trees. She had completed two purchases and three major sales in the past week. We smiled with the knowledge that the bills would continue to be paid for several months into the future.

Cary was relieved when calls to Montpelier proved that the staff there had handled matters admirably in her absence. She answered some questions about objects and areas of ongoing research before thanking the curators for their vigorous work, then followed up with a quick email to John Abbott complimenting his staff.

By 6:00 pm she was caught up with most of her daily emails and started to return the most important calls. I mixed our first cocktails of the evening and placed a nice roast in the oven. We were looking forward to a quiet dinner at home to catch up on all the nitty-gritty details of the past week. Besides, she had brought me some publications from the Hermitage on Russian decorative arts, including an English translation of the major catalogue on the metal furniture made at Tula. There were also heavily-illustrated books on several of the tsarist palaces, and I was dying to get some firsthand descriptions of the places she had visited during her trip.

"Okay, darling," I said, looking up from a catalogue from the Hermitage. "Let's hear about the way the *really* rich people lived. You know how I *adore glitter.*"

Cary had just answered her cell phone and wasn't listening. I had just started to explain the 24-carat gold surfaces of the architectural wonders in St. Petersburg, when she mouthed *It's VE.* I was getting ready to send my most jovial greetings when Cary's jaw dropped. The color drained from her face. She listened intently for a few moments and closed her eyes. Her body began to quiver.

I stood up in alarm and reached for her. Cary stood and dropped the phone, knocking over her chair in the process. She suddenly bent forward and put her head between her legs.

"What in the name of all the Gods is the *matter?*" I asked. I moistened a dish towel in the sink and, holding her steady, pressed it to the back of her neck. I had never seen Cary dizzy, much less ready to faint.

"Call Cal Rolfe! Now!" she gasped. She grabbed my arm as I reached for my phone.

"No! Not that phone" she insisted. "Use this one!" She shoved her cell into my hand.

Then she goose-walked me to the back door and shoved me out onto the patio.

"Go down the side street and through the backyards," she whispered. "You can't be here. Call Cal and tell him to send the police. Don't come back 'til the coast is clear." I did as she said, walking out into the backyard, hearing the deadbolt and main locks click behind me. I turned back and saw Cary and Lizzie sprinting away from the back door. I stumbled through the backyards and over fences along 26th Street until I reached Franklin, where I hunched under a tree and dialed Cal at home. He answered in his calm, cultured voice.

"Thank God, you're home," I blurted. "It's Connie. Cary's in danger. She's at her house now. *Send the cops please!*"

"Oh dear," said Cal. "Please hold."

I was speechless. *He put me on hold!* Here I was, cowering under a stranger's tree and calling for help, and all Rolfe could manage was a toneless *Oh dear*. It was like dire emergencies were an everyday occurrence for him. I began to hyperventilate and felt my heart thumping against my ribs. It seemed like forever before Cal returned to the phone.

"Connie, you *must* remain calm. The police are on their way. They'll arrive within six minutes. Where are you?"

Six minutes! Jesus, that's a lifetime! I spotted a house number on the backdoor beyond the tree and read it to him. The home owners did not appear to have returned from work and I couldn't see anyone else around. Somehow, Cal's voice remained calm as always.

"Connie, listen to me. I need you to walk over to 27th and go up to Broad Street. Head over to the Hill Café."

"Okay, then what?"

"Then I suggest that you sit at the bar, order a very large, industrial-strength cocktail, and wait for me to call you back with an *all-clear*. Got it?"

"Yeah, got it."

I stared at the phone in shock before dropping it at my side, then crept forward from beneath the tree, swiveling my head at the slightest noise. I climbed gingerly over a fence and stepped soundlessly onto the sidewalk. From there I beelined to the Hill Café and walked through the front door, casual as ever. A moment later I ordered the biggest, baddest bourbon that had ever been made.

Cal called back five minutes later to say that the police were at Cary's house. I polished off the bourbon and dropped my head in my hand, leaning forward at the wooden bar.

"Is she all right?"

"Yes. You can go home." He hung up as quickly as he had called.

CHAPTER 34

HAY ADAMS HOTEL, WASHINGTON – EARLY MORNING, JUNE 16, 2011
Cary, VE and Ray Goodson

Assistant Deputy Secretary of Homeland Security Bill Shaw knew how to make things happen fast when he had to. In this case, he really hustled. The suite at the venerable hotel had been swept only minutes before. The DHS official had arranged for a private jet to land at Andrews Air Force Base. A car was dispatched there to meet the flight. There were drinks and snacks available from the mini-bar. A bucket of ice and glassware had been set out.

Ray Goodson was admitted to the suite first. He greeted Shaw and took a seat on one of the two sofas in the living room. Shaw offered the NPS regional security chief a drink, which he declined. The drive from Philadelphia was made in record time. He glared at Shaw, then turned his head in disgust.

Shaw's phone rang a moment later. It was his agent dispatched to meet the flight, calling to report that the plane was on time and they were on their way.

Twenty minutes later, VE Shane sauntered into the suite, tossed her briefcase on a chair, and walked toward the bar. She located the Jack Daniels, grabbed a tumbler, poured herself a hefty drink, took a healthy swig, and turned to Shaw.

"Well, this is a goddamned mess, isn't it?"

VE introduced herself to Goodson with a gracious smile. "Cary's spoken so highly of you. May I call you Ray?'

Ray had stood at attention when VE entered the room. Shanes under full sail were always a formidable site. Ray beheld it at once. VE walked to the other sofa in the room and sat down. She reached into her briefcase and set two large photos on the coffee table. Ray and Shaw stepped forward to look at them.

"Secretary Shaw," VE said, "I will refrain from pointing out how difficult it was to reach you this evening."

Damned Texans know how to pull strings, thought Shaw. He wondered if sheer bull-headedness was in the water in the Lone Star state. The White House switchboard had located him at a private poker game in Bethesda, where he was having a banner evening with the cards. He had been instructed to call the chief of staff, pronto.

"Ms. Shane," said Shaw, "perhaps you will be good enough to tell us what this meeting is all about."

VE picked up the first photo. It was an enlargement of the one given to her by Reynaldo Mendoza in San Miguel only a few days earlier. She explained how and when she had obtained it. She pointed to Carlotta Franz and to the indistinct male in the photo.

"Why didn't your team have a copy of this image" asked VE, with sharpness in her voice.

"Where'd you get that?" Shaw demanded.

VE picked up the second image and both men stared at it. It was a digitally enhanced version of the first photo. However, in this rendering the faces of both subjects could be seen clearly.

"Do you recognize the man in this photo?" she asked. "Because I do."

"How'd you get that enhanced image?" Shaw asked. He glared at her and back at the photo.

"Secretary Shaw, my family owns a whole lot of businesses that perform a bunch of different services. We even have a rather sophisticated digital processing lab at our headquarters. The work was done there."

"Has anyone else seen these images?"

VE exhaled, waiting patiently for him to continue.

"Let me explain," said Shaw. He held his palms forward.

"*Explain, my ass!*" she said. "You'd better explain a lot more than this photo. It was taken on March 9 in Laredo, Texas. It shows that your agency had prior knowledge that this woman's body would later be doled out like dog food among thirteen historic sites, all of them supposedly under your protection."

Shaw's face reddened as he clenched his jaw.

VE reached into her briefcase and extracted another photo enlargement, this one taken on the recent trip to Russia. Shane pointed to one figure in the photo. "Recognize this man?"

"It's Ham Coles," Shaw said. "You know that."

"Your agency told the Constitution murder team that it had a mole inside the Zeta drug cell located in Grand Prairie, Texas."

Shaw nodded.

"Well, I found my own mole, gave him a copy of this photo, and asked him to let me know if anyone resembling him had ever showed up at that ranch. Guess who matched up?" She pointed to the photo taken in Sochi. "This same man was seen on more than one occasion entering and leaving the Zeta outpost there." She glared at Shaw. "Was Hamilton Coles your mole?"

"Yes," admitted Shaw, clearing his throat. "Who took that photo in Russia?"

"Cal Rolfe took it at the request of Cary Mallory. She was suspicious about several aspects of the murder case. Cal forwarded it to Cary, who sent it to me in Texas."

"Shaw, I think it's time for you to tell us the DHS version of what's been going on," said Goodson.

"That's need-to-know," said Shaw.

Suddenly, a voice emerged from Goodson's left jacket pocket. The security professional withdrew a phone and set it down on the table next to the photographs.

"*We* need to know, Bill," said the voice.

"Secretary Shaw," said Ray. "Of course, you recognize the voice of George Montgomery, the deputy secretary of the interior." Montgomery ranked two levels above Shaw within the government hierarchy.

"George, I can explain all of this," Shaw said, his voice quavering.

"We're waiting, Bill," said Montgomery. "By the way, I should explain that by *we*, I mean myself, the White House chief of staff, and Briggs Colonna."

The color drained from Shaw's face. He turned to face Ray before looking back at the phone. "Coles was CIA during the late 1980s and early 1990s," he said. "This was before we moved him over to landmarks. He did a lot of intel work before his wife was murdered. He's one of the brightest the agency's ever recruited."

"Was landmarks another cover?"

"He was simply too good to throw away after his wife died. We let him recover for a while, brought him back over landmarks, which was a safe environment, and slowly began to put him back into some special projects as the occasion arose."

"Tell us in a nutshell," said Montgomery, "exactly how and why did pieces of that young woman's body end up dumped on our turf in a line stretching from Massachusetts to Virginia?"

"It was a ploy to divert focus away from the disclosures coming in about Operation Fast and Furious."

"So, Coles gave the Zetas the security codes to bypass systems at the historic sites?" Ray asked. His cheeks had turned beet red.

"The plan was to blame the Zetas for the initial Constitution murder. It still is. No one was hurt; none of the sites were damaged. You people need to back off."

"And what about the bomb at the National Constitution Center?" asked Colonna.

"That was the Zetas working on their own. Coles' cover was blown, and the cartel retaliated."

"Who blew his cover?"

"It must have been the Franz woman. Ham was trying to get her to work as a double agent. She would do anything for drugs, for kicks. She was a real slut."

"Did you know she had *impressive* family connections, as it were?"

"Hell no. Coles intercepted her in Laredo to brief her before she met her boyfriend to continue on to Grand Prairie. The bitch suddenly waltzes him into a bank, sends a wire to Switzerland of all places, and picks up $10,000 like it was chump change. Then she tells him she won't play ball."

"Coles got her into a bar, slipped her a mickey, drove her to Grand Prairie, and made a hasty exit. Coles sensed that she might already have told her Zeta boyfriend of their planned meeting in Laredo."

"Go on," said Ray.

"May I ask why you all didn't move in then and bust up the cell?" asked Colonna.

"We were looking for more information on the pipeline. The internal distribution system that the cartel used to distribute the drugs from coast to coast."

"So, the bomb in Philadelphia was not a part of the plan?" asked Colonna.

"*Of course not!*" shouted Shaw. "We were trying to figure out our way ahead when the explosion took place."

"If the National Constitution center was not a part of your plan, then how did the cartel get the security codes for the building?" Colonna asked.

Shaw looked away from Ray.

"Did you ever really try to solve the Constitution murder?" Ray asked quietly.

"It was all tied into Fast and Furious," Shaw said. "The first disclosures about that fuck-up came out in March of this year. We wanted to coordinate the breakup of the cell with news about F & F and lay all the blame on the cartel. Surely you can understand the wisdom of killing two birds with one stone."

"Bill, I'm getting the picture that your position as head of National Infrastructure Protection is also a cover," said Montgomery. "Sounds to me like you actually work for the anti-drug arm of DHS."

"Oh, come on, George," said Shaw. "We all know that National Protection is pretty low on the totem pole at DHS."

"I would like to return, if we may, to the bombing at the National Constitution Center," said Colonna, with clinical guidance.

"We never gave the Zetas the green light on that action," blurted Shaw.

"Green light?" Colonna asked, his voice growing louder.

"I told you, when reports on Operation Fast and Furious broke in March, we needed to divert attention from that brouhaha immediately. Heads were going to roll over that fiasco."

"So, you allowed a hideous massacre of young Americans to buy enough time to link the ATF operation to the drug cartel?"

"It's fine for you guys," shouted Shaw. "You sit in your offices and don't have to make tough decisions. We must keep our borders intact and our nation free from drugs. Somebody has to take charge, damn it."

The room fell silent. A voice on the line cleared his throat.

"Okay, I need the names of the DHS security detail in the room," said the COS.

"Agent Mario" said one man.

"Agent Scollard," said another.

"Agents," said the White House chief. "You are instructed to arrest Secretary Shaw now and remove his communications devices."

Shaw looked stricken. He started to open his mouth, then slumping forward in defeat. The agent stepped behind him, and Shaw submitted without resistance.

"Now, where's Hamilton Coles?"

VE pressed a button on her cell phone and held the instrument out flat so the others could hear the voice on the other hand. "This is Cary Mallory, sir. VE alerted me by phone of her identification early yesterday evening. I sent Connie Taliaferro out the patio exit to get help immediately. Shortly thereafter I heard someone outside the house.

Where I live home invasions aren't totally unheard of. A while ago I created a small *safe room* in one windowless bathroom by replacing the door with metal and installing a special panic alarm. I was reaching to grab my dog Lizzie to go to the safe room, but she had heard the noises outside and ran out her dog door. I heard one gunshot less than a minute before the police arrived and surrounded the house. An officer with a bullhorn called to me to come out and get my dog, who was preventing them from reaching a suspect on the ground near the rear patio. Lizzie was lying on top of Ham Coles. I called her off and noticed that one of her ears was bleeding. When she attacked, Ham must have gotten off one shot that grazed her before she knocked the weapon from his hand and pinned him beneath her. I can assure you that the dog's injury was minor and has already been dressed."

"What about Ham?" asked VE. "Did Lizzie eat him?"

Cary laughed. "No such luck, VE. Ham's arm was chewed up and he had a few small puncture wounds at his neck."

Apparently, the dog was content to hold her prey alive until Cary showed up. Medics concluded that the minor neck wounds occurred when Ham tried to escape after she pinned him. The police arrested Ham while another unit delivered Cary to Rolfe's house. Connie had showed up in time to get a ride to Monument Avenue.

"Mr. Rolfe had asked the Richmond bomb squad to search around my house," Cary said. "Explosive-detecting dogs located one bomb on Ham and two others already wedged into the foundation. Technicians were able to diffuse them before they detonated."

"Is Coles in the hospital or in custody at the Richmond police station?" asked the COS.

"He was moved immediately to the jail after receiving medical treatment for his wounds at the scene."

Everyone present heard the White House chief barking orders to someone in the background. "I have instructed my office to contact the Governor of Virginia and the Richmond police and make sure that Mr. Coles fails to talk his way out of this situation. Mr. Rolfe, are you there?"

Everyone listened to the sounds of muffled movement on VE's phone. A moment later they heard a calm, genteel voice. "Rolfe here, sir."

"We are most grateful for your assistance, as always, Mr. Rolfe," said the COS. "I am sure the president will call to offer you his personal thanks."

"Please convey my ongoing respect and best wishes to the president," said Rolfe.

"Now, Ms. Mallory, will you share with us the factors that aroused your suspicions about this case," said Briggs Colonna. "I am not alone in being mystified."

Cary took a deep breath. "Well, sir, it's like this. When Ham and I first met in 1999, he came to me asking for leads on research into Edward Coles. At our third meeting, in Williamsburg, I gave him a microfilm of some original documents in a little-known public historical collection and advised him to read the manuscripts, which included some very revealing information about Dolley Madison's son, Payne Todd. Todd was something of a bad seed."

"So I have been led to understand, Ms. Mallory," said Colonna. "Tell me, did he read them?"

"Oh yes, most definitely. He quoted from some of the manu-scripts in his 2002 book about Coles."

"When did you smell a rat, as it were?"

"When he showed up at Montpelier and asked me to agree to work with his team on the Constitution murder."

"What gave you a clue?"

"Specifically, he asked me if I knew why Coles had gone to Russia at the request of President Madison in 1816. My research, as he should have remembered, was a search for information about Payne Todd's debts, specifically those that might have thrown light on the sizeable collection of art he purchased for Montpelier in Europe."

"Art?"

"That is my field of expertise, sir. However, such material is most often buried in the weeds. One must read everything to find nuggets of information. There was never any doubt about the rea-son that Coles went to Russia in 1816. I knew about the existence of a bastard child conceived in Russia during the negotiations to end the war of 1812."

"How?"

"Todd had recorded the information in one of his rambling di-ary entries included on the microfilm I gave Ham in 1999. It was in code, but quite frankly, it's not that tough a code to crack."

"So, you went into the affair of the Franz murder, knowing that something was fishy?

"Oh, most definitely. Ham Coles is far too intelligent to have forgotten. I kept pretending that I had either missed the diary en-try or forgotten it. As we went along, however, disclosures about the Russian genealogical connection from others must have made Ham wonder if I knew or remembered that obscure reference."

"I see."

"Now here we are in 2011," she observed. "After an absence of more than ten years, Ham suddenly appears out of nowhere, asking for my assistance on a matter of national security. He didn't need me, not really, sir. Most of my research is already in the Montpelier archives. Any forensic scientist with knowledge of the sources of genealogical DNA could have pulled the information from the collections files. Having me be included in his trip to Russia was the biggest clue."

"Why?"

"It's like what my late grandfather used to say, 'Keep your friends close and your enemies closer.' Ham obviously wanted to keep an eye on me to see if I was suspicious."

"Anything else?"

"His anguish didn't ring true that night after the bombing at the National Constitution Center. I almost felt like I was attending a second-rate play in suburbia."

"Go on."

"Ham was the most logical source for the letter fragment left with the body parts at Montpelier. Madison probably copied Coles on the letter, which ended up in some family file that Ham used in his research. He lifted it and kept it for future use."

"How'd you keep it from him that you were suspicious?"

"After the Constitution Center bombing, I was pretty sure I was in some danger. When Ham excused himself to use the restroom at Cal Rolfe's house, I confessed my suspicions to Cal, who told me to get some special phones that could not tapped easily by DHS."

"How'd you know Cal had worked for us?" This question came from the COS.

"Oh, please sir, the man knows everyone in all fifty states and forty foreign countries. He's well off, but I always knew somebody was paying his way on some of those busman's holidays to all parts of the globe. Rare books and antiques are expensive."

"Let's sum up, shall we?" said the COS. "Where did you get the phones?"

"VE had one of her people deliver them to me and Cal in St. Petersburg."

Then you, Ms. Shane, and Mr. Rolfe have had back channel contact since you landed in Russia?

"Yes."

"Did you realize that Ham Coles was outside your house?"

"I figured it was either Ham or someone from the cartel." Then Cary changed the subject abruptly. "Sir, I have to say that I don't think Secretary Shaw initiated the Constitution murders."

"What? The man practically sold his soul to wrap everything up into a package," said the COS.

"He may not be the brightest bulb on the tree," said VE. "But he's exactly what the government wants in these upper middle-level management positions."

"You're blaming us?" asked the White House chief, sounding surprised.

"Of course, I do, sir," said VE. "I think Ham pulled the wool over Shaw's eyes early on. I believe his motive all along was revenge for his wife's murder."

"Oh, come on, Ms. Shane."

"Bear with me, sir, if you will. Ham oversaw the landmarks unit within DHS. Therefore, he had control over the dissemination of information within his division and between landmarks and other branches of DHS. And NPS. Even Secretary Shaw remarked that the Protection Division is small potatoes. Ham's apparent lack of clout kept him above suspicion and gave him a great deal of wiggle room."

"You believe he knew in advance that Carlotta Franz was related to the Romanovs?"

"I think he found another document among the Coles family papers that pointed specifically to the tsar's sister as the mother of the child. Furthermore, I think the Zetas suspected Ham was a double agent and capitalized on his knowledge of security systems in historic buildings to carry out the initial scheme, and then later to activate the attack at the Constitution Center on their own."

"I thought you all got the genealogy from Princess Troubetzskoy," said Colonna, taking charge of the conversation.

"I was the one who contacted Natalia," Cary said. "But I alerted her to the possibility that the murder could lead back to DHS. Natalia had briefed Princess Troubetzskoy before she ever appeared in the NPS offices in Philadelphia. She arrived with a script already written."

"Then why bomb the National Constitution Center?" asked Colonna.

"It enhanced Ham's position. And Shaw's. This allowed Ham to branch out to effect damage in other departments within DHS."

"And Sochi?"

"Really, sir," interjected Cal. "Sochi was, and could well remain, a disaster waiting to happen. The trip was a pure red herring, and Cary and I knew it from the onset. Ellen Harriett could have handled the natural WHS habitat issues all by herself. We did not need to go at all. Most of the free world still distrusts the Russians. Every agency known to God and man will be looking over their shoulders until the ashes from the very last firework at the closing ceremony in Sochi have wafted to ground. Throw in a few diehard dynasts to muddy the waters; place the games in an isolated, politically unstable location that has to be fitted up with everything from electricity to flushing toilets, and paranoia grows like wildfire."

"What did your Russian colleagues think of your presence on the delegation?" asked Colonna.

"We said it was a typical political junket and that Cal and I were happy to be along for the ride. Everyone got a real kick out of it!"

"To be honest," said Cal, "we did not contact many of our colleagues lest we cause undue embarrassment to the United States."

Ray Goodson cleared his throat to speak.

"Go ahead, Ray," said the NPS director.

"Sir, we at NERO need a detailed briefing about how the government plans to handle the fallout from this fiasco."

"Ray, this one goes to the very top," said Colonna. "I can tell you that my instructions are as follows. First, reassure the American public that our treasured landmarks are safe. Second, honor the victims and their families. Third, keep the details firmly under wraps."

"May I make one suggestion, sir?" Cary asked.

"Yes, Ms. Mallory?"

"Throw some money at the problem in the best American tradition, and do a DNA test on Ham Coles. While we believe the gene passed through John Payne, it might have a connection to Mary Coles Payne, Dolley's mother."

CHAPTER 35

RICHMOND – JUNE 21, 2011
Connie

Cary, VE Shane, and I were having drinks in Calvert Rolfe's lovely garden on Monument Avenue. It was early evening on June 21, slightly muggy but not sweltering. The dog days of August were yet to come. Our host insisted on mint juleps, since he grew more varieties of mint in his garden than the Wrigley's spearmint gum people ever dreamed of. I even wore my *plantation white* suit and boater for the occasion. Cary said I looked like one of Tom Wolfe's poor relations.

"Are we going to have a different mint for each round?" asked VE. She was content because Cal preferred a recipe using bourbon, rather than the rye whiskey common in the Maryland version of the drink.

"Most definitely, my dear Virginia," said Rolfe, handing her an ice-coated antique silver cup filled to the brim with crushed ice, sugar syrup, and Makers Mark. A sprig of fresh mint rested on top. Cal explained that he always mixed some crushed mint into the sugar syrup to add *bloom* to the aroma and taste.

VE sipped delicately and smiled. "I believe this mint's even better than the last one."

The little garden table boasted ham biscuits, homemade cheese straws, and lightly salted Virginia roasted peanuts. Cary observed that nothing else to eat was necessary or desired, and everyone agreed.

We had all signed our lives away in confidentiality agreements with the government. It didn't matter though; we were all disinclined to discuss the Constitution murder affair with anyone who had not experienced the debacle firsthand.

Our conversation meandered and waned until a wry smile appeared on VE's face

"Did I tell you all the government has asked to see our prototype for the new spy phone?" she asked.

"Congratulations!" said Cal. "It really is a dandy little device. Apparently, no one had a clue we were chatting merrily about dark government secrets and emailing damning photos all over the world."

"Well done," added Cary. "Did you see the news about the Park Service? Congress is debating a $1 billion package to update all security systems at the nation's historic sites, including offering low-interest loans to National Historic Landmarks operating outside direct parks management."

We all raised our glasses and smiled.

"I had an email from Don José Ramirez," said VE, "telling me the extraordinary news that their adopted daughter Carlotta had apparently worked since she was a teenager as a secret agent infiltrating the Mexican drug world on behalf of theirs and the American government. I had no idea. She'll be buried with honors at Arlington in a few months. The Ramirezes want Princess Sasha and me to join them for the occasion. They're both so proud of her."

We all rolled our eyes in unison.

"Do you supposed the princess will come for it?" I asked.

VE laughed. "I've already heard from her. She wrote that it would be better to 'let sleeping dogs lie.'"

"What about Carlotta's police record?" I asked.

"Poof," VE said with satisfaction. "Up in smoke. What with the probable embarrassment about Operation Fast and Furious, the Mexican and U.S. governments are more than happy to rally around a false story about cross-border cooperation than a true one about 'screwing your allies.'"

"Wait a second," Cal said. "How does a non-citizen end up in Arlington?" He thought it unlikely that Payne Todd's native birth would open the gates to the famous cemetery.

"Done with a proclamation, no doubt," VE said. She knew that most of Carlotta's transgressions had taken place south of the border. The botched ATF operation should cost the U.S. the price of a burial, at the very least.

They all knew about the Reed National Prize scholarship program established in memory of the slain students from the high school in Delaware. They were disappointed that the innocent Missouri couple also killed in the blast did not get any laurels, but the family had received hand-written notes of condolence from the president and the governor of Pennsylvania, so that would have to suffice.

"The Schwartz brothers are casting new statues of Madison and Washington," Cal said. "I got pictures and they will look even better than the originals."

VE had gotten a report from Juan Hernandez about the explosion at the Zeta ranch near Grand Prairie, an incident that did not make the national news. Her source said there was widespread acceptance that the devastation was the work of a rival drug cartel that was battling the Zetas for control of that part of the border trade.

"So how *did* Carlotta get into the U.S.?" I asked. The idea of it was still confusing.

"*Darlin*, that girl probably walked with Ham Coles through one of the tunnels," sighed VE. "Y'all have no idea how bad the situation is down there."

They were on their third different variety of mint julep when Rolfe belched and giggled. The ladies giggled in turn. Then he brought up his own explanation about the NCC bombing. "It was a nut who was fired from his job as a custodian at NCC. Obviously, he's a Muslim with ties to the radical wing of Islam."

"I give it a four," said Cary, mimicking the scoring of Olympic judges.

To their amazement, Cal mimicked the South Philly jargon from the days of American Bandstand. "Dick, it's got no beat. The lyrics are nothing. I give it a two!" He even pretended to be chewing gum.

Cary smiled and motioned to her drink. "So, how did this lone Muslim rewire the security system at NCC?"

"China," said Cal. "Had to be China, since China is Communist and owns about one fifth of our debt."

"And he did it to protest," said VE and Cary simultaneously. Cary held up her hand like a reporter holding a microphone and pointed it in Cal's direction.

Cal gave a grim smile. "Who knows? Treatment of Muslim prisoners? The evils of Christianity? Capitalism? Support for one of their holy wars? Pork sausage? What the f**k!"

"Ain't that the truth!" said VE. She smiled in amazement at Cal, whose rare use of the F-word was a telling clue about how they all felt about the resolution to the Constitution murders.

Their host got up to prepare the fourth, and inevitably, the final round of drinks. They all knew two was the usual maximum in polite company. The girls and I knew we would have to take a taxi back to Church Hill, but nobody cared. For all I knew, the Shanes owned the cab company. I for one was pleased that the pieces of Carlotta Franz had found a worthy cemetery. Let the conspiracy theorists have a field day on their blogs, arguing in search of the truth about the deaths of JFK, RFK, MLK, and grousing about the evils of government intrusions into our daily lives. Despite her many flaws, the young woman had deserved a better ending.

"Okay, Cary," I said, trying to get in the last word. "Did Dolley know about her granddaughter or not?"

"*If* she read the packet of papers that James Madison left to her, and *if* it included Coles' note to President Madison, and *if* she included it in the carpet bag entrusted to her nieces –"

"It's possible, isn't it?" I said, thinking that the former first lady's knowledge of the child might have induced her to return to Washington to live permanently.

"Connie, my friend, anything is possible," said Cary. With that, she hiccupped and we all laughed.

EPILOGUE RICHMOND – 2018
Connie

The call came from Cal Rolfe after the Christmas holidays. I had answered the phone, yelled for Cary, and put Cal on speaker as soon as she sat down at the kitchen table.

"I have a report on the Fast and Furious investigation," he said.

Since Cary and I hadn't heard a peep from DEA since the previous spring, we were anxious to hear what Cal had found out from his network of government sources.

"Congress has decided not to pursue another investigation into the 2011 operation."

Before we could muster any questions, he continued. "The powers on high no longer see an advantage in exposing the actions of the previous administration, including its Attorney General."

"So, we don't have to testify? "

"No."

"And no one is going to dig up poor Carlotta Franz?"

"May she forever rest in peace at Arlington National Cemetery."

"What should we do now?"

Cal chuckled. "Put the report in another secure place off site. I will tell the others to do the same thing." Then he hung up.

APPENDIX I

Fact and Fiction in the Constitution Murders
Acronyms: (all real)
> APS: American Philosophical Society, Philadelphia
> ATF: U.S. Bureau of Alcohol, Tobacco, and Firearms
> CIA: U.S. Central Intelligence Agency
> COS: White House Chief of Staff
> DHS: U.S. Department of Homeland Security
> DOD: U.S. Department of Defense
> DOJ: U.S. Department of Justice
> FBI: U.S. Federal Bureau of Investigation
> INHP: Independence National Historical Park, NPS, Philadelphia
> MVLA: Mount Vernon Ladies Association of the Union
> NCC: National Constitutional Center, Philadelphia
> NPS: National Park Service, Department of the Interior, Washington, D.C.
> NHL: National Historic Landmark
> NHLD: National Historic Landmark District
> NERO: Northeast Regional Office, National Park Service, Philadelphia

POTUS: President of the United States
SBC: (Smithsonian Bering Center) New name for National Museum of American
History, Smithsonian Institution

Real People and Places:
This novel is a work of fiction built around four factual events. First, at the request of President James Madison, Edward Coles traveled on a ship of war as a special envoy to Russia in 1816 to meet with Tsar Alexander I. At issue was a diplomatic dispute relating to the misbehavior of the Russian Council. Second, in 1836 Madison is said to have prepared a packet of Payne Todd's debts he paid without his wife's knowledge and instructed his brother-in-law, John Payne, to give it to Dolley after his death. Third, on her deathbed, in 1849, Dolley Madison entrusted a carpet bag full of papers to two nieces, asking them to remove them. Finally, Operation Fast and Furious was a bona fide operation of the Bureau of Tobacco and Firearms that failed.

There is no evidence that Payne Todd impregnated a sister of Tsar Alexander I. The tsar did not have a sister named Natasha. The story is fiction.

Fictional Characters:
Many of the historical characters in this book are genuine. The following characters are fictional. Any relation to real people is unintentional. Major characters appear in Bold. Listing last names alphabetically, they are:

A
John Abbott, Director, Montpelier, National Trust for Historic Preservation, later President, Montpelier Foundation, Orange, VA

Bonnie Allison, NERO public affairs officer, NPS, Philadelphia, PA

Jim Andersen, CIA Central American anti-terrorist agent, Washington, D.C.

B
Selena Bagrationi, daughter of Nicholai, b. 1920

Angela Bagrationi, daughter of Selena, b. 1950

Davie Ballard, junior, Read High School, Centerville, DE
Jeannine Butler, Ephemera expert, Division of Political History, SBC

C

Anne Whiting Cary, late wife of Cap'n Johnny Mallory, Hampton, VA

Janet Casey, Assistant Director, DHS Landmarks unit, Washington, D.C

Barbara Charlton, DHS Landmarks staffer, Washington, D.C.

Agents Jones, Mario, Frank, Smith, and Scollard, DHS staff, Washington, D.C.

Hamilton Coles, landmarks coordinator, DHS, Washington, D.C.

Briggs Colonna, NPS Director, Washington, D.C.

Annie Cooper, Assistant Curator of Paintings, Colonial Williamsburg, Williamsburg, VA

George Curwin, NPS Independence National Park security agent, Philadelphia,

D

Steven Daniels, retired demolitions specialist, Orange, VA

Ned Donaldson, IT Executive, Dallas, TX

Sally Drennan, Assistant Curator, Montpelier, National Trust, Orange, VA

F

William Ferguson, art collector and creditor of Payne Todd, Washington, D.C.

Kim Field, Curator, Greensboro Historical Museum, NC

Carlotta Franz, murder victim. b. 1985, San Miguel de Allende, Mexico

G
Ray Goodson, NERO security chief, Philadelphia, PA
Donald Glenn, NPS security chief, Charlestown Navy Yard, MA
Antonio Guerrero, artist and father of Carlotta Franz, Mexico

H
Ellen Harriett, President, U.S. Nature Conservancy, Washington, D.C.
Juan Hernandez, Ranch Manager, Shane Enterprises, Joe Pool Lake, Texas
Nancy Hicks, murdered wife of Hamilton Coles

J
Amory James, chief archaeologist, Montpelier, Orange, VA
Billy Johnson, IT specialist, DHS, Washington, D.C.
Walter Johnston, Landmarks staff, DHS, Washington D.C.

K
Natalia Kruskov, Russian genealogist, specialist on Romanov family, St. Petersburg, Russia

L
Hans Lawson, student, Read High School, DE
David Leigh, Orange County Sheriff, VA

M
Cary Mallory, owner of Cary Mallory Antiques. Richmond, VA
Cap'n Johnny Mallory, waterman, grandfather of Cary Mallory, Hampton, VA
John the Umpteenth Mallory, son of Cap'n Johnny, father of Cary, VA

Ben Manheim, specialist on Russian Federation, DHS, Washington, D.C.

Alex McGehee, son of Maria Todd and Millard McGehee, b. Baltimore, MD

Millard McGehee, first husband of Maria Todd

Nicholai McGehee-Bagrationi, son of Sergei McGehee, b.1881

Sergei McGehee, son of Alex McGehee

Reynaldo Mendoza, Mexican anti-drug agent, San Miguel, Mexico

Bubba Montague, uncle of Cary Mallory, Texas

Elizabeth "Libby" Montague Mallory, Texas heiress and mother of Cary

Senior Montagues, parents of Libby Montague, Texas

George Montgomery, Deputy Secretary of the Interior, Washington, D.C

O

Nicki O'Reilly, DHS Landmarks staffer, Washington, D.C

P

Vladimir Popov, Russian architect, St. Petersburg, Russia

Gray Powell, NPS New York security agent

Dr. William Privale, historian, national Madison expert, university professor

Grand Duchess Natasha Pruskova, mother of Maria, sister of Tsar Alexander I, St. Petersburg, Russia

Prussian expatriate noble, San Miguel, Mexico

R

Don José and Francesca Ramirez, foster parents of Carlotta Franz, San Miguel de Allende, Mexico

Bob Read, Editor, Papers of James Madison, UVA., Charlottesville, VA

Elizabeth, "Liz" Rodgers, NPS NERO director, Philadelphia, PA

Alicia Rosen, student, Read High School, DE

Calvert Rolfe, architectural historian, Richmond, VA

S

Nancy Sayre, curator, (SBC)Smithsonian Institution, Washington, D.C.

Fred Schmidt, forensics DNA director, Dover Air Force Lab, Delaware, DOD

Don Schmid, Department of Justice Field Agent

William Searle, Director, Greensboro Historical Museum, NC

Bill Shackelford, security staff, Montpelier, Orange, VA

John P. "Paw" Shane, grandfather of VE Shane, Fort Worth, TX

John P. "Little Paw" Shane, Jr. father of VE Shane, Fort Worth, TX

Virginia Eliza "VE" Shane, former Sweet Briar roommate of Cary Mallory, Texas

William "Bill" Shaw, Assistant Deputy Secretary, Infrastructure Protection, DHS, Washington, D.C.

Patrick Shea, Orange County Fire Chief, VA

Julia Sheridan, DHS security officer, Philadelphia, P

Dr. Julius Stella, Director, National Constitution Center, Montpelier, Orange, VA

T

Conrad Taliaferro, administrative assistant to Cary Mallory of Cary Mallory Antiques, Richmond, VA

Maria Todd (McGehee Nicholson), natural child of Payne Todd. b. 1815, St. Petersburg, Russia

Princess Sasha Troubetzskoy, descendant of Romanovs, France

W

Harper Wade, curator, Virginia Historical Society, Richmond, VA

Lisa Walter, wealthy Texas ex-patriot in San Miguel de Allende, Mexico

Noel Weekley, Distinguished Professor of History, William & Mary, Williamsburg, VA

White House Chief of Staff

Ned Willis, head of security, Montpelier, Orange, VA

Suggestions for Further Reading

This novel was not written for serious historians, but for individuals who enjoy reading fictional mysteries set within a historical context. That said, anyone wanting to know more about the historical information herein can go on line and Google everything from James Madison to Operation Fast and Furious, from DNA to NPS, to find valuable leads and facts.

Two important Madison biographers are sited here:

Catherine Allgor. *A More Perfect Union.* Henry Holt and Company, New York, 2006. This volume is also available on Kindle and in other digital editions.

Ralph Ketchum, *James Madison: A Biography.* Charlottesville, University of Virginia Press, 1990. This is the best one-volume biography of Madison, and can be found in Google Books, Goodreads, and Kindle, among others.

ABOUT THE AUTHOR

Conover Hunt, a native of Hampton, Virginia, is a nationally known public historian. She has published seven nonfiction books on American history, John F. Kennedy, and James and Dolley Madison.

Over the course of her career, Hunt has worked on the preservation of historic sites and organized new museums and traveling exhibitions. She served as lead curator in the creation of the Sixth Floor Museum in Dallas, at the site of Kennedy's assassination.

Hunt received a bachelor of arts in art history from Newcomb College of Tulane University and a master of arts from the University of Delaware as a fellow in the Winterthur Museum's Early American Culture program.

The Constitution Murders is her first novel.

60431528R00155

Made in the USA
Middletown, DE
29 December 2017